D0021743

ALSO BY MASON DEAVER

I Wish You All the Best
The Ghosts We Keep

the FEELING of FALLING IN LOVE

MASON DEAVER

PUSH

Copyright © 2022 by Mason Deaver

All rights reserved. Published by PUSH, an imprint of
Scholastic Inc., *Publishers since 1920*. PUSH and associated logos are
trademarks and/or registered trademarks of Scholastic Inc.

The publisher does not have any control over and does not assume any
responsibility for author or third-party websites or their content.

No part of this publication may be reproduced, stored in a retrieval system,
or transmitted in any form or by any means, electronic, mechanical,
photocopying, recording, or otherwise, without written permission of the
publisher. For information regarding permission, write to Scholastic Inc.,
Attention: Permissions Department, 557 Broadway, New York, NY 10012.

This book is a work of fiction. Names, characters, places, and incidents
are either the product of the author's imagination or are used fictitiously,
and any resemblance to actual persons, living or dead, business
establishments, events, or locales is entirely coincidental.

Library of Congress Cataloging-in-Publication Data available

ISBN 978-1-338-77766-6

10 9 8 7 6 5 4 3 2 1   22 23 24 25 26

Printed in Italy   183
First edition, August 2022

Book design by Maeve Norton

FOR EVERY TRANS PERSON
WHO EVER BELIEVED THEY
WERE TOO COMPLICATED FOR
A LOVE STORY

Thursday

APRIL 14

"I love you," he says.

The sirens in my head start going off. At first I wonder if I've heard him right, between the heavy breathing, the sound of our kissing, the soft music he's got playing. In fact, I'm sure I heard him wrong. Maybe it was a line from the song instead?

But then I pull away from Josh, and he's staring up at me with those big brown eyes of his, like he's expecting some kind of answer from me.

That's when I realize I'm truly in trouble.

And here I thought this was going to be a nice visit, some making out, maybe fooling around before afternoon classes.

But no.

Instead, he's said those three little words, and he's waiting for me to say them back. Then we'll kiss and fall back onto the bed and probably miss class, but it won't matter because we're in love! And everything is perfect!

Except it isn't.

And now I have to have this conversation. So annoying.

"Neil?" He's still looking at me.

"Okay."

His face sinks, the smile gone in an instant. "Okay?" he repeats.

"That's what I said." I want to get off his lap, but his hands are still on my waist.

"I said 'I love you,'" he says again. Like I didn't hear him.

"And I said 'okay.'" I huff, pulling myself away from him, his hands retreating. He's always loved touching me, and usually I don't mind. A hand around my waist or up the back of my shirt, faintly scratching my back while we watch movies. He always gets frustrated because I fall asleep before the movie's over, but I can also tell he thinks it's cute. Movie night's the most we've ever allowed this arrangement to veer toward anything resembling us being boyfriends, and that's only because I get a nice back scratch out of it, or him playing with my hair.

Josh and I laid down the rules firmly when this entire thing started. It was just a bit of stress relief, and that's all it was ever supposed to be.

We'd both agreed to that.

"What else do you want me to say?" I ask him.

Josh still looks like he's in shock. "I'd like it if you'd say something besides 'okay.'"

"Thank you?" It comes out as more of a question than I mean it to.

All I can do is stand there awkwardly while he processes whatever is going on in that head of his. There's disappointment on his face, anger, sadness, pity—a whole range of emotions he's forcing himself through over three little words.

"I knew this was a mistake," Josh whimpers. I don't want to sound mean or anything, but he's getting pretty pitiful. "I knew it."

"If you knew it, then why'd you say it?" I ask him.

"I don't know." He hangs his head in shame. "I think part of me was just . . . I guess hoping you'd say it back."

"Not really, sorry . . ." I tell him. I glance at the Rolex on my wrist—Oyster Perpetual, the one with the nice black dial. If we don't wrap this up soon, we're both going to be late for class.

I should have known that something was up; I should have felt it. I mean, did I have a gut feeling that something bad like this was going to happen? No, not really, but still, I should have seen it coming.

The only reason I came here is because he asked, because there was an unanswered text from him on my phone telling me to drop by before Classic Lit. I figured, why not? Josh's dorm room was close to the English building, even if it meant that I'd be risking hickeys on my neck for the rest of the day. I imagined some fooling around would make the rest of the day a little more enjoyable.

"I thought . . ." Josh begins to say. Then he backs up and starts again. "You're telling me that you don't feel this? You don't think we have something real?" I think there might actually be tears welling up behind his eyes; they seem wetter than usual.

He reaches up for my hand, but I back away and let it fall.

"We had an agreement, Josh. No feelings, no dating, no emotions. Just fun. Look, I enjoy spending time with you, but that's because we were friends before this entire situation was even an idea. That's how I see us—two friends who happen to have sex every now and then."

It's been, up until this moment, an absolutely perfect setup. He has a single dorm room, so there aren't any roommates to worry about when we want to be together, and he isn't a half-bad kisser either; a little too much tongue, but that's his only real flaw.

When this whole situation started up at the beginning of this school year, we'd made things clear. This was just a friendly thing, just us hooking up, relieving some tension, and helping each other out. We even had a Pull-Out Clause—Josh came up with the name: If either of us ever started to get serious about another person, we'd call the whole thing off and move on.

This was never supposed to be about love, or feelings, or any junk like that. We're in high school, for fuck's sake. Who falls in love in high school?

And now, with three little words, it's all undone.

"I should probably leave," I say.

"No, wait!" Josh jumps up. "Please, wait!"

I just stare at him, his eyes wide after the outburst. In all the years I've known him, I've never seen him worked up like this. He isn't exactly the loud type. He's scrawny, with a little bit of muscle, and height that comes in handy when he plays basketball.

Maybe after things have calmed down a little, I can help set him up with someone, someone who wants the same things he wants. Let's just hope this other boy doesn't mind the amount of LEGO Star Wars sets that decorate his dorm room. My eyes avoid Josh's and instead focus on this huge thing he calls a Y-wing; it had been a bitch to find because apparently it had been "retired." I had to make an account on some LEGO-selling website just to find it, and we'd spent twelve hours total building the stupid thing.

"I'm sorry," he says softly.

"Josh." I close my eyes, pinching the bridge of my nose. "I've got to get to class."

"Can't I get anything from you?"

"I don't know what you want me to say."

"Anything,"

"I've said plenty and you didn't seem happy with that either, so forgive me if I'm a little confused." I glance at my watch, calculating the minutes it'll take to get to Mr. Johnson's English class. I think I've got three, and that's being generous.

"What if we go back?" Josh asks. "What if we just hit rewind, undo the last few minutes, and pretend like nothing ever happened. I take it back, okay? Seriously. Let's just forget it."

Oh, how I'd love for that to happen, to be blasted with some laser that would erase both of our short-term memories. But now that I know the truth, now that I know how Josh really feels about this entire situation, there's no undoing it. I need to pull the plug.

"Goodbye, Josh. I'll see you at dinner?"

He's known me for almost ten years, so he should know I'm not behaving any different than usual. He's always been one to appreciate my bluntness, my ability to tell the truth.

"You're joking, right?"

"What? It's not like we're broken up. I think it's better if we go back to just being friends without benefits. Or, like, the sexual benefits."

I know now I should've broken it off sooner. I take in the disappointment on his face, the sour expression, and I let out a low groan.

"Josh," I say, "let me ask you, what did you really think was going to happen?"

He finally looks up at me again, and he stares, contemplating his words for a bit before he opens his mouth. "I thought . . . I thought that maybe you'd change your mind, or that our 'rules' didn't matter anymore."

"How do you think that's going for you?"

Okay, maybe that was a little mean. But I'm getting annoyed, and I don't want to be late for class.

"You don't have to be a jerk."

"I'm not the bad guy here, Josh. You knew what this was."

"I'm not saying you're the bad guy," he tells me. "I was just hoping for a little compassion."

"I'll talk to you later, okay?"

His shoulders slump. I've never seen him look this defeated. "Yeah . . . sure."

I grab my backpack off his desk chair and slip out into the hallway as quickly as I can, walking as fast as my short legs will carry me. My mind keeps racing as I try to process everything that's just happened, and I rub at my forehead to calm the headache I can feel coming on. And of course, Josh just *had* to make his declaration *two* days before we're supposed to leave for Michael's wedding. Josh was going to be the buffer between me and my family, the safety net so I could protect myself, but now that's all gone up in flames.

An entire week spent in Beverly Hills surrounded by the awful people who make up my family. Josh was supposed to be there to save me, to drag me away from my grandparents when they asked about my surgeries, to distract me at the brunches and the rehearsal dinner.

Now I'm going to have to spend a week avoiding both him *and* my family.

That'll be fun.

Maybe this is my fault? Maybe I gave Josh too much attention, too much time, too much effort?

No. The more I think about it, the more I can see this as his fault. I never gave him any indication that we could fall in love, that we could possibly be boyfriends, that we'd drive off into the sunset holding hands. Jesus fucking Christ, we're teenagers. It isn't that serious.

This isn't my fault; it can't be.

Unless I'm just too lovable for my own good.

I think the day can't possibly get any worse, and of course it does. Between everything with Josh this morning, two quizzes in my final classes that I'm sure I failed, and being so distracted that I forgot to take notes in biology, I'm ready for this day to just end.

My stomach isn't helping either, growling low enough for the people around me to hear. If Josh hadn't dragged me to his room, I would've had time to eat lunch. Now I'm starving, and it'll be hours before the dining hall is open for dinner.

The iced coffee I bought from the campus café this morning is definitely gone. I'm already plotting on how to get back to the dorm and grab the box of granola bars hidden under my bed before Fowler gets there and forces me to *small talk*.

God, that's one more thing snatched away from me. Josh has one of the rare single rooms on campus, which means it's been a safe haven, a sanctuary where I can use the spare key he gave me to be alone if needed. Alone, and—most important—away from the annoying little Goody Two-shoes I'm forced to share this space with.

And now that's gone.

Fan-fucking-tastic.

The final bell rings, and I'm the first out of the classroom. Political science is in the Henry building across campus from my dorm, so it takes some time to get back there, but if I'm not mistaken, Fowler should be at the music club until five or six, so perhaps I'm in the clear for the next few hours.

When I get to my door, I reach into my pocket, looking for my key ring, except it isn't there.

I dig into my other pocket. Just my phone.

Wallet in the back right pocket. The back left pocket is empty like always.

Okay, Neil, don't panic. Don't worry because you always have your key in your right pocket, because that's where it always is and now it isn't for some reason. You probably just left it in your backpack, put it in one of the pockets.

Except it isn't there.

Even after emptying my entire backpack on the floor, there isn't a single key to be found.

I slowly bang my head against the door. How long will it take to concuss myself? I've seen guys in football games get smacked a lot harder and be . . . okay-ish? Maybe I should just do it harder? That'll give me an excuse not to go to the wedding this weekend.

Except when I go to smack my head again, the door opens and I stumble forward and trip, actually hitting my head on the floor before I can catch myself. The result is a sharp pain, and an instant headache that no amount of rolling over or rubbing my forehead will make go away. I open my eyes slowly, ignoring the pain, and I see Wyatt Fowler staring up at me. Or rather, down at me.

"Thank you," I say quietly.

"You were banging on the door."

"I lost my keys."

Wyatt looks at my nightstand and pulls something off of it. "Here they are." He tosses them toward me, but I make no effort to catch them, letting them hit my stomach with a jingle.

I pick myself up.

Wyatt's mostly dressed in his school uniform; the obviously secondhand blazer has been thrown casually on his bed to be hung up later. I suppose the music club is off if he's here already. I throw my bag on the floor and fall face-first onto my bed, relishing the feeling of the plush comforter. And then I let out the loudest groan possible.

"Yeah?"

I don't answer him.

"Rough day?"

"Stop talking," I moan, my voice muffled.

"Did something happen?"

"It's none of your business."

"Whatever you say," Wyatt drawls out. I don't know where Wyatt was born exactly, but I do know he's from North Carolina. He's said as much himself. And even if he hadn't, his accent alone would've told me he's as southern as the biscuits and gravy that seem to be on nearly every breakfast menu in Charlotte. His words are slow except when they aren't, when he mumbles so much that I can't understand a word he says.

"Just stop talking," I beg him again.

Wyatt whistles, turning up the same indie bullshit that he's always listening to or playing on his guitar.

"Turn that down," I tell him.

He ignores me.

"Hey, I said turn it down. Didn't you hear me?"

"I did," he says. "What I didn't hear was a 'please.'"

"I'm not going to beg you to turn the music down." I turn my head so I can see the smug smile on his face and that stupid gap between his two front teeth.

"It's not begging," he says. "It's called having manners."

"Whatever." I'm not going to fight with him over this. I just want to sleep. I don't even remember when I decided that a nap would fix the things wrong with today, but I'm deciding that now. Except the bass is kicking in on his song, and a beat comes in and it's super noisy, so I stand up fast and walk over to where Wyatt's ancient iPhone is sitting on the shelf (I mean, it still has a home button, come on) and I turn off the music.

"Hey!" he protests.

"I asked nicely." I get back in bed.

"That's the one thing you didn't do." He goes over and turns the music back on.

"I was trying to nap."

"What's up with you today?" he asks. "You never talk to me this much."

"You're lucky I'm acknowledging you at all," I mumble back into my pillow. "I'm just in a bad mood."

"Well, I don't know what caused your foul mood, but it isn't my fault, even if my last name *is* Fowler."

My God.

The worst part is that I know he's right. But it's the fact that he's right, and the way he's being so earnest and sincere about everything, that's driving me up the wall. That's what I can't stand about Wyatt, he's just so . . .

Good.

He's always asking me how my day was, if I did well on my exams or assignments. He asks me where I'm going when I'm leaving and *tells me to be safe*. And even though I never, ever ask, he tells me where *he's* going and if he'll be back late.

I'm about to get up to turn his music off again when I'm saved by my phone. Or, rather, Wyatt is saved by my phone. Samuel's calling.

"What?"

"Whoa, sounds like someone woke up on the wrong side of the bed." He laughs, and I can perfectly picture the way his mouth stretches into a smile while he does it. I wish I were there to smack the look off his face.

"What do you want, Samuel?"

"I was just calling you to see what's up."

"I'm in my room." I peer over at Wyatt, realizing for the first time that he's got an open suitcase on his bed. He's walking over to his closet now, grabbing one of the dozens of flannel shirts or worn-out band T-shirts he wears when we aren't required to be in uniform. The one he's holding has a picture of some blond lady on the back with the words TINY HOT TOPIC BITCH written on the front. Even after almost a year it's always funny seeing him outside of his uniform in this weird grunge guitar-kid aesthetic. The boy even wears *earrings*, tiny little hoops in his ears that he puts in every day so the holes won't close.

Samuel mutters to someone off the call before he comes back to me. "We're heading to the bridge; you want to come?"

"No."

The chances of Josh being there are way too high.

"Why not? One last hurrah before spring break. Josh isn't going to be there," he adds, like he's reading my mind.

I almost end the call there.

"Why would you say that? What difference does it make if Josh is or isn't there?"

"You two had a fight, didn't you?"

"Who told you that?"

"Let's see . . ." Samuel does a little *tut, tut, tut*. "I heard it from Julien, who heard it from Hoon, who heard it from Mark, who heard straight from Josh that you'd broken up."

I guess they had enough sense to not talk about it in our group chat.

"We didn't 'break up.' You can't break up if you're not dating." I realize I might be saying too much in front of Fowler, but he doesn't even turn around.

"Well, the posts Josh is making on Insta and Snapchat sure make it look like a breakup."

I pause.

"What?"

"Go check his stories—it's kind of sad. I feel bad for the guy."

"It wasn't a breakup; you shouldn't feel sorry for him!"

"Whatever. Just come down."

"I'm good."

Before Samuel can say anything else, I end the call, and a moment later I get a text from him.

SAMUEL: 😔

I ignore him and wonder if I should start packing now or if I can wait until tonight. I can't imagine what the wedding will be like without Josh there; then again, I really won't have to, because he'll still be there, sitting across from me.

I wonder how mad Michael would be if I backed out of being

a groomsman. It's not like we even talk that much. He doesn't text, doesn't call. He likes my Instagram posts every now and then and we see each other at holidays.

You'd probably never guess we're brothers.

He looks so much like Dad.

And I . . . well, pre-testosterone, I looked a lot like Mom. But then my shoulders got broader, my jaw filled out, and I started growing facial hair, no matter how sparse it looks. So now I don't look like her either.

If only 23andMe had some kind of service to wipe the rest of her DNA out of my gene pool.

I can't go to this wedding alone. I can't spend a week in Beverly Hills with Mom and Michael and them bickering with each other, and suits and family meals and parties, and Nana and Grandpa, who will most definitely ask me if I've "switched back to being a girl" or "gotten the down-there surgery."

I'd rather pull out each of my teeth individually. I won't be able to put up with Mother reminding me every chance she gets that I *ruined everything*, or the comments that my family will make about me behind my back.

I let out another groan before standing up and grabbing my suitcase out of my closet. Pants, shirts, underwear, socks, shoes—they all get stuffed inside, so stuffed I can't actually close the damn thing.

I pull the zipper, but it doesn't budge, because of course it doesn't.

"You've packed it too tight," Wyatt observes.

I step into his line of sight and pull the zipper again, and again, and again. It moves half an inch at a time, before it gets impossibly snagged.

"You're going to tear the zipper," he says. "If you packed neater, you wouldn't have this problem."

"*If you packed neater, you wouldn't have this problem.*'" I mock the drawl of his accent. "I don't need your help."

"Clearly."

I pull the suitcase onto the floor, sitting on top of it with all two hundred and twenty pounds of myself on top, pulling at it.

I pull, and I pull, and I pull, and suddenly I'm falling back toward my bed. My head hits the side of my mattress as I stumble, feeling the hardwood floor underneath my butt.

The reality of what happened only occurs to me when I'm sitting there, staring at the torn zipper, part still attached to the frayed teeth of the track and part in my hand.

"Fuck me."

"I told you."

"Just stop," I tell him. "Please, for the love of God, just stop."

I throw the zipper head down on the floor and pull my knees to my chest, hiding my face. Why won't this day just end? Why? It started off so well too: I got my iced coffee, the weather was nice, I took the long way to chemistry, Samuel wasn't a complete idiot and actually made me laugh a few times, and Hoon and I got some work on our Classic Lit project done.

Then Josh had to go and ruin it with three little words.

This is all his fault.

Everything.

"Don't worry, you can fix this easy," Wyatt says, picking up the broken-off part of the zipper.

"Leave it."

"I've got my sewing kit—"

"I said leave it!" I shout, cutting him off. Then I stand up, making the split-second decision to grab my phone and slip my shoes back on.

"Where are you going?" Wyatt asks.

"Out."

"Out where?"

"*Out*," I say, pulling the door loudly shut. I walk past my classmates, taking out my phone and dialing Samuel back.

"Hey—"

"I'll meet you at the bridge," I say before he can get another word out. And then I end the call.

I promise I don't make it a habit of hanging out underneath old bridges that no one uses.

I swear.

Hoon found this place first, near the south side of campus where no one really goes because it's so out of the way. Mark bought a couch from a thrift store and dragged it down here with Samuel, and Julien was always ready to provide something new to drink, typically stolen from his father's liquor cabinet.

Just like that, we had our own little clubhouse, perfect for two white gay trans boys (Samuel and myself), a bisexual Korean boy (Hoon), a Black bi boy (Julien), a Black kid who was supposed to be our token straight but is now going through his own adventure with his sexuality and gender (Mark), and a cis gay white boy (Joshua).

We're like our own gay Power Rangers, minus the color-coordinated rainbow suits.

"There he is!" Samuel shouts as I trudge down the steep dirt hill that we use as a walkway.

"Here I am," I say, making my way toward them. They've got

a fire going even though the sun is still out. Samuel and Julien are occupying the couch. Hoon brought the camping chairs from his room because, like me, he doesn't trust a couch that lives outside. "Where's Mark?" I ask when I notice that we're down a person.

Or two people, I guess.

"He left early with his parents," Hoon says.

Julien hands me a beer out of a bag that looks like it's from the CVS down the street. So that's new.

"No bourbon?" I ask.

"Dad was catching on," he says. "Gotta be careful. He won't miss his cheap beers, though." Julien's parents live in Charlotte, so he typically goes home on the weekends, always bringing back goodies for us.

"Sure." I open the can and take a sip, my mouth twisting at the bitterness. "This is awful."

"Big baby," Julien chides. "Don't like it, don't waste it." He holds out his hand to take the beer away from me, but I snatch it back.

"No way, I need this after the day I've had."

"Oh yeah, we heard about—" Hoon starts to say, but I cut him off.

"Don't mention Josh. This is a Josh-free zone tonight. I don't want to think about him, I don't want to talk about him, I don't even want to hear his name anymore. No more of that." I take my seat next to Hoon in the empty camping chair.

Suddenly, things get quiet, with nothing but the crack of the fire and some far-off cicadas making a racket. The guys are making a tremendous effort to not look at me. I can see where this is going from a mile away.

"So anyway." Samuel leans forward. "What happened between you two?"

"I told you not to say his name."

"Technically he didn't," Hoon cuts in.

I give Hoon a glare before I go back to my drink. I don't even really like alcohol in most forms—I don't think any of us do—it's just become a ritual of sorts. "Whatever. I don't want to talk about it."

"Are things going to get awkward now?" Hoon asks. His face is already flushed from however much he drank before I got here.

"I don't know, Hoon—why don't you ask Josh? He's the one who broke the rules."

"The rules?" Julien asks.

I don't answer him. Things get quiet again, and suddenly I wish I hadn't come here.

"Where is Josh?" Hoon asks.

I stare at him.

"In his room," Julien says. "I checked on him earlier, but he said he wanted to be totally alone. I think you really broke his heart, Neil."

"He'll get over it," I say. End of subject.

Only, Julien doesn't take the cue. He asks, "Did you see his posts? They're pretty depressing."

Ugh, I guess I should see what they're talking about. I go to Josh's Snapchat to look at the stories he's sharing. Broken-heart emojis, Olivia Rodrigo lyrics that imply that, while I didn't cheat, I still betrayed him somehow, a slide saying "i don't want to talk about it."

"In all lowercase too," I say. "That's when you know it's serious."

So melodramatic.

"You could probably be nicer about this whole thing," Julien adds. I'm starting to think he's enjoying this.

"What am I supposed to do?" I ask all of them. "This was just a hookup, friends with benefits. When this whole thing started, we agreed that we'd tell each other if feelings were getting involved, and that if that happened, we'd stop it."

This time it's Hoon who says, after a beat of silence, "Yeah, but . . . you made him cry."

I sit on the knowledge for a bit, a churning in my stomach stirring up every second I sit here. Then I say, "Okay, I'm leaving. I didn't come here to be put on trial." I leave my beer on the ground and start to walk away. If they want to make this such a huge deal, then they can do it without me here.

"No, wait . . ." Samuel stands up, racing over to grab my hand. This close up, I can see the peach fuzz on his face. "We were just talking. Don't be a party pooper."

Samuel most certainly isn't drunk yet, but I can't even tell if he's tipsy or not. He's almost always this bubbly, hyper, chaotic energy that's honestly very exhausting on the best of days.

Then again, he's one of six people at this school who go out of their way to talk to me. (Well . . . five people now.) I should probably do what I can to hang on to the friends I still have.

"No more Josh talk," I warn, looking at him and then the rest of the boys.

"Yeah, of course. No more." Samuel mimes zipping his mouth closed and throwing away the key.

The rest of the boys nod, except for Hoon, who also zips his lips shut.

"Okay." I take my seat again and sip on my beer, which is slowly getting better. Julien then pulls out a small Bluetooth speaker and blasts some music out of it, and we sit there. Just like that, the night has gotten back to normal. Samuel starts watching TikToks on his phone and convinces Hoon to join him on the couch, because Hoon is 100% whipped for Samuel; Julien starts doing his own karaoke; and after being down here for a good hour and a half, Hoon pulls UNO cards out of his bag and starts shuffling them carefully.

I'm out first, emptying my hand in a cruel move that leaves Julien with six freshly drawn cards in his hand.

"No stacking!" he shouts.

"No one said we couldn't stack." I laugh, opening my second beer can of the night.

We prefer to play for as long as we can instead of ending it at the first person out, which means the game lasts for another hour and comes right down to Hoon and Julien.

I don't know when things get so hot, but at some point, I unbutton the top few buttons of my shirt and roll up my sleeves. I feel queasy too. Probably should've eaten something before I came here.

"You look like you're thinking," Samuel says. He's definitely tipsy by now.

"Do not," I say. We've moved to the couch, not even caring about the mold or bugs.

"Yeah, you do." Samuel leans in. "You're getting that crease right there." His finger traces the skin between my brows.

"Stop." I pull away from him.

"You're going to get wrinkles!"

"And you're going to get smacked," I tell him.

Samuel holds his hands out defensively. "Whoa, okay, okay. Enough of that. No need to get upset."

"I'm not upset."

"Yeah, you are." Samuel scoots closer to me. "How are you going to handle this wedding? Josh is still going, right?"

"I don't know. His brother is Michael's best man, so of course Josh and his parents were also invited."

"You're going solo? That won't be much fun."

"Well, I don't exactly have time to find a date," I say. Nor would I want to if I did have the time.

"You know." Samuel wraps an arm around my shoulder. The only time he can get away with something like that is when he's drunk. "If I wasn't going with my parents back to New York, I'd totally go with you."

"As if I'd want to drag you along."

"How dare you!" he says with a sloppy smile. "I'm a catch!"

It's not that I wouldn't want Samuel to come with me. He'd probably provide a good relief from my family, or at least be able to keep me distracted. But there's no way in hell I'd subject him to that. Of course, they may be kinder about being trans to a stranger, but still, I'd rather not risk it.

"You could ask one of the boys."

"Like Hoon?" I tease.

And Samuel blushes right on cue. I should probably feel bad about making fun of his crush, but I swear, it's so obvious the two of them are in love with each other, but they just won't do anything about it. It's frustrating. Especially when I'm the one Samuel comes crying to about it.

"They're all busy," I say. "Besides, I'm not subjecting them to my family."

"What about your roommate?" Samuel asks, his voice a

little quieter due to his embarrassment. "I bet he'd help you out. Wyatt's a nice guy, charming, funny."

"Words used to describe most serial killers," I say. "And since when do *you* have such a boner for Fowler?"

Samuel sits for a beat. "You're being a jerk again."

"No, I'm not. Wait—*again*?"

Samuel leans in even closer. "You're being a jerk to Josh too."

"I don't want to have this conversation."

"But you gotta. You can't just dump him."

"I didn't dump him! We weren't dating!"

Samuel blows a raspberry. "You could've fooled me."

What is that even supposed to mean? I hardly let Josh touch me when we were out in public, and I sure as hell didn't touch him. How could anyone read into that? Unless Josh was telling them what we did behind closed doors . . .

I swear to God.

"I'm leaving." I stand up a little too quickly, wobbling my way away from Samuel.

"Wait, Neil! Come back!" he whines. "I didn't mean it!"

When I start to walk, it feels like I've got concrete shoes on. My feet feel so heavy, and I only make it five steps before I stumble and try to catch myself. Except I don't, and I land right in the dirt.

Shit.

Samuel laughs a bit before he walks over to me, hoisting me up by my arms. "Come on, let's get you back to your room."

"I'm fine. I can do it alone." Does my voice always sound this way? Suddenly my tongue feels very slippery.

"You're drunk," Samuel says.

"You're drunk too."

"Yeah, but I'm less drunk."

I look past him toward the rest of the boys. "Bye, guys!" I wave to the others still sitting around the milk box. "Have a good spring break!"

Samuel wraps one of my arms around his shoulder, and we make our way up the steep dirt path. I trip again, getting my shirt even dirtier. These stains are going to take so much to get out.

Once we're on flat ground, it's an easier walk, even with the uneven brick walkways all over campus. It shouldn't be a long walk, but it feels like it takes forever.

"Come on, Neil. You've got to help me here."

"Don't want to," I say. Because that's the truth. I don't want to walk, and I don't want to go back to my dorm room. I don't want to go to the wedding. I want to go somewhere far away, a cabin in the middle of nowhere with no one around. No Samuel, no Hoon or Julien or Mark.

No Fowler.

And no Josh.

"You had like three beers, you lightweight."

"I didn't eat lunch." Or dinner, for that matter.

"That explains it. Do you have your keys?" Samuel asks me.

"I dunno." Did I grab them?

"Check your pockets."

"You do it."

Samuel grunts, leaning me against the wall and running his hands along my pants pockets.

"Don't touch my butt." I push him away.

"Believe me when I say I want that even less than you do." He stares me up and down. "You forgot your keys?"

"Probably," I grumble.

"Fine." Samuel knocks on the door to my room loudly, again and again and again.

"Shhhh." I bat his hand away. "You'll wake the RA up."

"It's eight thirty."

I hear footsteps through the wood, and Wyatt unlocks the door, opening it slowly. "Yes?"

"Yes?" I mock his accent. "Why do you talk like that?"

I see his expression turn to disappointment.

"He's your problem now." Samuel wrangles himself out from under my arm and waves. "Bye, Neil. Have fun at the wedding."

"Wait, you can't just leave him here! Seriously?" Wyatt calls out, but Samuel is already down the hall with a spring in his step, his strawberry-blond hair bouncing while he moves. Then Wyatt turns to me. "You look awful."

"Shut up."

"You smell awful too." He looks at my shirt. "And you're filthy. Go take a shower."

"You're not my mom," I say, stumbling into the room.

"You need to shower; you can't go to bed sweaty and covered in dirt." Wyatt claps his hands together. "Where is your shower bag?"

I point to my closet.

"Come on," he says after he finds it.

"Where are we going?"

"To the showers, before curfew."

"You don't have to come with me," I say, trying my best to

stand back up. All I end up doing, though, is wobbling some more. Wyatt has to catch me. "I'm a big boy. I can do it."

"I'm more worried about me. Do you know how much trouble I'll get in if you drown yourself or fall down the stairs?"

"That's not going to happen." I wrestle his hands off my shoulders, but even though I told him not to, he follows me anyway. I slide against the wall a few times, catching myself before I fall to the floor.

"How much did you have?" he asks.

"Two beers."

"Wow . . . you really can't handle your alcohol."

"Right? You'd think with the amount of gin and vodka my mother ingests I'd have developed some kind of natural immunity."

"That's not how genetics works," Wyatt tells me, forcing me to stand up straight.

"It was a joke," I say bluntly.

"Forgive me. I'm not used to you making those."

It feels like it takes forever for us to make the few yards to the communal bathroom that all the boys on this floor share. Wyatt brings me to the shower area, stalls on each side of the room with a long bench running down the middle like a locker room.

Just like everything about Steerfield, it seems like the school never got past the original architecture from when it was built in the 1800s.

"Here, go shower." Wyatt shoves the shower bag and towel in my arms.

"Not going to hold my hand while I'm in there?"

Wyatt smirks, his eyebrows hidden by his hair. "Not unless you want me to."

I feel heat behind my ears. "Shut up."

I step past the first curtain into the small changing room where I can leave my filthy uniform as I strip down. I'm trying hard not to think about the idea that Wyatt is so close by, a thick piece of nylon protecting him from seeing me naked. I almost shower in my clothes, just so I don't have to look at myself, but then Wyatt would yell at me, so I step out of where my pants and shoes and underwear are pooled around my ankles and turn the water almost as hot as it'll go, the steam radiating off my body instantly.

I can't resist the urge to stand right under the stream of water, letting it run off me as I scrub at my face with nothing, knowing that it's just going to dry me out.

But Wyatt was right—this does feel good, so I really don't care.

For a bit at least, and then I start to trace my hands down my chest. I started on blockers *just* too late to avoid wearing binders or getting top surgery. I remember my doctors recommending me cream, saying that my scars would eventually fade on their own, but the cream would help. It did help at first, with how tender everything felt, but eventually, when I felt healed, I stopped using it. I don't really know why, maybe because I like my scars. I like showing them off . . . at least to myself.

Then lower, there's my stomach that hangs over my waist, and stretch marks on my hips. These parts of myself that I'm expected to hate so much, that are so ugly to other people whose opinions of my body shouldn't matter.

And they don't.

At least Josh appreciated them. The way his hands moved, it seemed like he couldn't get enough of my chest, and he never cared about my weight.

"You okay in there?" Wyatt's voice echoes off the tiled walls.

"Yes," I say. I reach toward the knob, turning off the water. I stand there for a bit longer, my soaked hair hanging on my forehead. I towel off, slip back into my clothes, and pull back the shower curtain.

"Better now?" Wyatt asks me.

That's when I feel it, the sudden heat in my stomach and the rise of the bile at the back of my throat.

"I'm going to vomit," I say.

"What?"

And then I empty what little contents are in my stomach all over Wyatt's shoes.

"I'll buy you a new pair," I say as Wyatt tucks me into bed, pulling my sheets up to hide my shame. I don't want to see the look on his face.

"It's fine," Wyatt says, though he sounds exhausted.

"Why do you even wear those things?" I ask him, peering over at the freshly scrubbed lime-green Crocs at the foot of his bed.

Seriously. Lime. Green. Crocs.

My vomit did them so many favors.

"Have you seen our classmates?" he replied. "I don't trust any of them to treat their athlete's foot properly."

"Fair enough." I turn over. "I'll still buy you a new pair."

"It's fine."

I know that it isn't; I can tell from the tone of his voice. And how am I ever going to live down Fowler having to take care of me while I was drunk? He'll never let me forget it, but he'll never actually use it against me because he's too nice. He'll just let the guilt hang there.

"This day has fucking sucked," I say, not caring one bit if Wyatt is paying attention.

"You're telling me."

"It's all Josh's fault."

"Is it?"

"Yes."

"Are you so sure?" Wyatt's voice is quiet.

"Yeah."

"Did you two break up?"

"I'm so sick of being asked that," I mumble.

"Okay, forget that I said anything. You're right. Josh totally ruined your day."

I should probably find it patronizing, but right now I don't think I could even pretend to care. "Thanks."

I hear Wyatt snicker, and the thud of him putting something on his desk. "For what?"

He wants me to thank him for taking me to the shower, for making sure I brushed my teeth three or four times, for cleaning up the mess I made.

He wants the moral high ground.

People like him like it there.

"For agreeing with me," I say.

He laughs again. "Good night, Kearney."

"Night, Fowler."

I lie there for just a little bit longer, my breath slowing, the alcohol finally wearing off a degree, the rancid taste in my mouth barely detectable thanks to the mint flavor of the toothpaste and mouthwash I used.

"I want a do-over," I grumble. Like one of those movies where the main character gets to live the same day over and over again. Josh made me watch one of those. *Happy Death Day*, that's what I want. Just without all the killing.

Well . . .

Maybe a little killing.

I want a do-over . . .

But no one will give me one.

Friday

APRIL 15

Everything hurts when I wake up.

My head, my jaw, my eyes, my hands for some reason.

"God, fuck me." I try to sit up slowly, but the moment I do, I regret it. The room starts to spin again, and there's something so bright that it's blinding me and making me see spots, the sound of a guitar from somewhere. "What the fuck?"

"Good morning to you too!" I hear Wyatt say from somewhere; I haven't dared opened my eyes again. All I know is that he's being far too loud for so early in the morning.

"What the hell?" I bury my head under the pillow. "Why are you up so early?"

"It is one in the afternoon."

"Fuck."

"Language."

"Shut up." I roll over, covering my eyes with my hands. "It's break, right? Classes are still off?"

"Yes."

I peek down at the floor, spotting a pile of clothes that are covered in dirt and grass stains. Wyatt's just sitting on his bed, guitar in his lap as he strums away, his fingers plucking the strings so effortlessly. I don't recognize the song.

"Hey, if you're going to go milk the cows or whatever, the least you could do is pick up your dirty clothes."

Wyatt looks at me, a slow grin spreading on his lips. "Those are yours."

"No, they aren't." Because if those are mine, that means that last night wasn't a dream. I stretch my arm, barely snagging the shirt by the collar and yanking it toward me.

Size XL, according to the tag. I'm fairly sure Wyatt is a large, but don't quote me on that. He might be fond of oversized flannel shirts, but his school uniform fits like it's been tailored.

So last night was real, but . . . how much of last night?

"What even happened?" I ask him.

"Samuel dropped you off, you showered because you were covered in dirt, then you threw up on my shoes and had to shower again, and then you passed out cold."

"I threw up on your Crocs?"

"Next time, if you think my shoes are ugly, you can just tell me," he says with a grin before he goes back to whatever it was he was doing before I woke up—still packing, by the looks of it. "I thought you might be dead there for a second. I had to make sure you were breathing."

"You watched me while I slept?" I ask him. "And you made me shower? Creep."

"Don't flatter yourself," Wyatt tells me. "And can you please do something about your phone?"

"Huh?"

"It keeps ringing, someone named 'Do Not Answer.'"

Fuck.

I dig around for my phone for a bit, finding it underneath my sheets. And sure enough, there are five missed calls, which won't be good for me.

"Do you need anything?" Wyatt asks. "Tylenol? Water?"

"What? No, just leave me alone."

"Good to see you're back to normal." He sighs. "I gotta pee."

"Thanks for the update."

My phone blinds me when I turn it on, and after a second or two of struggling with the brightness settings, I can finally see everything.

Wyatt grabs his wallet and slips on his shoes, and just as he opens the door, he straightens.

"Oh, hey, Josh!" he says.

Fuck!

"Hi, Wyatt. Is Neil here?"

The way the door swings into my room, it totally hides my bed, so Josh won't have seen me yet. Wyatt looks in my direction, as if that's not suspicious at all. But still, I mouth, "No!" hoping that he'll get the message.

Wyatt nods, understanding.

Thank God.

"Yeah, he's in bed. Why don't you come in?" Wyatt stands back, holding the door open like the gentleman he is, and Josh just strolls right on in. "This feels like a private conversation, so I'll leave you two alone."

"Yeah, thanks," Josh says.

Wyatt shoots me a finger gun, and I give him the middle finger. If looks could kill, Wyatt would be six feet under right now.

As for Josh—I'm not going to leave space for the awkward preamble. Josh is here for a reason, a glaringly obvious reason, and the sooner we get this over with, the sooner he'll be out the door.

"What is it, Josh?" I ask.

"I just . . . I wanted to talk to you."

This isn't going to end anytime soon, is it? I lean over, picking up a shirt off the floor and throwing it over my head. Yes, Josh has seen me 100% naked; I think he's probably seen me any percentage naked. But that was before, and this is now.

"I don't think there's anything left to talk about." I slip my arms through the sleeves. "That's that."

"Well, I didn't know if maybe we could . . ." Josh clears his throat. "I just wanted to talk, about what went wrong."

"Josh—"

"No, please. Just listen to me. I wish I could control my feelings, but I can't. I know we agreed that we'd stop if there were any feelings. But I didn't want to lose you."

"Well, you're not going to lose me. As far as I'm concerned, the two of us are still friends. So long as you want to be."

"You're so prepared to just move past us? What we had?"

"How many times do I have to tell you, there was nothing between us. No feelings, no romance. At least, not from my point of view." I look away from him. "We had a good thing going, but like all good things, it had to end. So it's over."

"I wish you'd just have a conversation with me about this."

"What would you say we're doing right now?"

"You're deflecting."

"Please, you're not my therapist, Josh."

"No, but I'm your friend, apparently."

I sigh. "Listen, Josh. It's over. That's it, and I, personally, am ready to move on past this whole situation."

"So, there were no feelings? You felt absolutely nothing for me?"

"Why is that so hard to believe?"

He shrugs. "I don't know. It seemed like things were . . . changing."

There's no going back.

I pause, clenching my teeth so hard my jaw starts to ache. I shouldn't listen to him.

But Josh is my friend. After things started to get bad, Mom was looking for a place to send me, a place to "build character"—which turned out to be code for *a place far enough away so that I don't have to deal with you.*

So she sent me as far as she could. She's known Josh's parents for years—they helped her build her empire of hotels and even managed a few of their own. It was an easy choice. A week later, I was enrolled in the same school as Josh, and a month after that, I was dropped off at the airport with three suitcases and a swift goodbye.

It was tough at first, new school, new city, new state. But Josh was there, and I was grateful. He introduced me to Samuel and Hoon and Mark and Julien, and for the first time in a long time, it actually felt like I had friends, not people who wanted to be friends with me for my money or my connections.

I want Josh to still be my friend. I'm already kind of missing what we've lost.

Why can't he just let this go?

I don't want to give him hope, but I don't want to ruin things.

"I just wish that you would talk to me," Josh says, walking toward Wyatt's perfectly made bed and taking a seat on the edge of the mattress. "Instead of shutting me down."

"What is there to listen to, though? I don't get it."

Josh opens his mouth . . . then he closes it again, the words lost.

I press on. "Exactly. What we had between us, it was nice, Josh, I'll totally admit that. But you read too much into it."

It's like I can watch his heart break in real time. He doesn't cry, there are no tears, but there's a light behind his eyes that vanishes.

"I still love you, as one of my best friends," I say. "But I want you to let this crush shit go, understand?"

"I don't believe you," he says.

The words actually surprise me for a moment, especially coming from Josh.

"What?"

"I don't believe that it was nothing to you. I don't believe that for a second."

"Well, I don't care what you believe." I keep my voice firm. "I know what's going on in my own head."

"Yeah, right." Josh clasps his hands together nervously.

"What does that mean?"

"I don't think it's that simple."

"Well, it is."

"You're telling me that you didn't feel anything for me? Not even a bit?"

Maybe he's right; maybe there were some feelings? I mean, who wouldn't fall at least a little bit for the small kisses on the forehead, being brought breakfast sandwiches in the morning, ankles connecting under the table while we studied, sharing AirPods on a walk, and listening to the same songs?

But I was never in love with Josh.

"Yes. Not even a bit."

Josh's head sinks, and it's times like this that I wish I could read minds. Not, like, permanently—that'd be a huge invasion of privacy. But right now, it'd been good to know what he's thinking, what's knocking around in that noggin of his.

I exhale slowly, rubbing the back of my head where my hair is sticking up. I probably went to sleep with it wet.

It's in this beat of silence that I think of my way out.

Clearly, the "it's not you, it's me" excuse won't work. And "it's not me, it's you" might make things too touchy. But there is one clause, one that Josh and I implemented.

Just in case.

"Okay, Josh. I didn't . . . look, it might be a weird time to spring this on you. But if you want to know the truth, I'm going to tell it to you. Something happened; I wasn't looking for it. It just . . . happened. And—I'm just going to say it. I've started to see someone. That's really why we have to stop." My monologue was probably a little dramatic, but I've got to sell the lie.

The Pull-Out Clause. Josh's own invention. The perfect way out.

He stares at me, and I can see the gears turning behind his eyes.

Sure enough, it's his turn to blurt out, "*What?*"

"I'm seeing someone. I've had feelings for this person for a while, but we made it official last night."

"When did it start?"

"We've been dancing around it for a few weeks now, but we sealed the deal last night. Which means that you're legally obligated to drop this whole discussion."

"I'm not *legally obligated*, Neil. This isn't a courtroom; there were no contracts. I still have questions."

"But we agreed," I gently remind him. "If one of us develops feelings for another person and things get serious, we end it."

"You're being such a dick."

"Can't be what you don't have."

The look Josh gives me tells me he doesn't appreciate the perfectly timed comment.

"All I want to do is have a conversation with you, and you can't even give me that?"

"I'm asking you to respect this boundary," I tell him.

"And I'm asking you to treat me like a person."

I pause, and we sit in the silence of the dorm room. I can't stop myself from biting the inside of my cheek, waiting for whatever's about to come next.

What do I have to do to convince him that we're over, we're done, that we'll go back to being friends and that's it, we'll just have to forget about everything that happened between us?

"I just . . . I don't like how things have been left," Josh finally says.

I'll admit, I don't like how we've left things either, but I really don't think that I'm in a place where I can have this conversation with him.

Josh keeps talking. "And some new guy? This is the first time I've heard about this."

"It happened very suddenly," I lie.

"Who is it? Do I know him? It's not Samuel, is it? Hoon?"

"No! Why was that your first guess? Doesn't matter, it's—" I stare around my room, almost as if my lie is going to materialize out of thin air.

And then, magically, he does. He walks right in the door. Six foot one, skin kissed from the sun, curly dirty-blond hair, with a sharp nose and a gap in his teeth, tiny hoops in his ears, dressed in an oversized flannel over a Bon Iver shirt, wiping his hands on his jeans. He glances around a bit before he asks, "Everything okay in here?"

My mouth forms the plan before my brain can.

Which, I'll admit, is probably my biggest fault as a person.

"It's Wyatt," I say.

"What?!" Josh gasps out, shocked.

"What's me?" Wyatt inquires, looking more confused than normal.

I leap off the bed, going over to Wyatt and doing my best to distract him.

"What's going on?" he asks.

"And actually, Josh, we've got to pack for the wedding—" I walk over to the door, swinging it open, forgetting momentarily that I'm only in my shirt and underwear.

"Yeah, right. Like I'd try packing with you again," Wyatt mutters. Then he turns to explain to Josh. "You should've seen him yesterday. He wouldn't let me anywhere near his zipper. Like fine, we could easily fix your problem but you want to keep stuffing things inside when nothing else will fit."

Josh has this look of confusion on his face, but Wyatt just keeps going. And me, well . . . I just stand there, dumbfounded at what's actually coming out of Wyatt's mouth.

"Next thing we know, he's on the floor, zipper burst open, everything spilling out."

"Yeah," I say, moving a little closer and touching him playfully, but not so playfully that he'll be suspicious. "You sure knew how to tell me 'I told you so.'"

It's clear from the way Josh is looking at us that he doesn't completely buy this, but he also isn't completely sure that he doesn't completely buy this.

If Josh asks Wyatt a single question, everything will fall apart. So, I walk over to Josh, give him a big hug, and whisper, "Thanks for understanding." Then I start to guide him to the door, grateful that the boy is light as a feather.

"Sorry to cut the visit short," I say once he's safely in the hall. "But yeah, packing!"

"Neil—" Josh tries to interrupt, but I don't give him a chance.

"We'll see you at the wedding," I say quietly through the small opening I've left between the door and the doorframe, so Wyatt doesn't hear. "I'll totally catch you up." I give him a smile that probably looks more like a grimace.

And with that, I shut the door. I press my ear to the wood, listening to the sounds of footsteps. A lot of kids are leaving today, packing their belongings for their spring break trips, so there's a lot of movement.

"What's going on?" Wyatt asks from behind me.

"Shh!"

"Don't shush me," Wyatt says. "If you wanted my help packing, you should've let me help yesterday before you broke your suitcase."

"Just shut up for a second. I need to think."

"Don't tell me to shut—"

I hold a finger to his mouth.

"Hush." I can do this; this will work out, I just need to think.

If Wyatt is this boy who I'm supposedly in love with now, then that means he'll need to come to California with me. I suppose it's plausible to sell Josh on the lie without Fowler being there, but it would cast doubt. Besides, if Fowler is there with me, he can act as a buffer, both for Josh and my family, even if that does mean spending an entire week with him. All I have to do is act all lovey-dovey with Wyatt, convince Josh that we're actually dating, then we're sold. He'll drop the feelings he has for me and move on to someone else who can give him what he's clearly so desperate for.

Flawless.

My finger still on his lips, I look Wyatt in the eye and say, "I need you to do something for me."

Wyatt finally bats my hand away. "What? You can't have my suitcase; I need it."

"Come to Beverly Hills with me for a week and pretend to be my boyfriend."

Wyatt stares at me, looking as confused as I feel. Ordinarily I'd make a joke about how that's the way his face always looks, but I want something from him now, so I probably shouldn't do that.

"I'm sorry . . . please repeat that."

"Come to Beverly Hills with me for spring break," I say a little slower. "Pretend that we're dating and in love so that I can prove to Josh that he and I are officially over and he needs to move on."

"You're not still drunk, are you?" he asks me before he puts the back of his hand to my forehead. "Or are you sick? Do you have a fever?"

"Stop it!" I slap his hand away.

"If you're going to vomit again, at least let me take my socks off."

"Just hear me out." I start to pace between our two beds; Wyatt steps out of my way. "Josh is hung up on me, which I should've seen coming because the dude is clingy as fuck. But we had this clause in our arrangement. If I'm dating someone else, he has to drop his feelings, and it just so happens the person I'm dating is you."

"Charming. Are we so sure Josh is the problem here?"

I shoot Wyatt a glare. "He didn't believe me when I said I didn't have any feelings for him. So, obviously, I have to prove him wrong. And moving on with you is my ticket to that."

"*Obviously,*" Wyatt says in a mocking tone.

"I bring you to Beverly Hills and he'll lose interest. He'll accept the breakup. It's perfect."

"I hate you so much," Wyatt says bluntly. "What kind of wedding even lasts a whole week?"

"Ever heard of those traditional four-day weddings? Yeah, my family believes that more is more. Because, you know, life is a competition against everyone else," I tell him. "It'll be easy, and all you have to do is come to California with me."

"Why would I do that?"

"Out of the kindness of your heart?"

"Yeah, no."

"Why not?"

"One, because it's a stupid plan and you're going to get caught. Two, because you're being mean to Josh, and he doesn't deserve that. And three, because I really don't want to, and even if I did, do you honestly think my moms will let me go all the way across the country with a stranger?"

"I'm not a *stranger.* We've lived together for months!"

"Name one thing about me." Wyatt crosses his arms. "What's my favorite color?"

He wears a lot of flannel, and his backpack is red.

"Red?"

"Song?"

Oh, I know this one! But what was the title?

"That Phoebe Bridgers song. The one where she's sad, but not really."

"Movie?"

"One of those Avengers movies probably. Everyone likes those."

"Food?"

"This one is obvious—you love Wendy's."

Wyatt starts counting on his fingers. "Yellow. 'All That' by Carly Rae Jepsen. *Chungking Express*. And Wendy's isn't a food. My favorite kind of food is a chorizo burrito with refried beans and rice."

"Okay, but I know lots of other things!" I declare.

"Like what?"

"You play the guitar."

"No shit, Sherlock."

"You hate algebra."

He always takes forever to do his algebra homework, and he's always complaining about failing his tests.

"Who would like math?"

"Oh, and you like anime! You're always rewatching that demon one."

"Jujutsu Kaisen," he corrects me.

"Yeah, that one. And I know that you like early Taylor Swift better than her new stuff, which is just such a wrong opinion."

Wyatt shrugs. "She peaked with *Fearless*. I'm not afraid to say that."

"But that's not the point. We don't have to know every little detail about each other; we can make all of that up later. What's important is that, if you're there and Josh sees it, he'll drop this weird crush he has on me."

"Okay, but what happens if we mess up? If we make a mistake or we aren't believable? What happens when we're back at school?"

"You don't think a week is enough for him to get over it?"

"You really aren't a people person, are you?"

"We'll figure it out. You can break up with me when we're back, and then if Josh makes a move again, I'll just tell him you broke my heart and I'm not ready."

"Can't break what you don't have," he quips, not even giving me time to respond. "It's messy, and you're going to get caught. So, count me out."

"I'll pay you," I offer.

That makes Wyatt pause. "What did you say?"

"I'll pay you," I say again, staring at the worn shirt Wyatt's wearing, with his frayed jeans and bare feet. He needs a lot of new things, like a new laptop, a new uniform, new clothes, a new phone. Money can get him all those things easily. "I'll pay you to be my fake boyfriend."

"You're lucky I haven't punched you yet."

"I'm just offering. You obviously need the money—"

"Oh, I obviously need the money?" He raises his voice, something I don't think I've ever heard him do. Clearly I've said the wrong thing. But I can still recover here.

"It's just to pay you for your time, I didn't mean anything by it."

Wyatt scoffs, finally stepping away to go back to his desk. "You did. You meant everything by it. And you can find someone else to help you."

"I don't have time," I tell him. "The flight leaves tomorrow."

"Then you'd better get to work."

"None of my friends are available," I tell him. "There is no time. Plus, I need a queer dude who won't mind holding hands or kissing a guy on the cheek."

Wyatt turns away from me. "You should still find someone else to help you."

I lean forward, putting my hands on his desk. "I didn't mean anything by the money comment, I swear."

"Well, you can't always get what you want."

"I'm on my hands and knees here, Fowler—"

"No, you aren't," he says.

"I'll do it if you want me to." I'm so desperate that I'm actually considering it.

Wyatt looks away. "I don't want you to beg. I'm not interested in that."

"Okay, then . . . what do you want?"

"Do you realize that the entire time you've been asking me to do this you never even said the word *please*? And that's the thing with you, Neil. You're so spoiled that you expect everyone to do anything you ask because you have money, or you feel like you have some kind of right to the people around you. You're asking me to do this huge thing for you, to lie for you, and you never even once said the word *please*." Wyatt stands up, grabbing the economics book that was open on his desk and sliding it into his backpack. "The answer is still no."

"Listen, I'm sorry for the way I've treated you. You're right, I've been a shitty person."

Wyatt shuts me up by holding up his hand. "Forget it."

He's walking away from me; this opportunity is slipping

from between my fingers. Maybe if I had more time to think about it, I could find an alternative, but the flight is in less than twenty-four hours. We're running out of time here.

"Wyatt!" I grab for his hand, and he stops.

His palms are warm, and I can feel his pulse in his wrist. Wyatt stops in his tracks and stares down at our hands. I look around the room for anything that I can use, anything that I can do to get him to stop.

The guitar.

Then it clicks.

"I'll get you an audition with my brother!"

Wyatt stops.

Got him.

At least for the next few seconds.

"What?"

"My brother, he's an executive at Periscope Records. One of his duties is finding new talent to sign. I'll get you an audition with him."

Wyatt blows a raspberry. "You're full of shit."

"No, look!" I grab my phone, going right to Instagram and typing in Michael's name. Right there, in his bio, Periscope Records. Then there are photos and photos of him with singers, both artists who are with Periscope and artists who aren't, him at awards shows, the Grammys, the recording studio. And there, a few pics down, is one of us both at the last Christmas at Mom's house.

"See, that's my brother! It's his wedding that we're going to. You come with me, and I'll talk to him. I'll get you an audition with a record label."

Wyatt pauses, biting at the inside of his cheek. "What makes you think that I want that?"

I could bring up the songs he's posted to Instagram and TikTok, which he obviously posted in the hopes of going viral. Honestly, when I discovered his accounts after some swift googling, I thought I'd have a night full of laughs, but I was surprised when he was actually pretty good. Wyatt's voice is smooth, like honey, and his fingers move effortlessly on the strings of the guitar. Not that I'd ever tell him that.

He's never sung that much in front of me. I don't know if it's stage fright, or if he's afraid I'll make fun of him. Which is probably a fair assumption, honestly.

"Because I know you love music," I say. "And this is a once-in-a-lifetime chance."

I drop his hand and it falls to his side. He's still thinking about it.

"I really need your help with this," I say, pressing him a bit more.

"Why me?" he asks.

"Because there's no one else who can do it," I say. "And because I'm asking you nicely. So please, help me with this."

Wyatt closes his eyes and breathes in deeply, letting the air out through his nose.

He licks his lips quickly. "I'll have to talk to my moms about this."

"You will?"

"If they say no, that's it. I'm done. I'm not going with you and you'll have to find someone else. Or go alone. I don't care."

"Yeah, of course," I tell him. "And the offer does still stand. I want to pay you for doing this."

"I don't want your money," he says. "And the audition won't be enough."

What more could he want? This is a free trip to Beverly Hills, a free stay in a five-star luxury hotel, free food, an audition that could make his future. What else could I possibly give him?

"I want you to be nice to me," he says.

"What?"

"I want you to be nice to me," he repeats. "I want to see if you can do it."

"Yeah, fine . . . sure."

"Seriously?" Wyatt eyes me, like he thinks I'm about to pull the rug out from underneath him.

"I can do it," I promise.

"You really think so?"

"You're doubting me?"

He snorts. "I think you'll last five minutes after we land."

"You're on." I'll be too busy with my family and avoiding Josh to even think about insulting Fowler, so this works out perfectly. I'll still pay him, though; anyone who is being forced to spend an entire week with my extended family certainly deserves some form of monetary compensation. "Give me your ID. I'll book your ticket now."

Wyatt grabs his wallet and tosses it to me. "First class, please."

"You'll take what I give you." I look down at the ID, spying his October 31 birthday. Huh, a Halloween baby.

"I'm going to call my moms. Remember—"

"If they say no, you won't go," I mimic. "I get it."

Wyatt sighs, grabs his phone, and walks out the door. I pull up the website for the plane tickets, and while all the available seats load, I figure now is as good a time as any for me to start actually packing.

But I don't see my suitcase.

After searching for a bit, I find it stuffed underneath my bed. I pull it out quickly, throwing it on my bed to inspect the damage from yesterday. But instead of the zipper being frayed and broken, like I remember leaving it, it looks like it's been repaired, and there's a new red thread that runs around the entire edge of the suitcase.

Did Wyatt . . . ?

No, he couldn't have. This seems too professional for someone like him. But didn't he say that he had a sewing kit that he could repair it with?

Did Fowler fix my suitcase?

I stare at the handiwork, inspecting every new thread and testing it out every which way to see if the zipper actually does work again. Then I glance toward his side of the room, at his made-up bed and the pillow where he rests his head every single night.

I stare at the door he walked out of just minutes ago.

Maybe there's more to him than I thought?

Saturday

APRIL 16

"Wake up!"

"Ah!" I gasp for air as my eyes shoot open and I get an excellent view of my sheets and folded-over pillow, breathing heavily, my chest heaving out of control.

"I literally couldn't have woken you up any quieter than that, and it still scared you?" Wyatt asks.

"I don't like being woken up," I say.

I roll over to face him.

"What's going on?" I mumble without really opening my mouth.

"We've got a flight to catch," he says.

"What?"

"Remember? The wedding, Beverly Hills, your brother. Any of this ringing a bell?"

"Yeah, yeah, yeah." I bat him away. "Five more minutes."

"You said that ten minutes ago, though now I'm starting to believe you were just sleep-talking." I hear footsteps on the hardwood floor, and suddenly my comforter has been pulled away from me. "Now get up."

"You're mean." I try to pull my comforter back up, but he must've left it on the floor. "What time is it?"

"Seven fifteen," he says. "Are you going to shower?"

"No, we'll have time at the hotel."

"Okay, well, I am, so be out of bed by the time I'm back."

"Yes, Mother!" I stick my tongue out at Wyatt as he grabs his shower bag and heads out the door. With him gone, I collapse back onto the bed, feeling the softness of the pillow underneath my head. I don't even care that it's cold in our room; I can sleep like this easy.

Even though I'd been counting on it, it was still a surprise when Wyatt told me that both of his moms had approved the trip. Something about them thinking that their son had never gotten a proper spring break—I hadn't really paid attention.

There were rules, of course. Wyatt had to call them every night, turn on the location settings on his phone, and not go anywhere without me there to babysit him.

Once the trip had been approved, I'd broken down every step of the week for Wyatt. The brunches, lunches, dinners, rehearsals, parties, reunions, the actual wedding itself, the reception.

Mother is bound and determined to make this a memorable affair. You'd almost think it was her wedding and not her firstborn's.

I shouldn't fall back asleep, even though we'll just be going through PreCheck, so I'm not sure why Wyatt is so pressed to get to the airport three hours early. I roll over and grab my phone, seeing the text messages from last night that I ignored.

A new group chat has been invented, sans Josh.

> SAMUEL: YOU'RE DATING WYATT FOWLER???????? YOU HATE HIM!!!!!!!
> HOON: What is going on?
> JULIEN: what?
> MARK: im gone one day and I miss so much.

SAMUEL: Josh just told me Neil's going to the LA wedding with Wyatt?

SAMUEL: Apparently, they hooked up the other night???

SAMUEL: Confirm or deny Neil

HOON: Dude what?

HOON: He's such a goody-goody

MARK: yeah what a dork, how'd that even happen???

JULIEN: are you sure Josh isn't just making it up? or maybe he heard neil wrong

SAMUEL: No! He told me!

The conversation kept going on for another hour, all without me sending a single response. God, this was going to be a pain in the ass to explain. I could just ignore them, wait the week out, then pretend that nothing happened, act like I'm too heartbroken to talk about it.

I finally pick myself up out of bed. Wyatt's bag is already packed neatly on his bed, all the clothing we picked out for him tucked away. We'll have to go somewhere to get him fitted for a suit, probably while I'm getting my own tailored. He really had the audacity to say he could just wear his school uniform to the wedding!

I couldn't tell if he was joking—but still, the idea was enough to scare me.

Wyatt comes back minutes later, just as I'm slipping on my Vans. "I ordered a Lyft," I tell him. "It'll be here soon."

"Okay." Wyatt runs the towel over his still-damp hair once again. When it's wet, the blond curls almost turn brown, and it hangs heavier on his head.

"All ready to go?" he asks, throwing the towel in his hamper and grabbing at his bags.

"Got everything?"

"I think so."

I grab my own bag. "Then let's go."

The Lyft meets us by the roundabout driveway near the front of the school. I sit comfortably in the back seat with Wyatt, unsure if I should talk to him or not. I'd much rather sleep.

I'm just about to close my eyes when he turns to me and says, "Do you think we should rehearse?"

"Rehearse what?"

"Our story, I guess?" He rolls his head back and forth like he's trying to choose his words carefully. "What if your family asks questions about me? What would you tell them?"

"I'd make something up, but I'll make sure you don't sound too interesting," I tell him.

"Maybe *they'll* find me interesting?"

"Don't take this the wrong way, Fowler, but my family is made up of some of the worst, most shallow people you're ever going to meet. They're needlessly cruel, mean, and selfish, so if they find you interesting, you shouldn't take that as a compliment."

"So they really are your family," he says.

I don't have the energy to do anything but glare at him.

"Still, don't you think we should have a story? Like what happened the other night and how we started dating? Don't you think Josh will be curious?"

"It's none of his business, but if he asks, we can just say I was tipsy, we made out, and the next morning we agreed that we liked each other enough to keep it going. Easy-peasy."

"You really think he'll buy that?"

"It's a story; it's not a big deal. How we act around each other is what's really going to matter. We have to sell the relationship."

"I still don't like it."

"We'll be fine. No one is going to care about when we started dating. Josh knows enough details to drive him up the wall."

Wyatt goes quiet, and suddenly all I can hear is the rush of the wind, and the other cars that are passing us. Even the talk show on the radio is at a low enough volume that I can barely make out any of the words. I pull out my phone, scrolling through Instagram for a few minutes, watching stories. Josh has some more melodramatic posts about his heart being broken.

There's some masochistic part of me that wants to message him, but instead I go to his profile, scrolling down a bit to get to the pictures of us. Some with the boys, some just the two of us, one of just me. I really hope that Josh can forgive me after all of this is said and done. He is my best friend—or the closest thing I have to one, at least—and I don't want to lose that relationship. Maybe this is all my fault; I was the one who instigated this entire situation, who made a move as we watched a movie one night. *The Conjuring*, of all choices.

"Do you ever think that you're being needlessly cruel?" Wyatt asks.

"Hmmm?" I don't look at Wyatt; I just keep staring at the screen.

"You're doing all of this, dragging me along with you, just to prove . . . what exactly?"

"That I've moved on."

"From what?"

I open my mouth, but I don't have an answer. "From . . . from us."

"But you said there was no 'us' between you two."

"I know that. I just have to get him to understand it too."

"But he loves you. Don't you think you could've loved him back?"

"No. Besides, we're in high school. It'd never last. It'd be dumb to think that."

"You don't have to be so cynical."

"I'm not cynical, I'm realistic. If you never have any expectations, you'll never be disappointed." I have my parents to thank for that lesson.

"That seems like a miserable way to live," Wyatt says.

"Yeah, well, nothing I can do about it." I put my phone back in my pocket, facing toward the window so Wyatt knows this conversation is over.

If I wanted to unpack all that, I would've stayed in therapy.

Because of Wyatt's guitar, we have to check something of his, and he refuses for it to not be beside him at every step of this flight, so he checks his suitcase, leaving him with the guitar and a backpack.

"What if they break it? I've had this guitar for eight years."

"It would've been fine," I say, setting my bag down for a moment. "You've got your ticket, right?"

Wyatt pulls out his phone and double-checks before nodding.

"Good, I'll see you on the other side, then." I pick up my bag and start walking toward PreCheck, but then a hand wraps around my wrist, yanking me back.

"Where are you going?" Wyatt asks.

"What?"

"TSA is that way." He points with his free hand. This early in the morning, there's only one line open, and it's stretched far past those retractable railing things.

"Yeah, well, I've got Global Entry, so I'm not standing in that."

"Then let me do PreCheck with you."

"It's a process," I tell him. "You can't just walk through with me. Do you even have a passport?"

"Why would I have a passport?"

"Okay, then, good luck. I'll meet you at the gate."

"No. I'm not going through TSA alone. You have to go with me."

"I really don't," I tell him.

"If I have to suffer with your awful family for a week, the least you can do is wait with me."

"You say that like I don't have to deal with my family either."

"Neil." Wyatt stands there, his arms crossed like he's scolding me for getting a bad grade on a test or something.

I breathe in aggressively, letting it out through my nose. "Fine."

"Good, let's go."

It takes half an hour to get through TSA because they're training a dog to sniff for bombs or drugs or something. Toward the beginning of the line, people have to go one at a time, letting the dog smell them as they pass. We finally make it, scanning our tickets and giving the TSA agents our IDs before we have to unload our laptops, take off our shoes, and Wyatt has to lift his guitar case carefully onto the conveyor belt.

"You don't have to do this in Global Entry," I tell Wyatt, standing there in my socks, and he gives me a look. "Just saying."

Wyatt goes first and is patted down lightly by security before he's passed on, and then it's my turn. My heart thuds in my chest when I see what the screen for the scan looks like, the areas of my body highlighted in bright red.

God, this is mortifying.

The agent directs me out and suddenly I'm surrounded by two other agents, all of them whispering to one another before one of them has the balls to ask, "Are you a boy or a girl?"

"What?"

"Boy or girl. We need to know so an agent can pat you down."

"What's wrong?" I ask.

"Our scanner detected an abnormality," another agent says.

An abnormality? What the absolute fuck is this scanner picking up on that it can tell I'm trans? This absolutely has to be some kind of human rights violation.

"I'm not abnormal," I say, feeling a heaviness in my head. "My ID says male—don't I look like a boy?"

"Sir—" The agent pauses, like he isn't sure if *sir* was the right word to use for me. "Just step to the side and pick an agent to pat you down. We don't want to cause any problems."

"Seems like you're doing a bang-up job of that already," I tell him, stepping to the side like a good little boy. I can see Wyatt standing a ways away, our bags and shoes already collected at his feet.

Then I make the mistake of looking back at all the people waiting, their impatient faces, counting down the seconds until their flight leaves, annoyed that I'm causing a stink about this. Because how dare a trans person ask to be treated with even just a bit of humanity? How dare I ask for just an ounce of respect in a fucking airport of all places? Do they think I've got an explosive in my crotch? Is that it? Am I going to blow up a plane with a cock bomb?

I pick one of the presumably male agents and stand wide as he pats me down, his hands getting too close to my crotch for comfort. Then he pats my chest, and I can feel his hand along my scars.

I want to disappear.

I want to vanish into thin air, never to be seen ever again.

This is so fucking humiliating.

In any other context I might be proud of the scars on my chest. I can remember not wanting to wear a shirt around the house for weeks after returning home—sure, it took some more courage to take my shirt off at the beach, or to walk to the mailbox without anything covering my chest. But now all I feel is shame. Even if the agent can't possibly see the scars through my shirt, I feel them there.

"Okay, you're good."

I give him my most condescending smile. "You're doing excellent work here, keeping our skies safe from the transgenders."

He shakes his head. "Just get out of here, kid, before I call security."

"Oh, so scary."

I walk across the floor with my socked feet, slipping into my shoes easily.

"What happened? Are you okay?" Wyatt asks, his hands on my shoulder as if he's trying to comfort me.

"It's fine." I'm probably being added to no-flight lists as we speak.

"That didn't seem fine. We should find someone and complain about—"

"I said it's fine, Fowler. Now drop it, please."

"Neil, you should—"

"I should what? Further embarrass myself just to be told that I misunderstood and that what they did wasn't transphobic as hell? That they were just 'doing their job.' I've been dealing with this for a while, Fowler—trust me when I say it isn't worth it. I'm not going to change the entire TSA in the Charlotte airport at eight in the morning." I pause. "Let's just go." I grab my bag and walk over to the large screen displaying our gates and times. "We're 7319, right there. Gate A-24." I point. Right on time too.

"Okay," Wyatt whispers, as if he's not allowed to talk anymore.

In silence, we make our way to the gate, which is already pretty crowded. We take some seats, and I lean back, staring at the ceiling, trying to calm myself down from what just happened.

"We can report the agents," Wyatt says.

"What agents?" He doesn't know what he's talking about. "It won't do anything."

"I am sorry, Neil."

"Stop apologizing. Just stop talking about it, please." I don't need his apology.

"I just didn't think they'd be such assholes about . . ."

"About me being trans?" I finish for him. "Yeah, welcome to my world."

I stand up.

"Where are you going?"

"To get some breakfast," I say. "You stay here with our stuff."

Wyatt looks like he wants to say something else, but I don't give him the chance. I just start walking, finding the nearest Starbucks. I get it; he didn't know that that would happen. Hell, *I* didn't realize it would be that bad, even though when I first started looking up information about transitioning, there were whole articles written by trans people about their awful experiences in something as simple as the TSA line, or when they were getting food or shopping for clothes in the men's section over the women's.

But Wyatt doesn't get it. He's cis; he's never had to deal with this. And the last thing I want is some cis dude breathing down my neck, making a big deal about apologizing so he isn't *contributing to the problem* or whatever's running through that frizzy blond head of his.

I just wish Wyatt would stop apologizing and stop trying to get me to fight back. That never does anything.

I'm just one person; what can I do?

I also know he didn't mean anything by it. He's just trying to help.

I peer over the crowd behind me, staring at the way he's sitting there. He looks sad, and suddenly I feel bad for calling him out. And not the kind of bad I felt when I was figuring out the trans stuff, scared of correcting people on my pronouns, making them feel uncomfortable even though they'd made me feel worse by misgendering me. I know what happened isn't Fowler's fault. And I shouldn't assume that he's fucking up just because he's cis.

That doesn't mean he's any less annoying, though.

Always getting high grades, correcting my French when I'm studying out loud, doing his homework and class projects like the perfect little student. I doubt he knows what it's like to disappoint his parents, who probably love him, who don't have a problem with him being queer because they are too. Wyatt's grown up only knowing that queerness is natural and not something surgical that's talked about like a disease with a cure.

I wonder if he knows just how lucky he is.

"Next!" the barista calls out, and I give her my order. When I've gotten the food and drinks, I walk back over to Wyatt, handing him an icy cup and a paper bag. "Here."

He looks up at me. "Hmmm?"

"You should eat something, and if you're anything like me, you're going to need coffee today."

He takes both, his black drink swirling around in the ice. He reads the label and gives me a small smile. "How'd you know I drink iced Americanos?"

"Because you can't go a single day without one," I say. Wyatt's trash can back at the dorm room is filled with these empty plastic cups, and he's always got a fresh one on his desk, ready to join the pile when it's empty. "Seriously, is your blood just espresso?"

"I need them; they help with studying," Wyatt says, biting on the end of the straw.

I stare at his hand wrapped around the cup. "Let me taste it."

He hands it to me, and I inspect the contents, as if it would've changed on the walk here from the Starbucks. It smells like coffee, but I usually never drink my coffee black; I like caramel flavors, especially when they're just a touch burnt and bitter. I sip the drink and—

"Blegh!"

I could vomit right here.

I like bitter, but the drink absolutely fills my mouth, coating my taste buds in an almost sour kind of bitterness. I swallow, just so I won't have to get someone to clean the spit-up coffee on the floor.

"That's the worst thing I've ever tasted."

"Pfft, big baby." Wyatt takes his drink back and sips again. "It's delicious."

"I'll stick with my own, thanks." I drink a bit of my Frappuccino to get rid of the taste in my mouth, but it still lingers there. "I can't believe you drink that."

"Well, I think they're delicious."

"Whatever, Fowler." I reach into my pocket and pull out my AirPods. "Wake me up when they call for Diamond members."

"Ohh, fancy."

I scoff, smiling a bit before I lay my head back and turn on one of my easier-going playlists. I don't actually fall asleep; I'm saving that for the plane. I just want to rest my eyes.

We get seated on the plane an hour later . . . but I only get a sense of what kind of flier Wyatt is when the flight attendant tells us how to buckle our seat belts, use the flotation devices, and all the normal airplane junk. The plan lurches as it begins to move, and Wyatt goes rigid, grabbing on to my wrist with a grip so tight it feels like he's going to cut off my circulation. "What was that?" he asks.

"What?"

"The plane just moved!" His eyes have gone wide, the black of his irises totally blown out. "Why did it move like that?"

"Because we have to go to the runway . . ." I stare at him. "What's the deal with you?"

"It's, um . . . nothing," he says, letting go of my wrist.

"This is your first time flying, isn't it?" The answer seems pretty obvious.

Wyatt stares down at his lap, holding his hands together. "Yeah. Hey, can we close the window?" He points, and I reach over to lower the shade.

"You've never flown anywhere?"

"Never had anywhere to fly." Wyatt jumps again when the plane turns and starts moving forward. "All my family lives in North Carolina or Tennessee, so we just drive."

"You don't go on vacation or anything?" I probably shouldn't ask that, but I don't stop myself.

"No," he says flatly.

"Well, I fly a lot, so you're lucky to have an expert here with you." I smile at him, and he looks a bit more relieved. "The worst part is taking off; after that you'll be fine."

"Define 'worst.'"

"It's fine, look." I take out one of my AirPods and hand it to him. "A distraction."

I shouldn't be embarrassed to show Wyatt my music—what do I care what he thinks? It's a mix of everything, mostly pop and rap, some experimental stuff in there, playlists with old songs from like a decade ago. I even have a few indie songs in there he might like.

"Can I play you a song?" he asks.

I don't want to hand him my phone, but if it helps him relax, then I guess it isn't the worst thing in the world and it justifies the ridiculous amount I just paid for wi-fi. He selects a song quickly, already knowing exactly what he's looking for.

This woman's soft voice fills one of my ears, sounding . . . I guess *tender* is the right word, with a guitar coming in a few seconds later.

"What is this?"

"Hayley Williams," he says. "That indie stuff you hate so much."

"I never said *hate*."

The song continues as the plane begins to move, coasting at speeds fast enough to finally launch us into the air. Wyatt holds his armrests in a death grip, and part of me is afraid he'll snap them right in half and I'll have to pay the airline for the replacements.

I put my hand on top of his, hoping that it just might calm him down in some way.

"I hated that," he says when he dares to open his eyes again.

"You get used to it."

"I'd rather not."

We sit there listening to the next song, and I take back my hand. Why did I even do that? What was I thinking? The album keeps playing, and I keep listening to the lyrics, the soft melodies. It strikes me that there aren't many more sounds beyond a guitar, a piano in some places. But the lyrics—

"These songs are depressing."

"Yeah," Wyatt says. His voice still seems filled with nerves, but he finally relaxes into his seat. "They're meant to be."

"Hmm."

"I like this album a lot. I listen to it when I'm sad."

"Jesus, wouldn't that just make your mood worse?"

"It helps, sometimes." He shrugs. "We can change it if you want."

"It's okay," I tell him. "I like that they're sad."

"Good." He smiles at me, his wide, gap-toothed smile. "Finally, you're getting some taste."

"Neil?"

"Hmm?" I roll my neck, closing my eyes tighter. I don't want to wake up. Just five more minutes, please.

"Neil." I feel a poke in my stomach, which makes me giggle. That's where Josh would always go for when he wanted me to laugh.

"What's happening?" I ask, still not opening my eyes.

"You were talking. In your sleep."

"What?"

I finally open my eyes, my lids feeling heavy.

"I was talking in my sleep?" I ask.

"A little bit. Nothing bad, but you mumbled some things I couldn't make out. You do that a lot at school too. I just wanted to make sure you were okay."

"It's nothing," I say. "How long was I out?"

"Maybe an hour? You were right—the takeoff was the worst part."

As if on cue, the plane shakes from a little turbulence and Wyatt grabs at my hand again.

"You've really got to stop doing that—you're going to leave marks."

"Sorry." Wyatt puts his hands back in his lap. "It's just scary. I think I'd prefer driving."

"You know, they say—" I start, but Wyatt cuts me off.

"If you say something like 'your chances of getting into a car accident are five times higher than flying,' I will smack you."

"Okay, okay. Driving would take so much longer, though."

"Last Christmas when we went to go visit my grandma in Nashville, the drive was, like, ten hours."

"Hmmm, so that sounds awful."

"It was actually pretty fun."

I cross my legs and prop up my arm, resting my chin on my wrist. "What do your moms do for a living?"

"Mama is a teacher, second grade. And Mom is a librarian, working on getting her degree."

"And you have just one sister?"

"Yeah. She's only four. Why are you asking?"

I shrug. "Can't I be curious? You're the one who said we needed to get to know each other better."

"That was for the lie."

"I know," I say. "So, your mom is getting the degree?"

Wyatt nods.

"What's the story there?"

He stares at me, and I can't tell what I've done wrong.

"I'm just trying to get to know you."

Wyatt sighs. "She was in college when she got pregnant with me, so she dropped out. She met my mama a few years later, after supporting herself by living at home, working odd jobs. The two of them fell in love, moved in together. Mama only felt good about going back to finish her degree when I hit high school."

Huh, you know, in all my time living with Wyatt, I don't think I've ever heard a single story about his parents.

"There's not a lot of money in teaching in North Carolina, is there?"

"It's not great," Wyatt says with this sense of bitter false pride. "And don't get the wrong idea; we live comfortably."

"I'm sure."

"Hey, just because I'm not going out to brunch every day and buying five-thousand-dollar coats and shoes doesn't mean that I'm poor. We just live within our means, and we appreciate what we have."

"I wasn't accusing you of anything," I say.

"Your tone implied otherwise."

"Apologies for my tone. I was just trying to make conversation." Though clearly this is a sore subject for him. "Why are you at Steerfield?"

"Because it's a good education? My moms wanted the best for me."

"That's not what I asked. I asked *why* you're at Steerfield." I've always found it suspicious that Wyatt managed to afford such a prestigious education when he couldn't even afford a new uniform. And not that it's any of my business, even now with this lie going, but my curiosity has been piqued, and if he's going to go ahead and tell me his whole life story . . . then why not ask?

Wyatt pauses, like he's confused or something. Perhaps I should've said that a little slower. No, no. That's mean, and I'm supposed to be nice on this trip. Nasty thoughts lead to nasty words.

"They offered me the scholarship, and I wasn't going to say no."

"For your guitar playing?"

Wyatt shakes his head. "It's academic."

"Academic?" Why does that surprise me? I know Wyatt is studious, and he works extremely hard on a nearly perfect GPA, but I'd never connected the dots together.

"Yeah, if my GPA slips below a certain number, I can be put on academic suspension from clubs and school activities, or they could take the scholarship away completely."

Oh.

I had no idea.

"Is that fair?"

"Not at all," he says. "What's worse, the bar for my GPA is higher than other students', ones who can afford to go to Steerfield without the help. All because my parents can't afford to buy a new building or a pool or pay to renovate the baseball field to get me out of trouble."

There's a bitterness in his voice that actually hurts to hear. It's clear that the school is important to him, but at the same time, it sounds like he hates it. I can't blame him—why go there if you don't fit in? If everyone around you looks down on you, if you don't have friends. I can't really recall a single time I've seen Wyatt hanging out with people outside of the music club. No one comes to our room to visit him; when he leaves the room, he leaves and returns alone.

"So why go?" I ask. "Couldn't you go to a public school?"

Wyatt waits a beat. "I could, but Steerfield has prestigious alum. Artists, CEOs, senators. When I got the offer, I couldn't turn them down. My parents wouldn't let me, and I didn't want to let them down."

I don't really know what to think right now. There's some pity, which I expect Wyatt would get angry with me about having, and some sadness. Then again, I like to think that I know how he feels.

"What about you?" he asks.

"Steerfield?"

He nods. "California to North Carolina is a long way."

"Well, if you must know . . ." I readjust in my seat. I'd rather not tell this story, and I can probably avoid a few details here and there. But if he was kind enough to share his story, the least I can do is share mine.

One version of it, anyway.

Because it means there's a whole country between me and my mother, and that way she doesn't have to take care of me. Because I was becoming a problem; I was embarrassing her; I was becoming stories on gossip sites; what I was doing was turned into whispers in her circle of friends, who all have very well-behaved children. I was the problem, so Mom decided to send me to the other end of the country instead of talking to me, instead of letting me continue seeing my therapist in person in California, instead of asking me what I wanted, what I needed.

All of that seems like a lot to dump on Wyatt.

So "Because my father went there" is what I say instead.

"So, you're some kind of legacy?"

"Yep, all the men in my family go to Steerfield. Ever since my great-great-great-grandfather."

"That's kind of cool."

"Yep." And it's also a total lie. My father went to Oxford Academy in Cypress; I'd bet money that Michael has never stepped foot in North Carolina, and I have no idea where my father's father attended school. I really couldn't care less.

I can sense that Wyatt wants to talk more about this, but I turn to face the window, hoping that'll signal an end to the conversation.

"Do you want to watch a movie?" Wyatt asks.

"Hmmm?"

He points to the screen on the back of the seat in front of us, the same one showing where we are in the air. "There are movies on this thing."

"I know that."

"Do you want to watch one?"

"We'll have to flag a flight attendant to buy some headphones."

"Nah, mine will fit." He pulls out the old analog-style earbuds that Apple hasn't sold in years.

"You seriously use those things?"

"What?" He looks at them like there's nothing wrong here. "They still work well."

"Pfft." I take the earbud he offers to me, and we scroll through the movie selections. Wyatt shuts down every single horror movie I suggest, so then I leave it up to him, and eventually we settle on this movie about a guy who's reincarnated as his girlfriend's dog.

It's almost sickeningly sweet; I want to puke.

"Are you crying?" I look over at Wyatt, seeing the tears well up in his eyes.

He wipes them quickly with the sleeve of his shirt. "No!"

"You totally were." I laugh at him. "Who knew you were such a sap?"

"Am not, it's just . . . it's sweet."

"Whatever."

"You don't think that was cute?"

"It's a movie, so of course everything works out in the end."

"Is that such a bad thing? I think it's nice when everything ends happy."

He would. Wyatt doesn't want to think about what happens after the camera stops rolling. The fights and the arguments, the passive-aggressive jabs and snide comments, the resentment that people grow toward each other as the years pass on, not caring if their child is witnessing it in real time, watching as the only relationship he's ever known crumbles around him.

"It's just not realistic," I say again.

"Well . . . does it have to be? What's wrong with a happy ending?"

I want to say something, but I decide to keep my mouth shut. I'm done with this conversation.

Two hours later, we hop off the plane at LAX.

I tried to sleep, but I couldn't. My brain just wouldn't turn off, and I have no idea why. So I loaded another movie and watched it without Wyatt.

Fowler actually did manage to sleep, though; I could just barely hear his soft snores through the headphones.

"Hey, wake up," I say to him now.

"Hmmm?" Wyatt opens his eyes slowly, sitting upright in his seat, hands on the armrests like he thinks we were going to crash or something. "Where are we?"

"Still on the plane, genius," I say. "We just landed."

"Really?"

"Yep."

"Huh. I thought it'd be rougher than that."

"It was," I say. We came in a little too quickly for my comfort. "But you were knocked out."

"I guess I didn't sleep well last night."

"Well, you'd better get over it. Once we're at the hotel, we won't have much time until we have to get changed and head to the first dinner."

"What time is it here?"

I take my phone off airplane mode, letting it catch up. "Three. Kind of."

"Ugh, gross."

With my phone back online, the missed texts and calls start coming in. There are a few from Samuel, and some new pictures in the group chat. Hoon is with his parents in Connecticut, and Samuel is back in New York. Mark was talking about the weather in London, but because of the time difference, no one else was awake.

Nothing from Josh.

Not here, at least.

There is one more missed call, though.

From Do Not Answer.

I'll have to call back at some point, but that can wait until we're at the hotel.

Part of me still thinks we might have time to book a flight back to Charlotte. I don't have to do this. In fact, skipping the wedding might lead to my excommunication from the family, and isn't that the dream? I won't have to deal with Michael, or Mother, or Josh.

Fowler and I grab our bags and make our way quickly down to the baggage claim, where we have to stand for his last bag to come out on the conveyor belt. I try not to stare daggers at him as we're forced to wait. The last thing I want is to be late for this dinner. I'll never hear the end of it.

My phone rings.

"Who is Do Not Answer?" Wyatt asks.

That's when I realize he's staring over my shoulder. I tuck my screen to my chest so he can't read it.

"No one," I say.

Wyatt shrugs and grabs his bag, and we make our way out to the pickup area.

"Are you parents coming to get us or something?"

"Bold of you to assume my mother would waste her time," I say as I order a Lyft.

"Your mom seems like a lovely person."

"You'll get to see just how lovely soon enough."

Fowler looks around, kicking his feet on the pavement while we wait. "You grew up here, right?"

"Why would I have been raised in an airport?"

He shakes his head, but there's this unmistakable hint of a smile on his lips. "Funny."

"Yes, I grew up in California. In Bel Air, to be specific."

"Is it nice there?"

"Nicer than Charlotte. I don't know how you deal with the humidity. It makes my skin feel awful."

"You get used to it."

"I suppose. Though given the choice, I'd rather be here."

"Really? You'd rather be back in California?"

"At least I know my way around here, and it's not just bank towers and bars."

"I suppose that would be a plus," Wyatt says. I wait for the inevitable next bout of painful small talk, but it doesn't come. Instead, we sit there in silence as the Lyft finally arrives, and we make the twenty-minute drive from LAX to the hotel. Though with LA traffic, that turns into forty minutes. Which gives Wyatt plenty of time to gasp in awe about all the new sights he's seeing.

"Where's the Hollywood Sign?" he asks.

"You can't see it from here," I say, pointing past the window. "It's about thirty minutes that way."

"Have you ever been?"

"What? No . . . why would I do that?"

"It seems cool."

"Pfft, tourists."

"Hey, what did I say about being mean?"

"You were excited about the Hollywood Sign; you deserved that one."

"I want to go see it."

"Maybe," I say. "If we have the time. This week is going to be busy."

"How many dinners can one person responsibly have for a single wedding?" he asks.

"Oh, you don't know the half of it."

When we finally arrive at the hotel, I'm hungry, carsick, my phone is dying, and I didn't shower earlier, so now I feel sweaty and disgusting.

"Oh, wow." Wyatt looks out the window, his mouth agape, staring at the hotel that we pull up in front of. "Is this where we're staying?"

"Yep," I say, tipping the driver again as he gets us our bags.

Then Wyatt sees the logo of the hotel above the drop-off area, and everything clicks. "Wait, this place is called the Kearney."

"Yep."

"That's you."

"My mother, actually," I tell him. "*Her* mother started the Hills Hotel franchise. They used to all be called the Kearney, but they changed it. No idea why. When Mom took over, she returned this one to the original name, since it was the first."

"That's pretty cool."

"I guess, if you find that kind of thing interesting."

We walk inside, and Wyatt stares at the lush decorations, the marble flooring, the tall columns, the original armchairs that are restored every six months to make sure they appear perfect. The main piece of decoration is the vintage-style sign from the fifties, when the hotel first opened. The bulbs are long dead, but even without them lit, you can easily make out THE KEARNEY in bold letters.

At the front desk, I say, "We're checking in, room should be under Neil Kearney. It's with the wedding party."

"All right, give me one second," the receptionist tells me.

While they're typing away, trying to find the reservation, I see her from across the lobby. Standing there, tall in her heels, her black skirt just below her knees, paired with her favorite black jacket.

Miss Do Not Answer herself.

And right now, her eyes are staring right at me.

The smile on her lips appears the second she spots me, ignoring whatever the bellhop was saying to her seconds before. She waves him off and starts to race toward me.

"Shit," I grumble.

Wyatt turns. "What?"

"Just keep your mouth shut," I warn.

"Is that—"

When most mothers see their children after months of being

away across the country, they probably hug them, embrace them, never want them to leave their side ever again. But my mother has never believed in hugs.

"Neil! You made it," she says, like there's nothing wrong. "I called you several times. I was starting to think that you'd missed your flight."

"No, Mom. I just missed the calls. My phone was off."

"Well, I hope that won't happen again this week. You're playing a big part in this wedding, Neil. I need this to go off without a hitch." She glances over me, already looking for something to comment on.

She then proceeds to lick her thumb and wipe away at some invisible mark on my cheek. I try to wrestle away, but she's still got an iron grip on my shoulder.

"Mother!"

"And who is this?" She sets her targets on Wyatt, and I wish that were a good thing.

"This is Wyatt," I say. "He's my date for the wedding."

"Nice to meet you, ma'am." Wyatt holds out his hand for her to take.

"Your date, and so mannerly!" Mom says with her plastic smile. "That's so wonderful. It's very nice to meet you."

She finally takes his hand, shaking it so violently that I'm afraid we'll have to pop Wyatt's shoulder back in its socket.

"Your accent is adorable," she says.

"Thank you, ma'am."

"And so polite too. What a gentleman." Then she freezes, turning toward me. "I thought you were coming with Josh? Oh, honey. Did the two of you break up? You remember, I told you—"

"We weren't dating, Mother," I interrupt. "So, we couldn't have broken up."

"Regardless. I hope this doesn't cause any needless drama. I'll have enough going on, planning every detail of this event."

I shouldn't even be surprised that she's planned this entire wedding herself. Why would she ever relinquish control for a single second?

"Well, Wyatt, we'll have to talk at some point. You'll have to tell me how you two met. And how you're treating my precious little prince here."

"Right, Mother, well!" I stop the conversation there. "It was nice to see you. But we're tired, so I think I'm going to go to the room and rest before we get ready."

"Okay, but don't be late." She points a finger at me. "I'm texting you the address. It's right down the street, so there's no reason to be late."

"Yes, ma'am," Wyatt answers when I don't. "We won't be."

And as quickly as she appears, she vanishes, like a ghost, except I doubt most ghosts wear red bottoms that echo on the marble floor of the hotel.

"*Precious little prince?*" Wyatt repeats.

I grit my teeth. "Call me that and I'll throw you off the balcony."

"Sorry—" The receptionist calls for our attention. "Here's your room key. Let me know if you'll need more than two. You'll be on the top floor, single-bedroom suite with a queen bed."

"Thanks." I slide my key into my pocket, giving the second one to Wyatt. "Here, don't lose it."

"I won't."

"Good, now come on. I want to shower."

• • •

"Whoa, this is nice," Wyatt says when we see the room for the first time. It's basic, a small kitchenette, double doors that lead to the bedroom, a large balcony that thankfully faces the ocean, so we'll have a nice view.

And, most important, there's a plush couch.

"You haven't stayed in many hotels, have you?"

"No." Wyatt drops down onto the couch, testing the springs. "Cozy."

"Good, 'cause that's where you're sleeping."

"What?"

"There's only one bed," I say, walking into the bedroom and throwing my bag onto the bed as if to say I'm claiming it as my own. "Plus, my family paid for this room."

"No one paid—it's your mom's hotel!"

"And don't you forget it." I leap onto the bed, letting the soft pillows and cushy comforter envelop me. If this bed wanted to swallow me whole, I wouldn't mind.

"Aren't you going to shower?" Wyatt asks. He's standing in the doorway to the room now.

"In a bit. I'm resting my eyes first."

There's a pregnant pause. "Your mom seemed nice."

"Don't let that fool you. Once she's got her claws in you, she'll never let go."

"Seemed okay." His accent is coming out again.

"A wolf in sheep's clothing, Fowler," I dare to sit up again so I can look him in the eye. "You'll find that's a required lesson for meeting my family."

"They can't all be bad."

76

"Prepare to be surprised," I say before I reach into my suitcase and pull out my shower bag. "I'm going to get out of these clothes."

"Should I get changed?"

"Yes, please. But we've got some time."

"What's this dinner for, anyway?"

"Michael and Ashley—that's his fiancée, by the way—their engagement moved fast, the wedding even faster. So this will be the first time she's meeting a lot of my family. Same for him meeting hers." I'm hoping all these introductions will keep people busy enough to simply ignore the both of us. Maybe we truly can just have a nice dinner to ourselves.

"Sounds fun."

"Right. Just wait until you meet my grandparents. Then again, they probably won't ask *you* what's in your pants."

"They actually ask you that?"

"They most certainly do."

"And you put up with it?" Wyatt asks.

"Put up with what?"

"Their transphobia."

I pause, staring at him, running my tongue along the top row of my teeth. *Be nice, Neil. Be nice.* "What do you mean?"

"I mean, I've seen how you act at school. Like nothing bothers you, not taking any shit from anyone. You kneed Riley Garner in the nuts when he was harassing you."

That was a good day, totally worth the weekend I spent in detention.

"You just don't get it," I say, hoping that we can leave the conversation there.

"Then explain it."

"This is my family—it's different. I can't just knee my grandpa in the nuts whenever he's transphobic toward me."

"But there are other ways to shut them down."

"You don't . . ." I shake my head. "You don't get it."

"Then explain it."

"I can't," I say a little too loudly. "Because you don't understand—you wouldn't understand, okay? So just drop it before I send you on the next flight back to Charlotte." I walk into the bathroom, and unfortunately it's a pocket door that slides into place thanks to the track on top of the doorframe, so there's no satisfactory slam to punctuate my exit.

He doesn't know what he's talking about. Just because Wyatt is queer, that doesn't mean he knows the shit that I go through on a daily basis, the transphobia, hearing every day that trans people have been killed, that entire countries have made people like me illegal, the gender dysphoria that I dealt with for years, that was supposed to go away when I got my surgery, when I finally felt like myself.

Except the surgery wasn't a magic fix. I knew that going in. My doctors told me that; the trans vloggers and bloggers I'd listened to said that. I learned that afterward, during the months of depression that I felt after my top surgery because of the dysmorphia I still felt, the fear of taking off my shirt anywhere outside my room because now there'd be no mistaking my transness in public spaces.

Wyatt just doesn't get it, and he probably never will.

I shouldn't let Wyatt get to me.

I need to calm down, and a shower is just the trick for that. I throw my sweaty clothes in the corner and jump right in. It's roomy in here, spacious, and I doubt the hot water will run out after five minutes. There's even a detached tub that goes deep and has jets in the sides, so maybe I'll take a nice bath on this mini vacation as well.

At some point I will have to get out and dry off, get dressed, do my hair, go downstairs to the restaurant, and see family members that I've been lucky enough to not have to see for a few years now.

But for right now, I'm content to just stand here.

Underneath the stream of hot water.

While I do my best to forget how awful the next seven days are going to be.

"Okay, so what are you comfortable with me doing?" Wyatt asks.

"What do you mean?"

"You said that I'm supposed to do 'boyfriend' stuff around you, but I don't know what that means."

"It just means you do the normal couple stuff. Hold my hand, kiss my cheek, get me drinks or food."

"That last part makes it sound like I'm just your servant."

"No, not at all. You'd make a terrible servant anyway."

"It'd give me more chances to poison you."

"Hmm, charming." I wrestle on my pants, pulling the belt tight around my waist. "Just do . . . whatever comes naturally."

Wyatt doesn't say anything from the living room area; all I can hear is the sound of him changing his clothes. I rear back on my bed, trying to get a look to make sure he heard me, but all I get instead is a view of his butt in his boxers.

The least he could do is warn me that he's half naked.

"Did you hear me?" I ask.

"Yeah, I heard you."

"And you don't have anything to say."

"I was thinking."

"Hmm, forgive me, I didn't see the smoke coming out of your ears."

Wyatt picks that moment to walk in through my door, his bare chest on display for the entire world to see, farmer's tan leaving some of his skin a paler white than the rest of his body. "What did I say about being mean?"

"My apologies; my mouth is quicker than my brain today. Must be the jet lag."

"No different than usual." Wyatt sighs as he walks into the bathroom to grab his deodorant before he pulls on a red-and-black flannel shirt.

"That's what you're wearing?"

Wyatt looks down at the shirt as he buttons it slowly. "Yeah, what's wrong with it?"

"So much. First, flannel . . . in California? You're going to die of heatstroke. And second, I know we packed dress shirts."

"Well, I don't have that many. I wanted to save the ones I brought for the important events."

"This is an important event. It's all important." I shake my head, grabbing my dress shoes. "Guess we'll add shirts to the list of things to get you when we go to get your suit."

"I keep telling you that I'm not going to let you buy me a suit."

"And I keep telling you that you need a suit for the wedding. I'm not going to be the one blamed when you're underdressed."

"What's so wrong with the shirt?"

"You look like a bumpkin."

Wyatt gives me a glare.

"Hey, you asked that time. I just told you the truth."

"Maybe your family won't mind?"

Oh, they'll mind all right. But maybe this is good; it can be a learning moment for Wyatt. Maybe after today he'll believe me when I say that my family is nothing but awful, terrible people. Well, awful, terrible people, and my cousin. Though she's awful and terrible in her own way. Maybe he could wear one of my shirts? It might be oversized on him, but that's the fashion.

Except Wyatt's got a good seven inches on me in the height department.

"Please, just go change. If you pick out a different shirt, I can iron it."

"Fine," Wyatt huffs, pulling out this hideous dark blue thing with small white dots decorating it.

Of course the label is branded Old Navy.

"Stop kidding around."

"Stop being a prick," Wyatt claps back.

"Fine, fine." It's better than nothing. I iron the shirt against my better judgment.

When I'm done, Wyatt throws it on, buttoning it quickly and tucking the tail into his pants. I spritz myself with some cologne, and just like that, we're off. In the elevator, down to the ground floor, and out to the street.

Volo Restaurante is this quaint, warm-looking spot that's been entirely rented out for the evening just for this dinner. By the time we make it to the front door and I give my name to the maître d', most of my family is already there.

"How do I look?" I ask Wyatt.

Not that I care about his opinion, but his is the only one I can trust right now.

"Your collar." He points. "In the back."

"Then fix it!" I whisper.

"Okay, okay. Jesus."

His strong hands pull on the back of my neck, flattening the collar out before he rests them on my shoulders.

"Good?" I ask.

He nods. "Good."

Thankfully, there are enough people here and everyone is distracted enough that no one really notices when we slip into the dining room. Each of the large, circular tables has been situated around the room, along with a few of the booths on the perimeter of the restaurant.

I lead us into a booth in the corner. Maybe we won't be noticed there.

The waiter comes over and, with a flourish, says, "The menu tonight was decided by the wedding party. Are there any allergies I should be made aware of?"

"No, we should be—"

"I'm allergic to shellfish, actually," Wyatt interrupts.

"Of course. There is an appetizer of crab cakes. I can substitute them for a different dish if you would like."

"That's fine," I say. "Just some bread."

I am starving. And crab cakes sound so good right now. But I have no idea how bad Wyatt's allergy might be. I've heard of people getting whiffs of shellfish and breaking into hives. I don't even know if that's true, but I'm not going to risk it in front of my family.

"Big crowd." Wyatt stares at the amount of people.

"And that's not even the full party. The guest list is, like, three hundred people. Maybe more."

"Jesus."

"Told you, you're in for quite the event," I say. Then things get quiet, like we've suddenly forgotten how to speak to each other. It's not like we have regular conversations; the ones we usually have rarely last more than ten words. "I didn't know you're allergic to shellfish."

"Yeah."

"Sorry for almost killing you."

"It's fine. My throat just swells up so much that I can't breathe. And I don't have my EpiPen with me, so you wouldn't even be able to do anything while I die in your arms."

I stare at him, more than a little dumbfounded. "Is that . . . ? Are you serious? Does that happen?"

Wyatt cackles. "No, it's not that severe. I just get hives. Over-the-counter allergy meds usually help."

"You're not funny," I tell him grumpily.

"Told you, we need to have some conversations about details."

I don't want to admit that he's right, but I can imagine this scenario in my head where Mom offers Wyatt a crab cake and he declines, and I have to pretend all along like I knew about the allergy and that his life wasn't potentially at risk.

"Okay." I straighten in my seat, the leather of the booth squeaking. "What do you think I should know?"

"Why do I have to go first?"

"Because you're my guest."

"That makes you the host," he says. "I learned in cotillion that the host should set the example."

"You attended cotillion?"

"They offered free classes at the YMCA near my house. My parents thought it'd be good for me to learn etiquette." Wyatt leans over the table. "They were fun. I liked learning to dance."

"You must've forgotten the first lesson," I say, looking at where his arms rest on the table. "Elbows? Very rude."

Wyatt moves them quickly, a blush creeping up on his cheeks.

"It's good that you can dance—you'll need it," I add, putting my elbows on the table. "What else is there?"

"What do you want to know?"

"Whatever you think I need to know."

He smirks at me, almost looking devilish in the orange glow of the lamp above our table.

"We've got plenty of time." Mom still hasn't noticed that I'm here. A quick glance toward the rest of the open dining space shows her sitting at a center table with Michael; his fiancée, Ashley; and two people who I'm assuming are Ashley's parents, alongside my grandparents.

On Mom's side, of course. I haven't seen my paternal grandparents in years.

Not for a lack of trying. I think Dad told them to stop talking to me.

"Let's start with what you know about me instead."

"Didn't we already play this game?"

Wyatt shakes his head slowly, still smiling. "I want to play it again."

I sigh. "Your name is Wyatt Fowler. You're sixteen. Blond hair, green eyes. Probably six foot one? Maybe a little taller."

"You're starting to sound like my driver's license."

"You're a Halloween baby."

"You definitely cheated."

"You gave me your ID to buy your plane ticket." I hold my hands up defensively. "I can't be held accountable here."

"You're really something, you know that?"

"You're afraid of flying," I continue. "You have a little sister; you play the guitar and want to be a singer."

"All of this is obvious."

I try to think if there's anything obscure that I know about Wyatt. I don't think the shellfish allergy counts. Something not so obvious.

"Oh, I know. You chew on the end of your pens when you're concentrating."

"You noticed that?"

"How could I not? You stole my favorite Micron once and you chewed the end to pieces. Those pens aren't cheap, Fowler."

"Oh, sorry . . . I didn't even realize."

It's whatever; I keep a stock of the pens because I love them so much. You never know when your most reliable brand might disappear one day.

"Okay, I played your game," I say. "Now what do you know about me?"

"You didn't know that much," he tells me.

"Stop changing the subject."

Wyatt folds his hands, covering his mouth, while he looks up at the ceiling. "Your favorite color is black."

"You've been through my closet?"

"Your wardrobe is like ninety percent black, dude. It's depressing."

I wave him off. "Next. Something less obvious."

Wyatt smirks again. "You hate olives."

"How do you know that?"

"Because every time you get a Greek salad in the cafeteria, you pick the olives out."

"You watch me eat?"

"Not of my own accord, I promise you. Plus, I can always tell when you eat a salad in our room because there are black olives left in my trash can."

"I don't like the smell," I say. It's too salty. "Your trash can is far enough away."

"You're unbelievable."

"I'll take that as a compliment."

Eventually our waiter comes back and we ask for water. Then both of us dive into the bread basket when it's left behind. I think we're hungrier than we realized. Even just the smell of the butter and the garlic is enough to make my mouth water.

"So . . ." Wyatt says, picking at a piece of bread chunk by chunk. "What do I have to look forward to the rest of this week?"

"Well, tomorrow we have a brunch with all my family who are coming in late. Then I need to get fitted for my suit, so we can get that done for you as well."

"I told you, I don't want a suit."

"And I told you, you're getting one. Even if it's a rental." Though, if it's going on Mom's bill for this whole weekend, I'd prefer it if Wyatt got something nice out of all of this. He'd probably appreciate a good suit. "You have to look presentable."

"Whatever."

"We're not busy tomorrow night or Monday. So maybe we can go out, see some sights." Thankfully, there's no reason for underage me to be involved in the bridal shower or the bachelor and bachelorette parties.

"That'd be fun."

"Another luncheon on Tuesday, then some wedding photos. The rehearsal dinner after that. Then the wedding on Thursday. Our return flight is on Saturday, so we've got some spare time at the end of the week. That's all."

"Oh, is that all?"

"Cool it, smartass." I pick at the bread some more.

The door to the restaurant keeps opening and closing, letting in this slight chill every few minutes. And every single time, I look up, expecting to see Josh. His brother got here shortly after us. But Josh wasn't with him.

Maybe he decided not to come. Maybe I'm in the clear.

The next time the door opens, I tell myself not to look up, even as whoever just walked in comes closer and closer to our table. I'm not going to let him mess up this weekend, and if I'm in love with Wyatt, then he should have all of my attention, right?

Except it isn't Josh. And I know it's not him because of three simple words.

"What's up, homos?"

Lindsay's standing there, in a white dress that comes down to her knees, an off-white/almost-gold jacket, her black hair down her shoulders, and her favorite red lipstick on.

"Lindsay!" I almost leap out of the booth to wrap my arms around her.

She hugs me back just as tight. "Neil!"

It's been too long since I've seen my cousin over something

other than my phone screen. There was a bit of a family emergency with her dad's mom last Christmas, so she missed the entire thing. Meaning I was left to deal with our family totally alone.

Worst part was that she didn't even feel a little bit guilty about it.

"When did you get in?" I ask.

"Like an hour ago? We checked in, changed, and came right down. I didn't even have time to shower."

"*That's* what that smell is."

She gets me back with a jab at my ribs.

"Ow!"

"That's what you get, assmunch." We both let go of each other, and she doesn't even bother with an invitation before she slides right into the booth, across from Wyatt. "I'm Lindsay, Neil's cousin."

"This is my, um . . ." Shit, what do I call him? Boyfriend? Date? Do I even have to lie to Lindsay? She'd probably think this entire thing is hilarious before she'd tell me how pathetic it is that I'm lying about having a date.

So no, I won't tell her.

"I'm Neil's boyfriend." Wyatt swoops in, throwing on his southern charm by offering Lindsay a handshake.

"Boyfriend?" She turns to me, a mix of surprise and excitement on her face.

I feel like this is going to go poorly.

At least, it's going to go poorly for me.

"When did this happen?" she asks.

"A few days ago." I slide into the booth beside her.

"Tell me all the details," Lindsay says to Wyatt and not to me. It's almost like I've been shut out of the conversation entirely.

Wyatt looks at me, unsure at first. "We're roommates at Steerfield. We were talking for a long time, going out to study and stuff, going to movies. And, then we kissed, and things kept going from there."

Oh Jesus. Seriously?

I look at Lindsay's face. I like to think that we've known each other long enough for me to know what she's thinking. But right now? I have no idea if she believes a single word that Wyatt's said so far.

"Keep going—I want the deets!" she says. "Mostly I want to know what my cousin did to convince you that he's worth your time."

"I'm right here!"

Wyatt looks at me again, almost like he's asking permission. I don't know what he wants me to do here. I've got nothing, and she asked him. This is his job.

"Well, we were walking back to the dorm one night. There was a student movie night in the auditorium. They were showing that *Emma* movie, the new one."

"With Anya Taylor-Joy," Lindsay adds. "Put respect on my girl."

Wyatt laughs and keeps going. "And you got extra credit in Classic Lit if you went and brought the ticket stub back to class."

I kick him lightly under the table, and he looks down.

Does this dude not understand the art of subtlety?

He's giving Lindsay too many details; he needs to keep the lie simple. I try to tell him as much with a look, but there's only so much a look can do.

"Sorry, um." Wyatt clears his throat. "The sun was setting; it was pretty romantic. And I finally worked up the courage to ask him out. Officially."

"Well, that's cute!" Lindsay cheers before she turns to me. "I thought you had that thing going with Josh?"

"That's over."

"Yikes? Break his heart?"

"I don't want to talk about it." I sip my water to give myself something else to do other than answer her questions.

But she just keeps asking them. "Is he coming this weekend?"

"No idea."

"His brother is Michael's best friend, right?"

"Yeah, and?"

Lindsay shrugs. "Okay, geez! No reason to get all rude. Is he like this with you?" she asks Wyatt.

"Oh, all the time."

"How do you put up with it?"

"I usually just ignore him until he forgets what he's angry about. Or a quick little peck on the lips—isn't that right, sweety-ookums?" Wyatt reaches across the table to pinch my cheek, and I slap his hand away.

"*Sweety-ookums?*" I glare at him, trying to decide if I'm more confused or angry. "I will make you sleep in the hallway tonight."

"Sharing a room already, my, my. This did move quickly."

"You can thank Mother for that," I tell her.

"Where is the puppet master, anyway? I should go say hello."

I turn to point over toward the table, and just as I do, I meet Mom's gaze, and the information that I'm here dawns on her as she stands very carefully, telling Michael and Grandpa that she'll be right back.

"Oh no," I murmur.

"Speak of the devil, and she shall appear," Lindsay whispers.

"Neil, how long have you been here?" Mom stomps up to the booth, her hair done in an elaborate bun. She's wearing a black dress that's actually pretty cute. "And, Lindsay, it's *so good* to see you again."

"Nice to see you too, Aunt Rebecca."

"We missed you at Christmas."

"Things got pretty intense."

"I was so sorry to hear about your grandfather—he was such a kind man. I wish I'd gotten to meet him."

Lindsay's voice sinks. "Yeah, we miss him."

Mom forces this frown. "Neil, honey. You need to come say hello to everyone."

"Do I?"

"Yes!" she demands. "Now come on. You too, Lindsay, Mom and Dad want to see you." Mom doesn't even wait for us to follow her; she just walks away, heading toward our grandparents.

"I thought your grandfather survived his surgery?"

"He did. He's kicking it down in Florida."

Wyatt and I both snicker.

"Neil! Lindsay!" Mom calls. "Come on!"

I shoot Wyatt a sympathetic glance. "We'll be back."

"I'll be here," he says flatly.

Lindsay and I walk down to the proper dining area, where most of my family is sitting. Michael stands up quickly, wrapping me in a head hold and giving me a noogie.

"You didn't tell me you'd gotten in, little bro!"

"Ow, okay. Let me go, please!"

I can't think of why I would've told him I'd gotten here. We've never been close; Michael "chose" our father in the divorce. Of course, he was nineteen when it happened, so it's not like it mattered; he could've gone anywhere he wanted. The fact that he still bothers to talk to that man, though, that Michael still wants him in his life, is enough for me to know that I don't need to talk to Michael.

It was a total surprise when he asked me to be one of his groomsmen. I even called Mom after I got the text asking if I absolutely had to be one, and she insisted. She said something about this wedding bringing us all closer or some bullshit.

"Have you gotten taller?" Michael asks me, doing his best to flatten out my hair.

"Probably."

"Right, right, those shots."

"Yeah."

"Oh!" Michael exclaims like he forgot something. "You haven't met Ashley before!"

"No, I haven't."

Ashley is in the middle of talking to the guy I guessed was her dad. Michael taps her on the shoulder, and she turns, and we introduce ourselves. I've seen Ashley in pictures on Michael's Instagram and she looks the same even without any filters. She's pretty, nice black hair, cute smile. I just don't know anything else about the woman except that she's one of those people who still have a Hogwarts house in their Instagram bio.

That's when I knew we wouldn't get along.

"It's so good to meet you, Neil. Michael's told me so much about you."

"Yeah, great to meet you too."

"Is that Neil?" I hear my grandfather shout my name. Then

he lets out this low, whooping laugh, which turns into a cough after a bit.

My grandmother is sitting right beside him, sitting at this perfect ninety-degree angle in her chair, her lipstick perfectly applied, not a hair out of place. Just like Mom. "Oh, Neil. I didn't realize you were here."

Except she doesn't say Neil; she uses a name that hasn't been mine for a very long time. Grandmother offers me a hand to shake.

"My name is Neil, Nana."

"Oh, right. I just expected for you to finally be out of this phase."

Shame fills my body, creeping up my neck.

"It's not a phase, Nana." I hate that my voice comes out quiet, like I'm afraid to ask for basic human decency. I look around for Mother, hoping that she's standing nearby to say something, anything. She *is* standing nearby, and there's no way she doesn't hear what her mother says, but she still just stands there, like she always does, saying nothing. I'm only glad Wyatt isn't here.

"Oh, she's kidding, Neil," Grandfather jumps in. Alone among my family members, he loves hugs and is hurt when he doesn't get one. He pulls me down to his level, wrapping his big arms around me.

"I see that you're growing your hair back out," Nana says, taking a lock of my hair in her fingers. "You got this color from your father, you know. You can blame him for this."

I'm not growing my hair out on purpose; I just haven't felt like getting a haircut. Besides, it's not even that long. The ends on the side just barely cover my ears.

"Okay, well, it's nice to see the both of you," I say quickly. "I'm going to get back to my table."

"Oh, right, your mother told us you brought your boyfriend."

I've never heard Nana say anything homophobic, but the way she says *boyfriend* sends a chill down my spine. Is she upset that I'm a boy dating boys? Or is she thrilled; does she see this as some fucked-up way of me reclaiming femininity?

Can her rotted brain even comprehend that sexuality and gender identity are two different things?

"Yeah, yep."

"I'd love to meet him." Nana stares daggers at me.

"Yes, ma'am."

Never in a billion years. I catch Lindsay looking at me from across the table, talking to her own parents, and I send her every signal I can.

She leans over the table. "Hey, Nana! Is that a new blazer?"

"Yes, dear. It's a part of the Chanel collection, brand-new, you know." She pats her jacket, so proud, you'd think she made it herself. "And get your elbows off the table. A young lady has manners."

"Yes, ma'am."

"You see, I was visiting some friends in Paris, and we went to the headquarters—"

Lindsay nods her head to the side, giving me the signal to leave.

God bless her.

I owe her so much In-N-Out.

I take my opportunity, slipping away from my grandparents while Nana tells a story about this café in Paris that dared to serve her the wrong kind of coffee, and I walk back up to our booth. I wish I could say that I'm home free, that Wyatt is waiting for me, that our food is already here so I can quell my grumbling stomach.

But when I get to our booth, I can see that Wyatt is talking to someone. And who could he be talking to? Who else at this god-forsaken wedding might he know? It's like a slow-motion reveal in a horror movie, when the identity of the true killer dawns on the audience and there's this collective understanding.

Josh is dressed in a nice black blazer and a white button-down that's hugging his chest in just the right way.

"Oh, there you are!" Wyatt smiles at me. "We were just talking about Mr. Daniels's last exam."

Josh turns to me as he comes down from laughing about something. I don't know what could possibly be so funny about Mr. Daniels or his AP History exams, but I don't like this. I don't like that Josh is talking to Wyatt.

Not. One. Bit.

"Hey, Neil."

"Hey." I keep my tone short, sliding into the booth next to Wyatt. I wrap my hand around his and keep us shoulder to shoulder.

Time to really put this lie to the test.

"Hi, Josh!" I grin when I say his name. "When did you get in?"

"Maybe two hours ago?" he says. "Had to reschedule my flight."

"Oh, that's a bummer."

"Yeah . . ." He sounds so dejected. What else did he expect? Coming here, talking to Wyatt behind my back. I'll have to have a conversation with Wyatt about what to say when I'm not around just in case Josh tries this again.

"Was the flight decent?" Wyatt asks.

"Yeah, there was a stop in Dallas, so it was extra long, but I'm glad to be here."

"That's nice." I clench my teeth.

"Is it?" Wyatt glances down at me. "I mean, our flight was already pretty long."

I squeeze his hand lightly.

"Are you excited to be here, Wyatt?" Josh asks.

What is he insinuating? That he shouldn't be excited to be here with me? Or that Wyatt should be on guard because Josh is here to win me back?

"Yeah, I've never been to the West Coast before. I'm hoping we'll have time to look around before the return flight."

"Right? It's a gorgeous city if you know the right places to go," Josh says. "Have you taken him to In-N-Out yet, Neil?"

"No. Not yet."

Josh smiles softly. "Neil loves In-N-Out. I got so sick of it last time we were here together. He wanted it for every meal."

Part of me wants to be angry at Josh for something as simple as talking, but I can't deny this weird comfort I feel from the moment. Almost like I enjoy him sitting here with us, having dinner. The fuck is up with that?

I shouldn't want to spend more time with Josh. If anything, I should be pushing him farther away. Once he's gone, I can stop getting all cozy next to Fowler. Though I'd be lying if I said I wasn't enjoying Wyatt's warmth.

"They don't have them in North Carolina," I mutter. "Had to get it while I was here."

That's when our waiter comes back to our table, two plates

of food balanced on his arms. It's just the starter salad, but it's Greek, the best type of salad.

"Will you be joining the table, sir?" the waiter asks Josh.

"Oh, no. I just stopped by to talk." Josh stands. And I almost have this compulsion to tell him to join us.

Almost.

"You guys enjoy." Josh gives us a wave, but then he doubles back. "Oh, and be careful, Neil; there are olives."

"Right. Thanks."

Of course there are olives in a Greek salad. It's literally a central element. A disgusting one, but still. I guess it's nice that he warned me, at least, even if I didn't need it.

"See you around, Josh," Wyatt says, and Josh goes to join his brother and mother at one of the other tables. Soon I see him laughing, talking with his family. He looks comfortable around them, at home.

I wonder what that feels like.

Thankfully, dinner is free of any other incidents. Lindsay eventually rejoins us, and I listen to her and Wyatt talk about some band called Day6 and its members. Then the soup comes out, and Wyatt doesn't touch a drop of it, followed by the pasta, which smells so good. The garlic and the sauce and the cheese

Pasta really is S-tier food.

There's even dessert in the form of pistachio cannoli, which kick ass. But we're both so stuffed that the extras come back to the hotel room with us. We're exhausted when we make it back, our bodies thinking it's well past midnight thanks to good ol' jet lag.

The second I get to the bedroom, I slip out of my dress pants and drag my sweatpants out of my bag.

"What if we split the bed?" Wyatt asks, already unbuttoning his shirt.

"What?"

"The bed. Can't we, like . . . alternate or something? You get it one night; I get it another?"

"Nope. It's my bed."

"How is that fair?"

"Because you're a guest, and it's my last name on the sign outside."

"You're a horrible host," he says. And it takes me a minute to realize that his voice has gotten closer. That's when I realize that he's been standing in the doorway, watching me get undressed like some kind of freak.

"Dude!" I cover up my crotch, even though I'm still wearing underwear.

"Pfft, what? We've been kinda-naked around each other before. Take a chill pill."

"That's when we're forced to share a room. There are *two* rooms here."

"Technically three," Wyatt says, walking right through to get to the bathroom.

The fact that the only entrance to the bathroom is through my room is an issue that I'm not ready to tackle just yet. I suppose it would be rude to ask him to use the public bathrooms on the lobby floor.

"What?" I sit on the edge of the bed, unbuttoning my own shirt, trying not to look at Wyatt where he stands in front of the bathroom mirror, shirtless, putting toothpaste on his toothbrush.

"Bathroom's a room," Wyatt says, goofy grin on his face. "Even has 'room' right in it."

I don't want to laugh, but I can't help the chuckle that escapes. "Shut up."

My eyes keep getting drawn to his bare back, which I've seen a hundred times before, but this time, there's something about the lighting. I wonder if Wyatt's ever dated any boys.

"I'm going to go out on the balcony, call my parents," he tells me when he's finished brushing his teeth.

"Okay." I lie back on the bed. I should brush my teeth too; I've definitely got garlic breath. I pull out my phone. There are a few missed texts, mostly ones from our group chat, the one that includes Josh.

I scroll for a bit; Samuel tells us about a man who got on the subway without pants on, and Mark's parents apparently decided to go visit family in Scotland, so he's taken some amazing pictures of rolling green hills. Julien tells us that he hasn't left his PC in at least ten hours and that he reached a new rank in *League*, and Hoon sent pictures of what he wore today when he went out.

And then there are texts from Josh, finally breaking his silence.

It's not much, not at first. Just that he landed in California safely. Then he and Julien get into some new skins that were released for this game they play together. After that, the conversations became normal again. All of them talking about everything and nothing at the same time. Hoon sending

TikToks, and Samuel liking every single one of them, like he couldn't make his crush on Hoon more obvious. Mark logging on to play games with Julien and Julien posting a video of Samuel's avatar diving off a cliff and dying just to avoid going down stairs.

And I haven't said a word.

They all sank back into normalcy, as if nothing happened, as if Josh and I hadn't had a huge fight, as if a foundation of all our friendships hadn't changed in some way.

Now it feels like it's not Josh who's the outsider—it's me.

Well, this isn't exactly a great feeling.

I want to send a text about the dinner, about how awful Mom is being, how terrible Nana was, how good the food was, how much I missed California. But every text feels pointless, and when more replies keep rolling in, each of them responses to other conversations I'm not a part of, it feels like there's no room to insert myself.

Like there isn't a place for me anymore.

That's overdramatic. I'm just in my feelings.

But still, it doesn't feel good.

I leave my phone to charge, stepping out into the living room. Wyatt's still outside, but he's not on the phone, not anymore at least. The balcony isn't a large one, even on the top floor. But it's enclosed, offering this peek out onto the city below us, and way, way, way past that, the rolling waves of the ocean. I can almost imagine the warm sand in my toes.

I slide open the door, listening to Wyatt's soft strumming. Usually his playing gets on my nerves, especially since he likes to do it when I'm studying.

But tonight, with the cool breeze rolling in from the ocean and the sounds of the city below us, it's a nice touch.

"How are your parents?" I ask, walking out, leaning against the iron railing.

"Good." Wyatt watches his fingers pluck the strings. "They were excited to watch *Jeopardy!* together for once, but they're dealing with it better than expected."

"Is that a song you're playing?"

"What else could it be?" he asks with a smile.

I give him a look. "You know what I mean."

"Yeah, it's a song."

"Which one? Sing some lyrics."

"I don't, uh . . ." It's hard to tell in the darkness, but I'm sure Wyatt's cheeks are going red.

"Come on, I've never heard you sing live before." I almost say *in person* but I feel like Wyatt knowing I've watched his videos will get me in trouble. "If I'm going to get you an audition, I need to hear what you've got."

"Okay, but . . . can you close your eyes?"

"What?"

"I get stage fright. Do you mind closing your eyes?"

"You get stage fright, but you'll post your covers online?"

Wyatt freezes. "You've seen those?"

I nod.

"You didn't tell me you'd seen them."

"Is that really information you would've liked to have?"

Wyatt waits a beat. "No, guess not." He pauses again. "It's different. When I'm singing to a camera versus in person."

"Fine," I tell him. "I'll close my eyes when you start to sing."

Wyatt sighs. He still looks timid, which is so unlike him, but I do notice this slouch in his shoulders as he starts to pluck at the strings again, playing the soft melody. The song starts off with this steady beat, and it's pretty fascinating to watch him play. I've always wanted to learn an instrument. Mom even made me take piano lessons when I was ten, but then I started skipping them, and she said she wasn't going to keep paying if I wasn't going to go. I almost wish she'd forced me to.

Wyatt's fingers move so effortlessly, almost as if the guitar is a natural extension of his body, something that he doesn't even have to think about. His foot taps along to another beat, the notes flowing softly. I close my eyes.

Then he starts singing.

"I wanna play this for you all the time. I wanna play this for you when you're feeling used and tired—"

His voice live is just as soft and warm as it was on the recordings I found online. There's also this edge to it. It cuts into me deep, in a way that I both love and regret.

I don't want to open my eyes, but . . .

I can't help myself.

I want to watch him.

Just a peek, that's it.

But when I open my left eye, I can see him sitting there, his own eyes closed as he plays without even having to look at the strings.

He doesn't play the whole song for me, though I wish he would. Still, after he runs out of words, he keeps playing his guitar. He finally opens his eyes, and he sees me standing there. The notes turn sour as he grips his guitar, this look of shock and horror on his face.

"You said you wouldn't stare!"

"Sorry, sorry!" I cover my eyes quickly. "I was just curious! But Carly Rae Jepsen's 'All That'—could you be more of a stereotype?"

Wyatt bends over, mostly so he won't have to look at me, I think. "Was it . . . was it good? Do you think that your brother will like it?"

What do I tell Wyatt? That I think his voice is beautiful? That I want him to sing more songs? That I want him to serenade me again? No, that's all too much. Even if it is the truth. His voice *is* beautiful; it's one of the most beautiful voices I've ever heard. And I *do* want him to sing another song. And if he sang just to me again . . . well, I wouldn't be upset.

"My brother has made some stupid decisions in his life," I tell Wyatt. "But he'd be a complete idiot not to love your singing."

This wild grin spreads on his face, and he looks up at me quickly. "Seriously?"

"I'm serious," I say. "It was really good, Wyatt. I mean that."

And I do.

I absolutely do.

"When do you think we can do the audition?" he asks.

Right. I mean, why wouldn't he be curious? That's what he's here for, after all.

"I'll talk to him about it tomorrow. I should have a chance during brunch."

"Okay, cool . . . yeah."

"Nervous?"

"A little."

"You're going to kill it, dude. Just relax. If you play half as good for him as you did for me, he'll want to see more. And if he doesn't, I'll just beat him up until he signs you."

Wyatt scoffs at me. "You couldn't hurt a fly, Kearney."

"Oh yeah?" I reach over, flicking Wyatt on the forehead. "How's that?"

"Ow!" He winces.

"Big baby."

Then Wyatt is standing up quickly. And you know, if he were anyone else, I might be afraid of him. It's probably the height, and the little bit of muscle. But I know he's a total teddy bear.

Still. For a second there, my heart skips a beat. The dark expression on his face; the way he seems to tower over me in this moment.

Then he flicks me in the forehead.

"Ow!"

"Not so nice, is it?"

"Shove it, Fowler." I push lightly against his chest, but he hardly budges. And we're left standing there, inches apart from each other. Me staring up at him, him staring down at me. He reaches up slowly with his fingers. Oh my God, is this happening? Is he going to try to kiss me?

What the fuck?

Why would he do that?

We're not acting right now; there's no one to pretend for.

Do I push him away?

Do I say no?

Do I duck away so he knows I don't want this?

But what if I do?

Wait, what? What am I thinking? Seriously? Kissing Fowler?

Wyatt's fingers move closer and closer, until he's reaching for my eye. He carefully plucks something from my cheek.

"Eyelash," he says, showing me the long black lash on the tip of his index finger. "Make a wish."

"What?"

"Never heard that? My moms do this all the time. When you lose an eyelash and you catch it before it falls to the floor, you blow on it while making a wish. Then it'll come true."

"Pfft, that's stupid."

I feel relief. And confusion. Why did I automatically assume that he was just going to kiss me?

And why do I feel a twinge of disappointment?

"Fine, then." Wyatt huffs in a lungful of air.

"Wait! That's my eyelash. My eyelash, my wish."

"Fine."

I think for a second, and then I blow. The eyelash flies off his finger, to God knows where.

"What did you wish for?" he asks me.

"Won't that make it not come true?"

"I think that's just with birthday candles."

I shrug. "I wished that we'd go to bed. It's been a long day and I'm beat."

Wyatt eyes me suspiciously before grabbing his guitar. "You know, something tells me that you're lying."

"Me? Lie? Never."

We both head inside, Wyatt packing his precious instrument away as I strip down in the bedroom, leaving my clothes in a pile on the floor. And just as I head to the door to close it, I watch him crawl under the blankets on the couch.

"Night, Fowler."

I flip the light switch, leaving us both in the dark.

"Night, Kearney."

I dive into my own bed, sinking under the comforter, and as I fall asleep, I think about Wyatt's song, his voice, and my wish.

I want to hear Wyatt sing again.

Sunday

APRIL 17

I wake up at six thirty the next morning.

Because of course I do.

I hate jet lag, and time changes. It's such bullshit, even if we do need them. What do time changes even really do? What have they ever done for me?

Worst part is that I don't even feel refreshed when I open my eyes. I have a headache, and my eyes are crusty.

God.

Fuck this day already.

I go right for my phone, scrolling through Instagram and Snapchat for a bit before checking TikTok. But there's nothing interesting going on anywhere, so I flip on the TV until I find the cartoon channels and just sit there with my brain off for a bit. Then, about twenty minutes later, my phone dings.

> SAMUEL: soooooo . . . .
> SAMUEL: you've seen Josh right?
> SAMUEL: like he's officially at the wedding festivities?

I could just ignore him. I should just ignore him.

> ME: Yeah.
> SAMUEL: how are you handling it?
> ME: What do you mean?

SAMUEL: well, it's probably pretty awkward, right?

ME: I haven't really noticed.

That's a lie. A complete and total lie.

And Samuel will probably be able to see right through it.

SAMUEL: i smell bullshittttttttttttttttt

ME: How are things going with Hoon?

SAMUEL: 😌

SAMUEL: low blow kearney

SAMUEL: have you talked at all?

ME: He showed up at dinner last night.

SAMUEL: with your family? how did that go?

ME: He basically cornered Wyatt and interrogated him.

SAMUEL: . . . .

SAMUEL: i meant the dinner part

ME: Oh . . .

ME: As well as you'd expect.

ME: Met my brother's fiancée for literally the first time.

ME: My grandmother asked me if I was out of this "phase" yet.

ME: Then she deadnamed me.

ME: But the pasta was good.

SAMUEL: where are you staying?

SAMUEL: i'm gonna go drop-kick that geriatric little fuck

ME: Be my guest.

For a moment, I feel like revealing the entire plan to Samuel, just so I have someone besides Wyatt who I'm not lying to, someone who I can talk to about this entire situation. Besides

Josh, Samuel was always the one guy who I felt like I could go to with anything. Not that I ever did—my business is my business—but the thought was nice. As far as I'm aware, he's the only other out trans kid at Steerfield. I'm sure there are others; at a school with three thousand students, there are bound to be other trans kids. It's just statistics.

But Samuel and I are the only out ones, so there are things that he understands. Like the strange way that some of our classmates will look at us, or sitting in the sex-ed course in Health 2 and not having to pay attention at all because for some reason the curriculum doesn't think education about vaginas is needed. Samuel's parents were a little more understanding, though, and never tried to bury that part of him when he was a kid. He's far from the youngest kid ever to really start on the journey to hormone blockers and testosterone, but he started young enough that top surgery was never going to be an issue for him. It always made me pretty jealous.

SAMUEL: you hear how paranoid you sound, right?
SAMUEL: about josh.
ME: No.
ME: What if he said something? What if he's plotting to break us up.
ME: Wyatt said he was talking about a quiz in Daniels's class. But I just know something else was going on.
SAMUEL: you're a dummy
SAMUEL: josh isn't going to do that
SAMUEL: he was literally just talking to wyatt. it's not that deep.

ME: I don't even remember Josh having Daniels this semester.
SAMUEL: he does
SAMUEL: he literally sits right next to me
SAMUEL: and wyatt sits behind him
SAMUEL: youre being paranoid

Deep down I know that Samuel's right. But I just need to be sure. I need to ask Wyatt if he'll tell me what Josh said last night.

It's just to make sure the plan isn't in jeopardy.

Wyatt wouldn't have outright told him this entire thing is fake.

But what if he slipped up, what if he messed up the story, what if he got details wrong?

After talking with Samuel for a bit longer about New York, I roll out of bed to pee, and after I'm done I slip on sweatpants and a T-shirt after remembering that I'm sharing this room, and that I probably shouldn't just walk out into the living room in my underwear.

I open the door, prepared to see Wyatt still asleep on the couch, probably snoring, drooling even. But he isn't there. His "bed" is made, pillows left to the side, blanket folded. He isn't on the balcony, and he definitely isn't in the bathroom.

He's gone.

It's fine; he probably just went to go get breakfast or something.

It's fine, it's fine.

That doesn't stop me from tapping my nails on the counter. Samuel's right—I'm being paranoid. Why do I even care about where he's gone? So long as he's back in time for the brunch, it shouldn't matter. And he can't get lost if his phone is charged.

It's fine.

This is fine.

He only comes back after I've taken a shower and I'm flipping through the channels on the television, where I find what—according to the TV guide—seems to be an all-day marathon of one of those sitcoms that people who don't have a personality make their personalities, but I sit there anyway and watch it because there's nothing else on and I don't have the energy to type in my Netflix info.

After a few minutes of suffering through the laugh track, I hear the beep of the card reader and the lock clicking, and Wyatt strolls in, a tray with two iced coffees in one hand, and a paper bag in the other.

"Good morning!" Wyatt sings, a little too chipper, one earbud tucked in his ear while the other hangs loose.

"Coffee?" I stare at the drinks he's presenting me.

"Yeah, figured you might want some." Wyatt's got his signature Americano, and what looks to be an iced mocha for me? "There's this little café down the street, really cute. They had a cat!"

"Right . . ."

"Your sandwich is bacon, egg, and cheese. I didn't really know what you'd want."

It's not until the smell of the breakfast food hits me that I realize how starved I am.

"You're the best person I know," I say, unwrapping the sandwich and taking the biggest bite I can manage.

"A compliment? That's new." Wyatt unwraps his own food and sips from his coffee. "When did you wake up?"

"Like thirty minutes ago." I talk with my mouth full. God, this sandwich is so good. I want to marry it.

"Same. This time change messed me up."

"You'll get used to it after a day or two."

Wyatt and I carry our food and coffee to the show playing in the background. I have no idea what it is, but it's decent background noise, filling this void so that we don't have to talk to each other.

"I don't get why people still love this show, it's, like, fifty years old," he says, breaking the silence.

"I dunno."

"It's not even funny, but the laugh track tries to make you think it is."

"Yeah." I share the same opinions, but I don't really know how to have a conversation with him right now.

I want to ask Wyatt about his conversation with Josh last night. I want to know every little detail, what Josh asked him, how Wyatt answered.

How do I ask, though?

I guess being direct is the best policy.

"Can I ask you something?"

"Hmm?" Wyatt turns to me, his sandwich stuck in his mouth mid-bite. "What's up?"

Except with the food in his mouth, it comes out more like *Wha ah?*

"What did Josh say to you last night?"

"Whadyo ean?" *What do you mean?*

"Did he ask you anything about us? Did he say anything to you about me?"

"Oh." *No.*

"Please just take the food out of your mouth. I'm being serious here. Did he say anything at all about me?"

"He asked where you were, and I told him you had to schmooze with your family for a bit. That's it, literally the only time you came up."

"Are you sure?"

"The conversation wasn't that deep."

"Can you give me the rundown?"

"Are you serious?"

"I just want to make sure he didn't tell you anything that you shouldn't have heard, or that you said something you shouldn't have said."

Wyatt lets out this sudden low laugh. "We're not spies, Neil. We're pretending to be boyfriends. It's not that big of a deal."

"I know, I know. I'm just . . . worried about what he might've said."

"Like that you're rude and abrasive and pretty selfish?"

"He said all that?" I'm going to kick Josh's ass.

"No, no! But I live with you. I've seen you at your worst. What is Josh going to tell me that I don't already know? Unless you've got a lizard tail, or if your family is secretly a cult and there isn't really a wedding, and I was dragged here for a ritual sacrifice."

I stare at him.

Wyatt shrugs. "It happens."

"It really doesn't."

But if those aren't things that Josh said, does that mean . . . ?

"Is that how you see me?" I ask.

Wyatt sighs, setting his food down on the coffee table. "You've got to admit, dude, you're not the easiest person to get along with."

"I try."

"Do you?"

"Whatever." I brush him off. "I just don't want Josh filling your head with ideas."

"What exactly is he going to tell me?"

"I don't know." I hate that I don't have an answer for him. I should have one, but I don't. "I just don't want him to mess things up with us."

Wyatt raises an eyebrow. "With us?"

He eats the final bite of his sandwich.

"You know what I mean."

Wyatt relaxes back into the couch. "You're worried about nothing. Josh just wanted to talk about Daniels's class and this book we're reading. It was small talk, you know. Normal stuff."

"I just want you to be careful."

"You're making him sound like an anime villain. Isn't he your friend?"

"Yeah! I think, I don't . . ." Really know where we stand. "I just don't want you to slip up, forget that we're here to make him get over me."

"No worries there." Wyatt balls up the paper his sandwich was wrapped in, and then he takes mine. "I'm a good actor."

I watch him as he walks into the kitchen, dumping our garbage. He's right, we've got nothing to worry about. I was being paranoid. Josh has no reason to doubt that this relationship is real, and we've got six whole days to prove to him that I've moved past what we had, that we can go back to being friends with no bad blood between us.

For now, though, we'll have to convince my family we're together as well.

Brunch is in the hotel garden. There's a man at the entrance, standing in front of the sign that marks the gardens as closed for a private party. I wonder how the influencers of LA feel about their prime photo location being closed for the day.

There are vertical gardens filled with flowers of every breed and color, a gorgeous fountain, these tall hedges that provide the perfect backgrounds.

If there's one thing Mom has an eye for, it's gardens.

She loves her gardens.

"Fancy," Wyatt whispers as we step past the gate. Because we're tucked in the shade, the temperature drops what has to be, like, ten degrees. "So, who is this brunch for?"

"Mostly just my family. People who arrived late last night, this morning."

"Is this entire week just going to be us eating at different places in Los Angeles?" Wyatt asks. "I gotta say, I wouldn't be mad about that."

"I wish it were going to be that simple."

We walk through the archway covered with blooming roses. Right in the middle of the garden, in front of the gorgeous fountain, there's a white tent that's already half full of my relatives. Mom, Michael, Ashley, and my grandparents are at the head table, of course. Lindsay and her parents are a few feet away at another table. The rest of the tent is populated by family members and people I haven't seen in years. Other cousins and second cousins who I like much less than I like Lindsay.

Uncles and aunts, nieces and nephews, some of Mom's best friends and their younger children, who are off playing in the grass, staining their shirts. And there are some people I don't know—probably from Ashley's side.

Mom sees us from across the yard and motions us over, pointing to the opposite end of her table, where there are two empty chairs just waiting for us.

"Is it too late to run away?" I ask Wyatt.

"It won't be that bad," he promises, reaching down to hold my hand.

Right, we're dating.

"You got off easy last night, Fowler. I'll go ahead and apologize up front for whatever they might say to, through, or about you."

We make our way to the center table and take the empty seats.

"Aren't you going to introduce us?" Nana says before I even have a chance to open my mouth.

"This is my boyfriend, Wyatt."

Grandpa reaches across Nana. "Nice to meet you, son," he grumbles while offering Wyatt a handshake.

"Nice to meet you," Wyatt replies, shaking Grandpa's hand. Thank God Wyatt already has good manners. The less ammunition he gives them, the better.

"Quite the handshake you got there, son," my grandfather says admiringly. "What sports do you play?"

"Oh, none, sir. But I play the guitar."

"I see." Grandpa stares at Wyatt, this unsure look on his face.

"How did you boys sleep?" Mom asks.

"Fine," I reply. "We slept fine."

For what it's worth, brunch isn't that bad. Everyone seems more preoccupied with talking to everyone else. No one makes comments about my weight or my gender or my surgeries. Grandpa tries to occupy Wyatt in conversations about baseball and soccer, the two things he knows most about in this world. And poor Wyatt just has to sit there and endure it, even when he admits that the only baseball team he knows anything about is the Yankees.

Then Nana starts asking her questions.

"So, Wyatt. What do your parents do?"

"Oh, well, one of my moms is a teacher. And my other mom is a librarian."

"Mothers," Nana says slowly. "Two mothers?"

"Yes, ma'am."

I need water.

"No father?" Grandpa asks. "A boy needs a father figure, don't you think?"

"Well, my father can't really parent from his urn on the mantel." Wyatt lets out this soft chuckle, and I have to resist laughing while my family sits there in their discomfort. "But both my moms raised me pretty well, so I've been just fine without a father figure," Wyatt says matter-of-factly.

I barely have time to aim away from everyone in front of me as I spray the water out of my mouth.

Between that and what Wyatt just said, no one really knows where to look. We all kind of just sit there, staring at him for hours. Or it feels like hours at least. I had zero idea that Wyatt had a dead parent, that that was something he was carrying with him. But at the same time, seeing the reactions from the rest of my family, it's pretty hilarious.

Then I can't stop myself from laughing.

"Right then." Grandpa clears his throat. "Maybe that's why you don't know much about baseball." He brushes it off like a joke, but I know that tone. The discomfort of Wyatt's joke is still so obvious on everyone's face, and as embarrassed as I am, I can't help but feel a little proud of Wyatt in this moment.

"Actually, my mama is a big baseball fan. I just don't find it that interesting."

"Hmm . . ." Grandpa hums, and goes back to nursing his mimosa.

After that, they're gracious enough to leave Wyatt alone. I do put my hand on top of his to get his attention when I notice how rigid his body goes, how quiet.

"Sorry," I mouth to him.

He just gives me a sympathetic look and a shrug.

The rest of brunch passes quickly, with another set menu of omelets and bacon and quiches and waffles and fruit salads.

When the final course has been served and eaten, and everyone else seems tipsy and buried in their own conversations, I nod to Wyatt, motioning for us to take our chance to get out of the tent. We're nearly out of the garden too when Mom calls my name.

I turn, and she's standing by the tent, waving me back over to her.

"So close," I whisper. "Wait here. I won't subject you to her any more than you have to be."

"Fair." Wyatt tucks his hands in his pockets and sits on the brick half wall around the entrance as I race back toward Mom.

"Where are you going?"

"Back to the hotel. I thought we were done eating."

"Is food all you care about?" she says with a certain level of venom in her voice. Like how dare I eat food at a brunch.

"I just thought—"

"You didn't even say goodbye to your grandmother. She's very upset with you."

"I don't want to talk to her."

"Neil, please. I'm asking you nicely. And do tell Wyatt not to mention his parents again. You know how your grand-parents feel."

"You mean I know how homophobic they are? Yeah, I'm fully aware."

"They're just from a different time."

"Such bullshit," I mumble.

"What was that?"

"Nothing." I keep my head down.

"I want you to go get fitted for your suit. Your appoint-ment is today. Does Wyatt have the appropriate attire for the wedding?"

"I was going to get him fitted for a suit too." I don't want to admit to basically stealing from her right in front of her face, but she doesn't seem to mind actually.

"That's fine; you can have them put it on the same bill as your suit. But I was also talking about the other events."

Her voice has taken on this sudden trepidation. Almost like she's afraid to say what she's saying. Which is extremely odd coming from her.

"What do you mean?"

"Look at how he's dressed," Mom whispers.

I turn to look at Wyatt, typing something on his phone. He looks nice; he's wearing a button-down and khakis. Not exactly the outfit I would've picked out, but this was brunch with my family; I wasn't going to make him put on his Sunday best.

"His clothes are faded, Neil. And the shoes look like they're from Target."

"Is there something wrong with that?" I ask. Sure, I've made fun of Wyatt's clothing before, but that's something *I'm* allowed to do. Not her.

"Just buy him some decent options. My friends were staring at him when he walked in. And maybe convince him to get a trim while you're out. Put it on the emergency card." Mother stares at me intently, and something about her gaze just makes me shut down.

"Yes, ma'am," I say.

If my entire family hates Wyatt's clothes, that's all the more reason to let him wear whatever he wants. Hell, he could come to the rehearsal dinner naked, for all I care. If it pisses off Mother, it's worth it.

"Good." She brushes something off my shoulder, and then takes some of my hair in her fingers. "Maybe you should get a trim too."

"Yes, ma'am."

With a smile and a nod, she turns around and goes back to her mimosas and our family. I turn, walking past Wyatt and out onto the Beverly Hills sidewalk.

"Neil! Wait up!" Wyatt shouts behind me.

I just want to walk. Somewhere, anywhere. The farther away from my family the better.

"Neil!" Wyatt grabs my hand, stopping me in my tracks. Anger swells in my stomach for a second before I remember he's not the person I should be mad at right now.

"Sorry, sorry. I just had to get away from them." I try to slow my breathing a bit. I need to relax.

"Yeah, that was . . . something."

"I'm sorry for what they said to you."

"Are your grandparents always that charming?"

"Honestly? Count yourself lucky they didn't say something worse." Then I remember. "Sorry about your dad too. I had no idea."

"Why are you sorry?"

"I . . . I don't really know. It just feels like the appropriate thing to say after learning something like that."

"He died when I was a baby, so I never really knew him."

"What happened?" The second I say the words, I suck in my bottom lip. "Holy shit, don't answer that. I'm so sorry."

"Dude, what are you freaking out for?"

"Because you might not want to talk about your dead dad?"

Wyatt actually laughs. "You're taking this way more seriously than I am. It's not a big deal."

"It's still weird, though, right?"

Wyatt shrugs. "I don't know. I was, like, two when he died. He was diagnosed with pretty aggressive prostate cancer. It all happened pretty quick."

"Damn, that sucks."

"Yeah," Wyatt says quietly, staring down at his feet. "But, ya know. There's nothing I can do. And my mom is happy now, so I guess it all worked out."

"Is that really the healthiest way to think about it?"

"You're one to talk about healthy coping mechanisms." Wyatt finally lets go of my hand. "What did your mom want?"

"We're getting fitted for the suits, and she wants me to buy you new clothing. She hates how you're dressed."

"What's wrong with my clothes?" Wyatt looks down at himself.

I could point out how the pants are last season, how the shoes have scuff marks on them, how the shirt looks faded, but I keep that all to myself.

It won't get me anywhere.

"Let me put it this way: The woman doesn't understand the concept of wearing something for comfort or wearing something more than twice, and that's only if she *really* likes it. She cares a lot about appearances—that's her whole thing. If she thinks you look bad, she also thinks it makes *her* look bad."

Everything I did as a kid, she thought it would color how people saw her. How I dressed, how I behaved in public, even the grades I got in school. She thought it all came back to her.

Imagine her surprise when the articles started to pop up.

Mother is just the right level of famous to not have to worry about paparazzi out in public, but she's also a topic of interest whenever anything scandalous happens around her. So, my wild nights, sneaking into the queer clubs that populate Los Angeles, I never actually drank or did any drugs or things like that, but it was enough to just be seen in these clubs and for people to connect the dots.

It all came back to her.

"Where do we have to go?" Wyatt's calming question draws me back into myself.

"Rodeo. The Gucci store there does fittings."

"Right." Wyatt shuffles uncomfortably. "How far?"

"More than a walk," I tell him before I pull out my phone and order a car. Might as well get this over with as quickly as possible.

"Do you have a suit style in mind?" I ask Wyatt after we're dropped off and we approach the Gucci store in the middle of Rodeo Drive.

He looks at me like he's surprised I've asked him the question. "What do you mean?"

"I mean what kind of suit do you like?"

"Oh, um . . . I don't really know?" It comes out more of a question than an answer. "Is there more than one kind?"

I shouldn't even be surprised; it's my fault for assuming he'd know anything fancier than his school uniform.

"You'd probably look good in a slim fit," I say, giving him a quick glance over. "Or maybe a shawl lapel? We'd have to be careful, though—you're not in the wedding party and I don't want you to look like you're in a tuxedo."

Wyatt stares ahead. "Right."

"You have no idea what I'm talking about, do you?"

"Not one bit," he says with a lopsided grin.

The moment we step inside the Gucci store, I feel at home amid the smell of the perfumes and the leather.

"Hello, gentlemen," the store associate greets us at the door. "What might we help you with today?"

"I have an appointment for a fitting, Kearney wedding. I'm Neil. And I was hoping to get him scheduled for a fitting as well? This is Wyatt. My date." I put my hand on Wyatt's shoulder.

The associate goes to check his records and returns quickly. "We should have the time. Which of you would like to go first?"

I volunteer, and we follow the associate to the back of the store. I get up on a platform in front of these mirrors so he can take my measurements.

"Our notes say that you're in the party, correct?"

"Yeah, I'm a groomsman."

"The color of the jacket is a deep violet."

Of course Michael would go for a purple wedding; the color feels cool and relaxed, like him.

"Are you in the party as well, sir?" the associate asks Wyatt, but I answer for him.

"No, he's not."

Wyatt gives me a stink eye. "What color should I pick?"

"Deep navy or dark gray are traditional for men," the associate tells him. "Though lately forest green has been popular."

"I think you'd look good in something between slate and charcoal," I say.

"Oh, do you?"

"Shove it, Fowler."

He sits there with a grin while my measurements are finished. Then the associate steps to the back and grabs the suit I'll be wearing. The color is a lot darker than I imagined. More fashionable than the clown suit I predicted.

I change, stepping back onto the platform with the arms and legs of the suit too long on my body. The associate pins the areas of the suit that will need to be adjusted, which thankfully isn't in too many places, and I'm told to go change, and to be careful of the pins.

Then it's Wyatt's turn.

It's obvious that he's never been measured for a suit before because he stands there uncomfortably while the measuring tape is wrapped around his arm, thigh, chest, inseam. Though I can't exactly blame him for being uncomfortable for that last one.

"We have a few different styles that you can try on," the associate tells us. "What were you thinking?"

"Something simple," I say. No way in hell is Wyatt picking his own suit. "I was thinking a slim fit; let's try charcoal first."

"Yes, sir." The associate heads to the storeroom.

"Is knowing a lot about suits a rich-person thing?"

"You don't have to be rich to know about style," I scoff.

The associate brings out a deep charcoal suit and Wyatt stares at himself in the mirror as he slips the jacket on. "Isn't this just black?"

"Charcoal," I say. "There's a difference."

"Would you like to try the pants on?" the associate offers.

"Yeah, if that's okay."

"I'll show you to the dressing room."

A minute later, Wyatt comes out wearing the jacket and the matching pants, his pink shirt on underneath, and black socks on his feet. I expect him to look good—like, that's totally a thing, thinking that people look good in suits.

But Wyatt looks *really* good, and I don't know how to feel about it.

Even if it hasn't been tailored yet, the suit fits him well, and the pink brings out his tan. Even with his unruly hair and those stupid little hoops in his ears, he looks more handsome than I've ever seen him.

"How do you feel?" I ask.

"It's soft on the inside."

"Fully lined to prevent catching," the associate tells him. "It may be warmer in the heat, though we were informed this would be an evening wedding, so you should be fine."

"How do I look?" Wyatt asks me, giving a quick turn. Both articles need to be hemmed, obviously. The fitted part hasn't exactly had time to be applied yet, but I have no doubt he'll look fantastic when it's done.

"I think that's the one," I say.

Wyatt smiles as he steps on the platform again, giving the associate time to pin everything in place, which takes a bit longer than my own.

"Bow tie or tie?" the associate asks.

"Bow tie," I say.

"A bow tie? Really?" Wyatt glares at me.

"It'll look good."

"What if I don't want to wear one?"

I rear my head back. "It's the style."

He sticks his tongue out at me as the last pin is slipped in, and with that, he's directed to change back into his old outfit.

When he returns, I say, "Come on, we should look at shirts for you while we're here."

There are a few cute options that I immediately grab without even knowing Wyatt's size. A nice striped cotton shirt, a simple blue cotton poplin shirt, and a soft pink with the Gucci logo printed in a slightly lighter pink, though I don't think that last one would be appropriate for another brunch.

"How much even is this stuff?" Wyatt tugs at one of the tags on the shirt. "Seven hundred and fifty dollars?" He stares at me, his mouth agape.

"Don't sound so dramatic—it's tacky."

"I'm not doing this," he says.

"They're just shirts. You'll even get to keep them afterward."

"I'm not going to keep them."

"Well, you can't return them, and they're not my size, so I don't know what you want me to do here."

"Not buy them."

"I have to."

"No, you don't."

"Wyatt, please."

"Why can't we just go to Target? They have those here; I saw three of them on the drive over. They've got nice shirts that don't cost a mortgage payment!"

I pull away from him. "You're getting nice clothing for free. Stop complaining."

"I didn't ask you to do this."

"No, you didn't," I say. "My mother did. And she's paying."

He stands in this empty spot between racks, leaning against the wall with his arms crossed, like a child who's restless after being forced to come shopping. I ask the associate to confirm Wyatt's size, then pick out shirts that he'll be able to wear for the next five days, as well as a simple white button-down that he can wear with the suit.

He follows me in silence to the cashier, where I pay for everything with the credit card that Mom gave me when I left for Steerfield. We're instructed to return in two days to try on the suits again, to leave time for any last-minute adjustments.

By the time everything is bagged up, Wyatt's outside, sitting on a nearby bench.

"Hey." I have to keep myself from shouting, so people won't

look at us. Why is he acting like this? Usually, I get to be the petulant child, not him. "What's your deal?"

He crosses his arms, staring down at his shoes.

"So you're just going to ignore me?"

"I'm not ignoring you."

"Then what happened in there? You were acting like a child."

"Let's just go."

"No." I stand my ground firmly. I won't go anywhere until he admits what's wrong.

"Now who's the child?"

"Dude, just tell me what's wrong. How are we going to survive this week if we aren't honest with each other?"

"I just . . . Do you know how that felt?"

"What? The suits?"

"The suits, the shirts, hearing that your family makes fun of the way that I dress."

"Wyatt." I slump down next to him on the bench, and he scoots away from me.

And I scoot closer.

"Neil." He sighs.

"Wyatt."

"Just give me some space, please."

"We need to be honest with each other," I repeat. "You have to mute any comments my mother makes. That's what I do. It's the only way you'll survive this week."

He stares down at his feet again, his arms still crossed.

"It's not just that. It felt weird, the fact that you just bought me all that without asking if I was comfortable."

"But I wasn't making you pay!"

"Exactly." He finally looks at me. "You basically just spent what my mom makes in a couple months teaching on clothing that I don't even want. Do you know what seven thousand dollars would mean for my family? We'd have extra food; we could make repairs to our house; my mama could knock off a bit of her student loans or their credit card debt."

I sit there, more than a little shocked at what he's telling me.

I'd never even considered that, not until he said something. Hell, I'd never even batted an eye at the idea of spending that much money on anything at once, how I didn't have to worry about my bank accounts, and that I was able to just assume that Mom had plenty for me to spend.

We'd always had more than enough, never scared of not being able to afford anything like a home or food or school.

"I didn't think about it that way," I admit.

"And you never do. All the months of you making fun of my clothes, my uniform, how old some of my stuff is." Wyatt hesitates, his breathing a little irregular now. "You know, I never really cared when you made fun of me, but when you'd insult my clothes, my phone, things that my parents worked hard to get for me—that was when your words really hurt me."

It's like Wyatt stabbed me, right in the gut, and each word is him twisting it just a little more.

I say, "I didn't . . ."

Think of it that way.

I can't just say that again, but it's the truth; I never thought about how Wyatt might feel, or how he got those things, that he might not have the ability to have nicer, newer things, or that he was perfectly content with them.

I breathe in and out, slowly.

"I'm sorry, Wyatt."

"It's whatever."

"No, it doesn't have to be whatever. I am sorry."

"Remember how at the airport, you said that I couldn't understand what you were going through when the TSA agents harassed you?"

I don't say anything, and I let my silence be my reply.

"This is like that for me. You're not going to understand what I've experienced. How hard I have to study to stay at Steerfield, and the relief I feel that, since I'm not home, that's one less mouth my parents have to feed. You don't understand what they have to do to put clothes on my back, and my sister's back, or to get me a phone that works. And the worst part is that I don't care—I don't care about what I don't have. But so many other people at that stupid fucking school do."

I don't say anything.

I don't know what I could possibly say to make this any better.

And maybe that's my answer, that I can't make this better. I can't just pay Wyatt to forget about this and move on. I can't buy him clothes to make him forget. I can't do anything but sit here and take it.

Because honestly, that's what I deserve right now.

Wyatt continues. "When we were assigned roommates, there was this hope I had, that you might finally be different. But you weren't, and I bit my tongue, I didn't say anything, because if I make too many waves, then my place at Steerfield might be jeopardized, and then everything I have put my family through and everything I have put myself through will be for nothing. Absolutely nothing."

There are tears behind his eyes, and his hands are starting to shake.

I reach over carefully, unsure if he even wants me to touch him right now. I grab his hand in his lap, and I rub small circles in the space between his index finger and his thumb.

He says, "The only reason my moms let me go on this whole trip with you was because they felt bad. They didn't tell me that, but I could hear it. They knew this might be the only way that I'd ever get a trip like this, especially for spring break. So they let me go."

"Wyatt . . ."

"Whatever." He wipes his eyes with his free hand.

"No, I told you—not whatever." I try to keep my breathing steady. "I'm really sorry. I really am. I didn't realize that I made you feel that way."

"How else was I supposed to feel, though?"

More than anything else he's said, that question takes me aback the most. Because he's right. I saw these things about him and decided to make snap judgments. I decided to ridicule and tease him.

Because that's just who I am.

I thought that was reason enough.

My perfect little bullshit reason.

"There's no excuse," I tell him.

"No, there isn't."

"I'm sorry you sat with that for so long."

"Sorry I blew up at you."

"I mean, I deserve it."

He finally looks at me. "Yeah, you do."

There's something about his tone—I can't explain it, but it makes me want to laugh. I can't stop myself from smiling, and then he starts to smile at me, and we both laugh at each other, and at ourselves.

Wyatt takes his hand back, covering his face and brushing his hair away from his forehead.

We both sit there for a moment, in silence, a few people staring at us after our little Hallmark moment.

"For what it's worth, I really am sorry," I say. "I mean it."

I don't know what to do next—if I should promise to be better, that I'll think before I say something, that I'll stop being so judgmental. But saying all of that feels so shallow, so disingenuous.

Maybe Wyatt sees me struggling, because he says, "For what it's worth, I forgive you."

I lean into him a little more. "Not to be cheesy, but when this is all over, when we're back at Steerfield and we're broken up or whatever you want to call it, I'd like to be your friend."

Wyatt smiles slowly. "I'd like that."

"Good." And this is probably the wrong thing to say, but it feels right all the same: "Can I take you out to dinner tonight?"

Wyatt glares at me, as if we didn't just have this whole conversation.

"Not like—" I struggle to find the right words. "I want to take you out as a friend, not as fake boyfriends or whatever. I just want to treat you to a nice dinner. But not too nice. Moderately nice. A Target dinner, not a Gucci dinner."

Wyatt chuckles, and for a moment I think he might turn me down, which would just be the icing on the whole cake of today. But when Wyatt turns to me, he's still smiling.

"Yeah, I think I'd like that," he says. "But it's only one o'clock right now."

"Okay, what do you want to do until tonight?"

"Well, you promised me that you'd show me around your city."

"Pfft, my city."

"You know it better than I do."

I smile at him, and he smiles right back. "Fine."

I hold out my hand, and when he takes it, we hoist each other up.

If he wants to see my city, then I'll show him my city.

"Let's go."

I want to take him to the observatory, to the Getty, to the Science Center. There are all-ages queer bars and clubs that I bet he'd kill to see, and even some twenty-one-and-over places I could probably still get into, but it's too early for any of them to be open. There's the boardwalk, and so many amazing hiking trails with killer views. I want to take him to so many restaurants like In-N-Out or Bob's Big Boy. Hell, I'd even settle for getting dropped off in a random neighborhood and just showing him some of the cool houses.

But we'll have more time for all of that in the days after the wedding.

So the question becomes: What do I show him first?

Everything we pass seems antithetical to where I want to start with Wyatt. The high-end stores and boutiques, the classy eating joints where you pay three times as much for a quarter of the food you could get anywhere else.

We keep walking, and I'm looking around, desperate. A

stupid landmark would do, but there's nothing around that seems interesting enough, or that I know enough about.

I'm scared to look at Wyatt for how pissed he might still be at me, probably thinking that he shouldn't have come along with me.

Except when I do look at him, he doesn't look angry at all.

There's a slight smile, not that goofy grin he usually has or anything like that, but there's a smirk, and he's looking around at all the buildings, the signs, the restaurants and bars, the trees and the birds on the sidewalk.

He doesn't seem to be having a bad time at all.

"I have an idea," I say.

"Age before beauty." He motions for me to lead him, and I ignore the jab.

It's just up the block, but the closer we stretch toward the afternoon, the hotter the sun is getting, so I can feel the sweat down my back and under my armpits. It makes me feel gross, and I'm definitely going to have to take another shower back at the hotel room. But I've finally got something to show Wyatt, and I don't want to give up this chance. He might hate me, but I don't want him to hate Los Angeles.

I lead Wyatt up the block and across the street toward Beverly Gardens Park, the bronze—almost gold—letters shining on the blue sign, and I take in the bright green of the lily pads on the small fountain in front of the sign, the smell of the grass and the trees, and the slight breeze that's blowing.

I've missed this place.

"A park?" Wyatt asks, looking around. His expression is kind of hard to read, but he doesn't sound disappointed.

"Yeah, I thought it'd be nice to take a walk."

"I'm down." Wyatt smiles a little bit wider.

"My parents used to bring me here a lot."

"Really?" Wyatt looks around. "Doesn't seem like the kind of place a kid goes for fun."

I shrug. "Don't laugh, but I kind of had this plant phase as a kid."

"Seriously?" Despite my request, he still lets out this laugh he tries hard to hide.

"No, there's a playground. I was all about that jungle gym life." I laugh, and I only realize a few seconds later that Wyatt's staring at me. "What?"

"Nothing—it's just cute to imagine kid Neil."

The words set off sirens in my head. What does he mean by that? Is he calling me cute? Is that what we're doing here? Is he being serious, or just pulling my leg? If I'm being honest, I'd rather Wyatt not think about kid Neil—being forced to wear dresses and grow my hair out so it could be tied in little bows, being called a girl, having a name that I didn't like, that never felt like it belonged to me. It's bad enough that Mom still has some of those pictures hanging up in our home, that some of those pictures will forever live on the internet because of Mother's status.

"What?" he asks, and that's when I realize that I've been staring a little too long.

"Nothing, just . . . thinking," I say.

This close I can see how unfairly long his eyelashes are; I can see the faintest of freckles, the trail of moles that begins under his left eye, and then to his ear, down to his neck, to vanish beneath his shirt, a half-finished constellation. There's the crack in his lips where he clearly hasn't worn ChapStick properly, even the sparse acne scars on his cheeks that suddenly make me feel less self-conscious about the acne on my own face thanks to the testosterone shots.

I never noticed how pretty he is up close.

I feel my pulse jump a little.

"I like this place. The plants are cool," he says.

"Yeah, it's really pretty."

"We should take a picture."

"You want to take a picture?"

"Yeah, I mean, if we take a picture of, like, a day out or something, won't that make Josh jealous or whatever it is you're trying to accomplish?"

"Oh, yeah. Right."

I pull out my phone, and we stop near this walkway, leaning against the half wall.

"Here." He holds out his hand. "I've got longer arms."

"Are you insinuating my arms are short?"

"There's no insinuating," he says, a smile on his face. "You have short arms."

"You're lucky we're friends now, or I might take that as an insult."

"Whatever, Kearney." We stand beside each other, and he snaps a few selfies. "We need to act more like boyfriends if these are going on your Instagram."

"Right, what should we do?"

Wyatt wraps his arm around me, pulling me in close. With his hand around my waist, I feel that skip in my heart. There's an odd sense of comfort, and then I realize that I'm literally pressed right up against his body.

Holy shit.

"Lean your head on my shoulder," he tells me.

I do it without a second thought.

I hate how perfectly my head fits in the crook of his shoulder. I give my best lovey-dovey eyes to the camera as he takes a few more pictures. Then, without warning, he leans down, kissing my forehead and snapping more pictures.

I feel like my brain is short-circuiting.

"I— Why'd you do that?"

"For the picture. Gotta sell the boyfriend lie, right?" Wyatt hands me my phone, the pictures we just took pulled up. If someone from the outside saw these, I think it'd be easy for them to imagine we're two teenagers in love, having a nice day out together. Then I scroll to the last one, where he's kissing me on the forehead, and there's no doubting the shock on my face.

I hover over that picture, almost deleting it.

I want to delete it.

And at the same time, I want to keep looking at it.

"Right," I say.

Got to sell the boyfriend lie.

"Wow . . . how did you get so red?" Wyatt asks as I apply aloe-vera-infused skin cream to my cheeks.

"I've been out of the LA sun for too long," I tell him. "And I forgot to apply my sunscreen this morning."

And unfortunately, I don't tan. I burn.

"Can you get my shoulders?" I ask, turning around.

We only walked around for an hour after we had our little heart-to-heart, but that was enough for the sun to get to my cheeks and my arms below the elbow. I didn't even realize it had gotten bad until Wyatt looked at me, shock on his face. It's not nearly as bad as it could be; it looks like I maybe got a little too excited over some blush. Well, that and the sting when I blink or when I brush my arms against something.

Wyatt's hands feel nice as he massages in the cream, the cooling sensation giving me goose bumps. I feel him trying to pick at something, his nails scratching into my skin, threatening to force me to fall asleep right here, right now.

"What are you doing?" I finally ask him.

"You've got a weird mark here. I thought I could rub it away or something, but it's not coming off. It looks like ink or something."

"Oh." I feel the heat hit my cheeks again. "That's, um . . . that's my tattoo."

"What?"

There were only three other witnesses to this story, and I don't speak to any of them anymore, so I always figured this could be my little secret. But now it feels like I'm an open book of sorts to Wyatt.

"You have a tattoo? It's a *line*."

I can't stop myself from laughing—whether the story is actually funny or I just want to prolong him knowing the truth, I have no idea. "I was at this party one night when I was, like . . . fourteen."

"Fourteen?"

"Listen—we all make mistakes," I say. "They had a tattoo guy and my friends convinced me to get something, but when the needle hit my skin, it hurt too much and I chickened out."

"What was it even supposed to be?"

"No idea. The tattoo artist was just doing whatever, I never even saw the stencil."

"Oh my God." Wyatt laughs. "This is golden."

"If you tell anyone, you're toast," I tell him. "Not even Samuel knows about it."

"Wow, I feel so honored." Wyatt takes his hands away, and I have to resist the urge to ask him to put them back. "Do you still want to go to dinner? We could just order room service or something."

"No, no, the aloe is working. I'll be fine."

It's not like I'm lobster red the way that some tourists get.

"Besides, I promised you."

"It can wait, dude." He keeps massaging.

"No, I'm hungry. We'll just go to the hotel's restaurant downstairs; that way we can bail if it hurts too much."

"Whatever you say." Wyatt chuckles softly. "I'm going to take a shower real quick."

"I'll be here," I say, lying back on the bed to stretch my body out. The aloe is definitely working already, my body feeling a few degrees cooler after just a few seconds. I grab my phone, still hooked on the charger.

I posted the pictures to Instagram while we were on our walk, nothing too elaborate, a touch-up here, orange filter to get that golden-hour vide, sun emoji as the only description. I debated about posting the one with the kiss, knowing if I posted it, Josh would definitely see it.

So I kind of had to, right?

There aren't that many comments; most of them are from the guys. Hoon and Julien both left kissy faces, and Lindsay commented with a heart emoji.

Samuel texted me right away.

SAMUEL: um . . . .
SAMUEL: that picture
SAMUEL: you're both so cute omg
SAMUEL: not gonna lie, I was sus about this whole thing.
SAMUEL: it screamed "elaborate plot to get back at josh"
SAMUEL: but y'all are cute or whatever
SAMUEL: does wy-guy have a cousin? or a brother? we could be in-laws!
ME: No brother, but he has a sister.
ME: She's four.
SAMUEL: 😔
SAMUEL: i just want a boy of my own with a southern accent and cute green eyes
SAMUEL: what are you two doing tonight?
ME: No wedding events to attend, so we're going out to dinner.
SAMUEL: dragging him to in-n-out? gonna break his animal style cherry?
ME: That's gross
ME: And no, we're going out somewhere nice.
SAMUEL: whateverrrrrrrrrrrrr

He stops responding, so I guess our conversation is done. Samuel's like that, at least over text. When he's done, he's done.

I go back to my Instagram, looking at the picture, the two of us together, having a nice day out. I wonder if it's believable to other people. Obviously, Lindsay, Samuel, Hoon, and Julien believe it.

But none of them are the person I'm really trying to fool here.

I listen to the water running in the shower, the low music from Wyatt's phone. I'd swear that I can hear him singing as well, but I can't tell if I'm just imagining that. I should get dressed; I know that I should. But I just want to sit here for a little bit longer, staring at the photo of him and me together.

This picture of two boys who are in love with each other.

Even though it's all a lie.

The restaurant attached to the hotel is a funky little place, raised dining areas, lit fireplaces because a breeze rolled in and with the sun gone it's gotten cool, a full bar where we have to wait for a bit because I definitely didn't have a reservation.

"You should've pulled that 'my name is on the sign outside' card," Wyatt says as he plays with one of the coasters.

"You're not funny." I spin on my stool.

Eventually, our waiter comes to take us to the table, right beside the window so we have this pretty awkward view of people walking by. And the restaurant doesn't have actual dining chairs, but leather chairs meant for lounging that make eating awkward.

But I figured this would be nice enough, and we wouldn't have to walk far.

"What are you going to order?" I ask.

"I don't know. It's been a while since I had a steak—that might be good."

"Prime rib is always good if you're going for steak. I've heard the marinade is excellent and the restaurant is Michelin-rated."

"Pfft." Wyatt covers his face with his menu.

"What?"

"You sound so hoity-toity."

"Shut up!" I kick him under the table, but we're both laughing now. He looks pretty handsome in the blue Gucci shirt that I pushed him to wear for the night; the color is nice and soft, and it goes with his eyes. If he doesn't want to keep the clothes after the wedding, then that's fine, but I at least want him to wear them enough on this trip for the price to have been worth it.

"What about you?" he asks. "What are you going to get?"

"I have no idea. No lie, I've been thinking about drowning myself in a basket of fries."

"It'd still beat the food at Steerfield."

I whip my menu down. "Oh my God, right? Like we pay how much to that school every year and they're still serving us cheap-ass hot dogs that are the wrong color and pizza that tastes like wax."

"Or chicken sandwiches where there's no breast, just two chicken strips."

"Disgraceful."

We're both laughing, and I have to say, I like this version of us where we're friends. To think that a week ago I couldn't have imagined even having a meal with him.

"God, it was mortifying," Wyatt says, finishing a story about how his first official performance with his guitar happened when he was thirteen and his grandmother volunteered him to play at her retirement center. "All these old people just staring at me, most of them asleep. I have a theory that one of them was dead and no one knew."

"Please tell me you're joking."

"That's the thing, I have no idea. He was just passed out in his seat, slumped over! I wanted to tell a nurse they should check on him."

"Why didn't you?"

"I didn't know! I didn't want this old man yelling at me for ruining his nap!"

We both laugh, picking more at our food. I ordered a burger, mostly for the fries. Wyatt got his steak with a baked potato on the side.

"How did you even start playing the guitar anyway?" I ask him.

Wyatt chews quickly, covering his mouth awkwardly with his hand. "The answer is going to make me sound like a dork."

"Wyatt, I've got news for you," I say. "I already think that you're a dork. But that's fine. Dorks are cute."

His cheeks go red. "I, um . . ." He's doing that thing where he's laughing to waste as much time as he can.

"Well?"

"It was One Direction," he mutters.

"I'm sorry." I lean in, knowing exactly what he said. I just want him to admit it again. "What was that?"

"One Direction, okay? They were performing at some award show and Niall pulled out his guitar and . . . it made me feel things."

"If you're admitting to me that Niall Horan was eight-year-old Wyatt's gay awakening, I might leave this table right now."

Wyatt bites at his bottom lip. "Then I guess I'll see you back at the room. And I was seven, for your information."

"Oh my God!"

"He wasn't . . . it wasn't my gay-wakening or whatever you want to call it. But looking back, things start to add up."

"Like?"

"Like me picking up the guitar because I thought girls would scream at me like they were screaming at Niall or Harry."

Girls?

"I was always more partial to Harry than the rest," I interject.

Wyatt plays with his food for a bit. "But my moms thought it would be a good outlet for me, so they let me sign up for lessons at the community center in town."

"So did it help you get girls?"

He shakes his head. "No way, not with my stage fright. Besides, I've had to spend the last few years unpacking whether I wanted to be Niall singing to all those girls or if I wanted to be one of those girls Niall was singing to."

I stare at him, taken aback by the shift in conversation.

"Sorry," he says when he notices my expression. "That probably doesn't really make sense."

"It makes perfect sense," I say to him. "Can I ask you something?"

"You just did."

I glare at him, so he knows that he isn't funny.

Wyatt grins, taking another bite of his food and talking through a piece of baked potato. "Go for it."

"What do you identify with?"

"What do you mean?"

"Like . . . sexuality wise, I guess?" God, I couldn't have asked that in a weirder way. "Like your labels."

"You know, I haven't really thought about it a lot."

"Really?"

"No, I think about it all the time." Wyatt sets down his fork and covers his forehead with his hands, and then he leans back and lets out a huff of air. "Sometimes I think about just not identifying with anything at all, just being myself."

"You can do that."

"Yeah, I know. But I'd still like to have something, you know? Even if it's just for myself."

"Who are you attracted to?"

"I don't know; I don't think it really matters," he says. "Like I've had crushes before. Girls, boys, people whose pronouns I didn't know, plenty of out nonbinary people."

"It sounds like you're pansexual."

"Maybe." He picks up his fork and starts playing with his food again. "And don't even get me started on the whole gender thing."

"What about gender?"

He smiles. "Didn't you hear what I said?"

"Oh, right. Sorry."

"Don't apologize." Wyatt looks away at a different table. "I just . . . I don't think I'm quite ready to have those conversations. Even with myself."

"Well . . ." I sigh, wishing I could do a bit more to comfort him. "I'm here if you ever want to talk. I've got experience in the gender department."

He finally looks at me again, another smile on his lips. "Thanks, Neil."

"Okay, okay, let's move away from the gender talk."

"Thank you."

"If your stage fright is so bad, why do you want to be a singer?"

Wyatt puts his napkin down after wiping his mouth, and he stares at the lit candle, flickering in the middle of the table in a glass jar. "To be honest with you, I don't even know if I want to be a singer."

I mean, I guess that was just sort of an assumption I made when I offered the audition. "Then what do you want to do?"

"I want to be in music—don't get me wrong. And a record deal could do so much for me and my family. But then I look at how pop stars are treated, how their fans act, how everything they do is under this microscope . . . it seems scary."

"Well, getting a recording contract doesn't guarantee you'll be some ultra-mega-famous singer with millions of stans who stalk you on Twitter."

"Yeah, I know. But there's the unpredictability, you know? Honestly, I think I'd rather bomb than be ultra famous."

"I can understand that." My few experiences with the paparazzi and tabloids writing about me haven't been fun. You wouldn't even think the child of a hotel mogul would be that interesting, but the world loves to watch a fuckup.

"I'm just trying to do what I can to help my parents," Wyatt tells me.

"Okay, but what do *you* want to do?"

"I don't really know; I haven't thought much about it."

"Kind of sick that we're expected to know what we want to do with the next sixty years when we're sixteen, huh?"

"No kidding. I've already had to start submitting college applications, drafting scholarship essays, making sure I've got enough extracurriculars and volunteer hours for the admissions people to even give me a second glance."

He really has to do all of that? Like I've heard of kids in, like, TV shows and movies having to work themselves to death just to get into a decent college, but I didn't think that it was real.

Mom never really talked about college before, but it's sort of an inside joke at Steerfield that a graduate has enough money to go to whatever college they want.

I guess not for Wyatt, though.

"Oh, ten o'clock."

"What?" I glance at my watch. "It's eight."

"No." Wyatt chuckles. "My ten, your four."

"What?"

"Like a clock face?"

"What the hell are you talking about, Fowler?"

"Just look over your right shoulder!" he whispers.

I turn slowly, trying not to attract attention to myself, and I see Josh sitting at a table, another boy seated across from him. I don't recognize the guy, but he's conventionally attractive, with black hair and light brown skin. Josh looks head over heels for him; he's totally got that puppy-dog look in his eyes while the guy is telling some story.

I don't want to feel jealous; that's not what this is, the heat in my stomach is nothing, the bitterness I feel doesn't have anything to do with this. It's just—well, I'd like to just blame it on my period, but I don't get those much anymore.

Who even is this guy? And what's he saying that's got Josh so hooked on his every word?

"Do you know who that is?" Wyatt asks.

"No, why would I?"

"I didn't know if they might be a mutual friend or something."

"No. Never seen him before in my life."

There's a beat of silence while I stare at the two of them.

"You're going to burn a hole in the back of his head," Wyatt cuts in.

I turn back quickly toward Wyatt, confused by whatever the hell he just said. "What?"

"You've never heard that expression? Staring at someone so hard you'll burn a hole in their head."

"No," I say, still distracted as I turn back around. "Never have."

"Can I ask you something?"

"Didn't you just?"

Wyatt smiles, stealing another fry. "You learn fast."

"What's your question?" I slide my plate out of his reach so he'll stop stealing my food.

"How did the whole thing with you and Josh start?" he asks. "You keep saying you weren't looking for a boyfriend—"

I open my mouth, but before I can say anything, Wyatt corrects himself.

"And I'm not saying he was! But just hooking up seems like the first step on the boyfriend journey, you know?"

"Yeah, I mean . . . it was only ever supposed to be stress relief. Plus, my T shots make me pretty horny."

Wyatt almost chokes on his water.

"He was kind of my first friend—" I say, but then I double back. "Actually, he was my first friend at Steerfield. Our moms are friends, so we only kind of knew each other. Then he went to Steerfield and I didn't see him for a year."

Wyatt doesn't say anything.

"That story is also pretty dorky. Josh admitted to never having kissed anyone, and I have a lot of experience kissing people, so I volunteered to help him out. And he was actually surprisingly good at it for someone with no experience, so we kept going and going and, well . . . one thing led to another."

"I see." Wyatt's voice has gone firm. He stares down at the table again, his fingers playing with the end of his fork.

"The next day, we both agreed that we liked it, but that we weren't interested in relationships. So, we kept it casual, until . . ." My voice trails off.

"Until he said that he was in love with you."

I nod.

"Wouldn't it have been nice, though? To be in love?" Wyatt leans forward on his elbows.

"It's just not for me."

"Did something happen?"

Yes. "No, I just . . . I never felt that way for him. Josh was a friend with benefits, not a boyfriend. Besides, I'm sixteen; I've got my entire life to fall in love. Why bother with it in high school? Those relationships always fall apart anyway."

"You don't think it might've been worth a try, though?"

"Listen." I don't know why Wyatt is lingering on this subject, but I'm ready for a topic change. "I watched my parents fall out of love. I watched them argue and fight and resent each other. And I saw pictures; they were college sweethearts, so in love, they couldn't get enough of being together."

At least, that's what Mom told me.

"But they got angrier the older they got, and it tore our family apart."

Wyatt stares at me, unsure of what to say.

"Josh is my friend. One of my only friends. Falling in love means falling out of it sometimes, and I didn't want to do that to him."

"You could argue that rubbing his face in a fake relationship might make him angrier."

"Maybe, but at least then my heart won't be broken." I take a sip of water just to give myself something to do. "Okay, subject change, I'm over this."

"Fine, fine!" Wyatt holds his hands up defensively, smile on his face. "Can I ask you one last question?"

"Is it about Josh?"

"No."

"Is it about my family?"

He doesn't answer.

"What is it?"

"You don't have to answer."

Well, now I'm curious. "No, ask."

"Is there anyone in your family who isn't awful?"

"Besides Lindsay, no. I mean, there were my grandparents—"

"Seriously? They could've fooled me."

"Not the maternal ones you met. My dad's parents."

"Oh, were they cool?"

"Yeah." I can't help but smile when I think about them. "They basically raised me for the first few years of my life. I spent nearly every weekend with them. My grandma would make me watch all these super-old movies that she loved like *Singin' in the Rain*. And my grandpa was the person who taught me how to swim, and we'd garden in his yard, and I'd get really sunburned."

"That sounds sweet," Wyatt says.

"Yeah, they're good people."

"Why aren't they here? Or are they coming later?"

"Well, after my parents got divorced, they kind of picked my mother over their son. He didn't like that very much, so he told them to stay away from us. I'd still sneak out to see them, though. Go get some fresh-baked cookies and sit down and watch movies with them. But Grandpa died a few years ago. And Grandma moved all the way up to Red Bluff. I think she wanted to come to the wedding, but since Dad said he wasn't coming, I think she decided it was better to stay on his side. It's complicated."

"That's awful, Neil. I'm so sorry about your grandfather."

"He had a hard fight, and we knew where it was going, so we just tried to make him comfortable. Dad had the balls to tell me that I couldn't still see him, but Mom stepped in. I basically lived with them the last two months he was alive."

Wyatt remains silent.

"He was actually the first person I came out to," I say, because the faucet has been turned on and now I can't stop myself. "I was so scared of what he'd think. I know it's not fair to assume, but you just kind of think a lot of older people won't understand gender or being trans.

"I told him how I felt, how my outside didn't feel like my inside, how it felt almost like I was two different people, and how confusing and scary it was, and how good I felt when I wore T-shirts and jeans and sneakers and when I pulled my long hair into a ponytail and hid it in a hat or behind my head.

"He just told me that he loved me, and that I was always his favorite grandson. Then he asked me about my name, and I didn't have an answer for him. I hadn't decided what I wanted my new name to be. I hadn't found one that I'd connected to yet." I remember feeling so bad for not having an answer for him, a different name he could call me.

My old name, the one that was given to me, wasn't mine; it hadn't felt like it belonged to me for a long time.

"He made me promise that I'd tell him my new one before he died. He wanted to be able to know his grandson's name."

"So you picked Neil?"

I nod slowly, trying to stop the shaking of my hands under the table. I don't know why I'm telling him this, and I feel like an idiot.

"What was his name?" Wyatt asks.

"Neil," I say. "Neil Kearney Jr."

He smiles softly, and there's so much comfort in the look that he's giving me. At least with Wyatt, I feel like my story is safe. That this is something that's just between the two of us. I've never told this story to anyone. Of course, Dad figured it out, and he wasn't happy. So did Mom. Grandma just hugged me when I told her my new name, and she promised that she loved me.

"Sorry, I didn't mean to get all gushy there." I snatch my napkin and wipe the tears away.

"No, no, I—" Wyatt seems to think for a moment. "Thank you for telling me that."

"If you tell anyone I cried, I'll tell them about how you didn't report a dead guy in a retirement home."

He lets out this loud laugh. "I don't know if he actually was dead! It could have just been the Ed Sheeran song I was singing—lots of people have narcoleptic responses to Ed Sheeran."

"Still, you couldn't have called a nurse?"

"Oh my God." He falls back in his seat, covering his mouth as he laughs some more. And then I start to laugh, and we stare at each other from across the table, just looking at each other. He looks so happy, and his laugh is so warm.

Yeah, I think I like being friends with Wyatt Fowler.

Monday

APRIL 18

"You're joking, right?" Wyatt says.

"What?"

"Cupcakes?"

"But it's a cupcake ATM! Isn't that amazing?"

I drag Wyatt down the block, to the nearest Sprinkles Cupcakes ATM. It's this metal mesh wall painted like a rainbow with straight rows of colors. And right in the pink row, there's a futuristic-looking little kiosk.

The world's very first cupcake ATM.

As far as I know.

It's also one of the most popular. At ten thirty in the morning, there's already a line.

"Couldn't we just go inside?" he asks. "The bakery is right there."

"That takes away from the fun," I say as we get in the back of the line. It moves pretty fast, thankfully, the cupcakes coming out in record time. "What flavor do you want?" I ask Wyatt when we're finally at the front.

"What do they have?"

"The usual. Vanilla, chocolate, dark chocolate, strawberry, black and white, salted caramel, carrot cake, red velvet."

"So, lots of choices."

"Come on, Fowler—we've got people waiting."

"Okay, okay! Strawberry!"

"A good choice." I pick salted caramel and swipe my card. A minute later, the boxed cupcakes are delivered from this sliding cylindrical door that I'm guessing leads into the bakery itself.

"This better be the best cupcake I've ever tasted."

"They're pretty good."

"Just pretty good? All that hype for pretty good?"

"It's not the cupcakes to get excited over. This came from a *cupcake ATM*. How cool is that?"

"I'll admit, that's pretty cool."

We stop to enjoy the cupcakes in front of this art installation that was all over Instagram a few years ago. Is *installation* even the right word? It's just one huge wall painted a sunflower yellow. I swear this thing used to be in the background of every single selfie tagged in Beverly Hills. It's seen better days now, but I still think it's got some character, and the yellow is nice. There's a couple taking pictures there right now, both of them squatting down to the pavement to get their golden retriever into the frame.

"Okay, taste test."

We both unbox our cupcakes, biting into them at the same time. Mine's moist, and the flavor is good. The salt gives it that kick that really complements the icing.

"Oh my God," Wyatt mutters, his mouth full. "This kicks ass."

"Told you."

He glares at me. "You said it'd be pretty good."

"And isn't it at least pretty good?"

"It's more than that." He swallows, then takes another bite, not noticing the strawberry frosting he's left on his nose. I accidentally let out this snort when I see it.

"What?"

"You've got some . . ." I wipe my own nose.

Wyatt scrunches his nose, going cross-eyed.

"Here." I grab one of the napkins left for us in the cupcake boxes and wipe it away for him.

"Thanks."

"You're so gross."

"Whatever, Kearney." Wyatt purses his frosting-covered lips and leans toward me, doing his best to leave a strawberry lip print on my cheek.

"Oh, gross!" I shove him away, making sure my cupcake remains safe. "Stop it!"

We down the cupcakes and buy some bottles of water because we're both incredibly thirsty after that much sweet stuff. There's a bit more walking as we make our way back to Rodeo Drive to try on our suits. I make it a point to show Wyatt Anderton Court, the Frank Lloyd Wright–designed shopping center that's maybe my favorite building simply based off the aesthetics.

A brand-new sales associate greets us at the Gucci store and gets our suits.

"You try yours on first," I say. "I want to make sure there are no more alterations that need to be made."

"Okay." Wyatt shuffles uncomfortably to the changing room. With any luck, this will be the last time I have to subject him to Gucci. After a few minutes, and some assistance from the store associate, Wyatt walks out to the main floor.

I can't stop my jaw from dropping.

The charcoal suit hugs his body in all the right places, the fit defining his chest perfectly, the pants hugging his thighs.

Then the boy does a spin and I get a firsthand look at how good his ass looks too.

What the fuck?

When did this happen?

Since when is Wyatt Fowler hot?

Like, he looked handsome yesterday, but today . . .

"Does it look good?"

"Mhmm," I hum, my brain and my mouth no longer working in tandem to pronounce proper nouns or adjectives. "Yeah, I mean . . . you look really good."

Fuck, was I drooling?

"I like it." Wyatt stares at himself in the mirror, still looking mildly uncomfortable. I wonder if the price is still an issue.

"Every guy should have a nice suit," I say. "It's the backbone of a decent wardrobe."

"You don't own a suit."

"I own several; I just don't keep them at school."

"Sir, would you like to try yours on?" the associate asks me.

Unlike Wyatt, I don't need help. I've always liked suits; I don't really know why. When I was younger, and before I realized that I'm trans, I thought suits were way cooler than dresses. Now I recognize that dresses and skirts are stunning—they're just not for me, not like a suit. I just like the way it hugs my body, the way that it seems to make me present.

It almost feels like I'm baring my chest proudly to the world even though I'm wearing two whole layers.

And I have to give it to Michael and Ashley—the purple isn't bad at all.

Wyatt's still looking at himself when I walk out. Then he stares at me, taking it all in.

"Well?" I ask.

"You look great," he says with humor in his voice.

I wonder if he's being genuine.

"Would you like to make any alterations?" the associate asks, and after several long seconds of looking at ourselves and each other, Wyatt and I both determine that our suits are ready to go. The associate packages them and offers to have them delivered to the hotel by the end of the day, so they're totally out of our hands.

I'm still thinking about Wyatt in his suit when we're walking outside. Does he even realize how hot he looked? I have to direct Wyatt to stand straight, to push his shoulders back. He almost seems slumped over, and I understand his discomfort, but we need to make sure he looks good.

And he certainly does. Something about boys in suits . . .

But also, why the hell am I so obsessed with how he looked in that suit?

What is going on with me?

"Hey?" Wyatt's voice pulls me out of my thoughts. When I look at him, he's staring down at me, his smile out in full force, that slight gap in his two front teeth worn like a badge of honor. "You okay?"

"Yeah, yeah, just . . . hungry, is all."

"I am too. Can we grab lunch?"

"Sure."

"You have anywhere in mind?"

I give him a look. "Oh, you have no idea."

Of course, I have to take Wyatt to In-N-Out.

Not just so he can experience it, but because I haven't had

it in months and I'm going through withdrawal. The red-and-yellow interiors almost feel like home when we walk through the door.

Which is super dorky, yes. But I don't care.

I guide Wyatt through the menu, forcing him to order everything Animal Style, and wait impatiently as he takes his first bite.

"Well?"

I watch him chew.

"It's . . . fine."

"Fine?"

"It's a burger."

"You can't just say it's fine! What do you mean it's fine?"

"That it's fine!"

"It's In-N-Out. It's *not* just fine."

"I don't know what to tell you. It's fine!"

I'm not proud to admit that I spend the next ten minutes explaining how superior In-N-Out burgers are, beating out Wendy's, McDonald's, and Five Guys by miles. But Wyatt doesn't relent; he actually has the gall to tell me he prefers Shake Shack. A lost cause.

After that little moment, we head back to the hotel for some rest after walking around so much. We're barely in the hotel room for twenty minutes before there's a rapid knocking on the door. Wyatt's in the shower, and I'm flipping through the Netflix app on the TV, still bitter about what Wyatt said about In-N-Out while also definitely not thinking about him in that suit at the same time.

The knocking is fast and panicked, so I shoot up off the couch and race to unlock the door. When I open it, Mom is standing there.

Note to self: Always check the peephole.

"You're here; good. I was worried you might be out with your boyfriend."

"Yeah, we just got back. I wanted to show Wyatt some of the city."

"Did you get your suits?"

"Yes, ma'am. They'll be delivered tonight."

"Good." She looks over my outfit, confused. "Aren't you getting dressed?"

"Dressed?"

I changed into my favorite white Gucci T-shirt and Fendi sweatpants the second we got back to the room.

"Well, you can't wear sweatpants to Gordon's, Neil."

"Gordon's? We're not going to Gordon's."

"That's where Michael is having his bachelor party."

"We weren't . . . we weren't going to go to that?"

"Why wouldn't you?"

"Because we're sixteen. We can't drink."

"It's a steakhouse, Neil. You don't have to be twenty-one to go in."

"But we weren't invited," I tell her.

She stares at me like I've grown a second head. "Of course you're invited—you're a groomsman. Besides, Michael and his friends will need a designated driver for the night."

"I don't even have my license!"

That's when Wyatt chooses exactly the wrong time to walk out of the bedroom, his sweatpants on, still using a towel to dry his hair.

Mom gets this wicked grin, like she's an evil mastermind. "Which is why I wanted to talk to Wyatt."

"What did I do?" Wyatt stares.

"I wanted to talk about the bachelor party with you."

"We're not going," I cut in.

"Neil, don't be silly. Of course you're going." There's no hint of a question in her tone. We're going to this party. "Do you have your license, Wyatt?"

"Yes, ma'am."

"Are you permitted to drive with multiple people in the car?"

"Yes, ma'am," he repeats. "I drive my moms all the time. They say I should get as much practice as possible."

"Perfect!"

"What's going on?" Wyatt asks.

"We were going to have a nice night in," I tell her.

She stares at me. "Neil, you're a groomsman—it's your responsibility to attend events like this."

"I don't mind driving," Wyatt says, like his opinion matters right now.

Mother claps her hands together. "There you go. Michael and his friends will meet you downstairs in thirty minutes. You two get ready."

Before I can even get another word out, she vanishes as quickly as she arrived, slamming the door behind her.

I glare at Wyatt. "Why?"

"They needed a driver."

"They could've just hired one!"

"Come on, it'll be fun," he says. "We were looking for something to do anyway."

"We were going to order food."

"Well, now we can go out." Wyatt throws his towel at me. "Go get dressed."

• • •

I could've stayed in the room. Had my own movie night, ordered room service or gotten dinner from the Chipotle down the street. But no, as much as I resent him right now, it's probably not wise for Wyatt to go driving around in a city he's never been in, being led around by four drunk dudes.

At least we can try to keep each other sane.

"Hey! Neil and Wyatt!" Michael cheers our names when he sees us walking out of the elevator. He's surrounded by his friends: Josh's brother, Zach, one of their roommates from their college days—I want to say his name is Ricky—and another guy I've never seen before in my life.

"We're here to drive you around," I tell him, ducking away from his hand when he tries to rustle my hair.

"Yeah, we super appreciate it, dudes. Not that we're planning on getting schwasted, but better safe than sorry."

"'Schwasted'?" I hear Wyatt repeat, his voice quiet.

"Hope we didn't fuck up your plans," Michael says as we all walk toward the black SUV that one of the guys owns. It certainly isn't Michael's; I don't know if he'd ever be caught driving an SUV.

"Well, you kind of did," I tell him.

But he doesn't quite hear me. Ricky—or Richard?—makes a joke and pulls out a flask, and then they're all laughing with one another.

We climb into the front seats of the SUV while the rest of the guys pile into the back. Just as Wyatt ignites the engine, there's a knocking on my window. I almost jump out of my skin, it scares me so badly.

But that's nothing compared to how I feel when I realize who is on the other side of the window.

Josh.

Wyatt rolls the window down.

"Hey, sorry. I was getting changed," Josh says.

"You're coming?" I ask.

"Yeah! I was invited."

Josh's brother cheers from the back seat, which then gets the other guys cheering, all while Josh opens the door to the back seat, squeezing in beside Michael.

Great.

Just fucking great.

"Okay, so let's figure out how this works." Wyatt presses the touch screen a few times, trying to get the GPS to work, but he keeps opening up menus and settings and radio station lists.

"You don't even need that. I know where the restaurant is," I tell him.

"Just in case."

"Tap there." Josh leans forward, his fingers nearly touching the screen.

Wyatt follows and the GPS comes right up. "Thanks."

"You're going to take a left out of the parking lot."

And at the same time, the robotic voice of the GPS says, "Take a left."

"Here." Wyatt hands me his phone. "Pick some songs."

It doesn't strike me how odd it feels to have Wyatt's unlocked phone in my hands until it's actually in my hands. When you think about it, someone's phone can be their entire life. Their pictures, their information, their contacts and text messages, their songs and other apps. All that information about Wyatt is at my fingertips. Even his phone background, some hi-res photo of an overturned car with rose petals spilling out, seems *so* Fowler.

I open up his Spotify, staring at the playlists made by both him and the app. I can tell instantly which ones are Wyatt's too because Spotify names their playlists things like *Summer Rewind* or *Release Radar* and Wyatt's are named things like *cool jam time* or *sappy sad sack songs*.

I chew on my bottom lip to keep from laughing.

"God, could you be more of an indie dork?" I ask him.

"What do you mean?" Wyatt asks as he finally pulls out onto the road. I can tell he's nervous by the way his hands are tight on the wheel at ten and two, and he keeps checking his rearview mirror like he's expecting blue lights to pop up out of nowhere.

I don't know how he normally drives, but it can't be like this.

I scroll through his *On Repeat* for a bit.

"Ew . . . country?"

"What?"

"You can't be serious."

Wyatt shrugs a bit. "Some of it's good."

I resist the urge to say something I'll regret and turn on Taylor Swift's *Fearless* rerelease.

Ricky pops his head over the center console. "Hey, guys . . . can we get something a little more . . . exciting? And less about fifteen-year-old girls?"

"Ugh." I grunt, handing the phone to the back seat.

Josh takes it, our hands touching for the briefest of seconds.

"Oh, sweet, you've got Wallows." Josh picks a song, and this upbeat guitar melody kicks in. The rest of the guys in the back seat cheer.

"Come on." Wyatt reaches over to pinch my cheek. "Don't be such a sourpuss. It's gonna be a fun night."

I spare him a glance. "Sourpuss?"

"People say it."

"Whatever, grandma." I lean against my window and count down the seconds until the night is over.

The touch of his hand feels sudden and unexpected, but when I look down at my left hand in my lap, Wyatt's right is right there, on top of it. I move so that our fingers can intertwine. I've never been one for physical affection; it's just not my thing. When Josh tried to hold my hand or kiss me in public, I always recoiled away from him.

It wasn't Josh exactly, it was more . . .

More this feeling of someone touching me. It felt constrictive, and it made my skin crawl. But with Wyatt? It doesn't feel constrictive at all. His palms are warm, some of the skin on his fingers rough.

I like holding hands with Wyatt.

Probably more than I have any right to.

Josh is out of view of the rearview mirror, but I can hear him laughing at a joke, and there's a tapping along to the beat of the song. Maybe that doesn't have to matter, though. Maybe what matters is that just for a few precious minutes, Wyatt and I get to pretend to be boys so madly in love with each other that we can't go a second without touching.

When we get to the restaurant, we're seated in a private room near the back.

Michael's at the head of the table; the two guys I don't know sit next to him, and then Wyatt next to me. Directly across from us sit Zach and Josh.

Perfect.

"I thought most bachelor parties were, like . . . going to bars and stuff?" Wyatt whispers to me.

"Michael always loved a good, expensive steak; give him a nice prime rib and he's putty in your hands."

The table fills with small talk. Michael talks about some of his clients, new people he's signed, some award one of his singers won last month, and a full bottle of whiskey gets delivered to the table along with baskets of bread, so that pretty much shuts us out of the conversation entirely.

"So, what did the two of you do today?" Josh asks across the table.

Would it be mean to just ignore him?

"Well, we went to a cupcake ATM," Wyatt replies too quickly.

I put my hand on Wyatt's thigh as a signal for him to stop talking to Josh, but he doesn't understand, instead putting his hand on top of my own and keeping it there.

"Sprinkles?" Josh perks up. "How'd you like it?"

"Oh, it was amazing! They were so good. Then Neil made me try In-N-Out for the first time."

"And?"

"It was okay. Neil got pretty upset with me."

"Yeah, he loves In-N-Out."

I hate that they're talking about me like I'm not here.

Like, hello?

"What did you do?" Wyatt asks him.

"Pfft, nothing." Josh sticks his tongue out. "My parents were busy, and I didn't have anywhere to go, so I just hung out at the lounge by the pool for a bit. Saw some friends."

I wonder if the guy we saw him with at dinner is one of these "friends."

"Oh, well, you should've come out with us. We wouldn't have minded."

I almost kick Wyatt under the table.

"Well, I think Neil might've," Josh says with a smile. "It's okay, though. I've got some homework I've been putting off. I have to write an essay on *The Grapes of Wrath*."

"You're in Mrs. Nelson's English Three?" Wyatt asks.

"How could you tell?"

"She loves giving out essays over spring break. Last year we had to do *East of Eden*."

"I swear she must have such a crush on John Steinbeck, it's freaky."

"My working theory is that she never wears short sleeves because she's got a giant John Steinbeck tattoo on her arm."

Both of them laugh. I want to throw myself into the conversation along with them. But there doesn't seem to be a place for me to fit in. I hate that Wyatt slides so easily into conversation with people. Like, how does someone do that? Does it just take practice; is it natural?

"Just be grateful this wasn't at a ski resort," Josh says.

I have no idea what they're talking about now. I completely shut them both out of my brain.

"That's oddly specific." Wyatt laughs, turning to me. "Why not a ski resort wedding?"

Josh looks at me. "Do you want to tell the story?"

"We don't have to," I say through gritted teeth.

We don't need to tell the story of last summer.

"Well, now I have to know." Wyatt grins. "What happened?"

"I'll tell it if you don't."

I bite the inside of my cheek. "Last summer, we went skiing in the Alps."

Josh looks at me, patiently waiting for me to get to the "funny" part of this story.

"And I broke my ankle, okay? It's not that big of a deal."

"No, what was a big deal was that you broke your ankle doing absolutely nothing."

"You just won't forget it, will you?"

"Well, it was pretty hilarious." Josh laughs. "We're on the slopes maybe ten minutes, all bundled up, our skis on, and Neil just starts sliding away from me mid-conversation."

"No one taught me how to stop."

I don't want to give Josh any indication that I do actually find the story pretty funny, regardless of how embarrassing it is. I don't want to give him a win.

"He spent the rest of the trip in the cabin with his foot in a cast."

"Shouldn't they have taken you home?" Wyatt asks through his laughter.

"What makes you think my mother is going to cancel an entire trip just because I broke my ankle?"

"We tried," Josh says.

"Walking in snow on crutches wasn't easy."

"God, that sucks." Wyatt stops to catch his breath. "Are you that bad at skiing?"

"Have you ever been skiing?" I ask.

"Well, no, I—"

"Okay, then." I smile so he knows that I'm telling a joke. "Don't judge me."

Thankfully, the waiter chooses this moment to interrupt. Dinner at Gordon's isn't a set menu, so we get to order whatever we want. Then again, this is a steakhouse, so the options pretty much fall between what part of the cow you want. I order the prime rib with a basket of french fries, which isn't the classiest side, but if I'm going to suffer through this night then I'm at least going to get french fries to make it better.

"So, Wyatt, how are you liking our sunshine state?" Michael asks from his spot at the head of the table once the food arrives and we've all gotten to it.

Wyatt pauses mid-bite, putting his fork back down on the plate. "It's been a lot of fun. A lot busier than I'm used to."

"Oh yeah. You guys pretty much only have banks out there in Charlotte, right?"

"Yes, sir." Wyatt's voice is a murmur. "I don't really live in Charlotte, though; my parents live in Mint Hill. I just go to school in the city."

Michael and all his friends chuckle at him being called *sir*, and Wyatt's ears turn red.

"He's, like . . . twenty-six—don't call him *sir*," I whisper.

"I'm used to calling adults *sir* and *ma'am*. It's called having manners!" he hisses low.

"So"—Michael keeps talking—"I've been wondering about you two. How'd you manage to woo my little brother, Wyatt?"

"Oh, well—" Wyatt starts to talk.

But this is the real test; this isn't some lie that we're telling Lindsay. The person this entire lie revolves around is literally sitting right across from us.

I can't afford to let Wyatt fuck this up.

I cut him off. "We were just talking a lot, over the last few months. And then, before the break started, we made things official, I guess."

Great.

A totally believable, and more importantly—simple—lie.

No way for Josh to find it weird that in the twenty-two hours after our breakup, I just so happened to catch Wyatt on the rebound and manage to drag him across the country for a wedding.

Wait, did I just say breakup?

Shit.

"I was bummed when I heard you broke my little bro's heart," Zach says with a smile, and out of the corner of my eye, I can see Josh doing his best to hide his face. "But I've got to say, I think Wyatt is an upgrade."

Zach laughs, mostly to himself, while everyone else chuckles awkwardly around us, but that's enough to kick off the conversation.

"You know, I'm surprised anyone had the patience to put up with Neil," Michael says. "And we've got two people right here!"

God, when the fuck did this become about me?

"Yeah . . ." Wyatt doesn't even bother with a fake laugh. He just looks at me, unsure of what to do.

"I'm kidding, I'm kidding," Michael continues "I love you, little dude."

"Yeah," I say.

You know, you wouldn't think that ten years between siblings would be that big of a gap, but it is. When Michael turned seventeen, school became less of a priority for him. He got Mom's permission to move out with his friends in the hopes that he could achieve his dreams of becoming a producer.

She agreed, but he only had a year to make something of himself, or else he was going to go to college, follow in her footsteps, maybe take over the hotels one day—as if she'd ever let them go.

Within six months, Michael was interning at Periscope, and knowing the right people and being at the right place at the right time, he found himself with a permanent position as an engineering assistant, then second lead, then first.

All in a year.

So ever since I was seven, he's been an irregular presence in my life, coming back to Mom's house maybe once every few months. I guess it never actually felt like I had a brother, more like a cousin I saw infrequently.

I never even came out to him. He just returned home one day, saw how short my hair was, and figured it out.

To his credit, he never once slipped up after I told him to use he/him pronouns with me, so he's got that going for him.

"I'm just glad to see that he's calmed down." Michael takes a sip of his whiskey. Halfway through dinner and all four of them have already made their way through three-fourths of the bottle.

"Oh yeah!" Ricky gasps. "I remember all of that—God you were so young, running around Los Angeles like that."

Wyatt has this visible look of confusion on his face, and even Josh looks uncomfortable, probably because he knows the stories.

Jesus, not now. Can we not discuss this now, please?

"Let's just drop it, Michael," I tell him. "No need to bring it all up."

But Michael goes right ahead and asks, "Wyatt, you ever heard the stories about this kid?"

The worst part is that he doesn't sound malicious when he asks it. If anything, Michael's always been a nice guy. Conceited and selfish, sure, but after being raised by our mother, there are loads worse ways a person can turn out.

"Our little Neil here was quite the party animal a few years back," Michael says with a smile on his face. "Sneaking out of the house, getting into clubs."

"I remember reading some of those articles online, those drama channels on YouTube talking about you." Zach chuckles. "You really rocked the headlines on the no-news days."

I slink lower in my seat.

"Mom kept trying to reel you in," Michael says, "but you'd just find new ways to sneak out of the house. All the drinking and partying, stealing that car, you were a little hellion. I was actually pretty proud of you. Seeing my quiet little brother come out of his shell finally. It was sick."

Please, shut up.

As if you were even around enough to know me as a kid. As if you've been paying enough attention to know me now.

Please just shut the fuck up.

I clench my fists underneath the table.

"You know we don't have to talk about this, right, Michael?" I say.

Michael throws his hands up defensively. "I'm just saying, Wyatt should know what he's getting into, you know. Before he gets too deep."

"Dude, I always hate that shit," Ricky says. "Dating a girl just to find out she's, like, a super-clingy psycho. Best to get all the wild shit out in the open, my dudes, even if you're . . . you know, both dudes." He downs the last bit of whiskey in his glass.

Wyatt's face is still a deep, shameful red.

Why should any of that matter right now? And where is this even coming from? Is this because Michael's drunk?

"You managed to be both homophobic *and* misogynistic in one go, wow!" Josh cuts in, and his words surprise me.

"Oh, come on, we're just kidding with you," Michael tells us both. "Always so serious."

"It's still a pretty shitty thing to say." Josh continues to be the knight in shining armor. "And Neil is clearly uncomfortable, so I think that we should just drop it and move on."

I want to appreciate what he's doing, but I also can't stand the idea that I'm being talked about like I'm not sitting right here, that I don't have any kind of agency in this fucked-up situation. I just want it to stop. I want to stand up and walk out of this place. I want to walk away from all of it, order an Uber to come and pick me up, take me back to the hotel to spend the rest of the night inside just like I wanted.

I want to vanish.

Wyatt glances at me, and then he clears his throat.

"I mean, it doesn't really matter to me what Neil has done in his past. I like him for him." He smiles this awkward smile that shows off a little too much of his teeth, that stupidly adorable, cute gap on display. "You know, as long as he didn't, like, murder someone."

He tries to laugh, and Michael and his friends are drunk enough to think it's the funniest thing they've ever heard.

Michael claps his hands together in laughter. "I like this kid. You can keep him, Neil."

What the fuck is happening right now?

"Ah, I'm sorry, Neil. But you know I've got to embarrass you, right? It's my job as a big brother!"

"Right, yeah." I turn away from him.

Wyatt is still looking at me, and I feel his hand fall on top of mine, his touch so close to the inside of my thigh.

You okay? he seems to ask with just a glance.

No, I'm not. I didn't exactly expect Michael to bring all of this up now, especially not in front of Wyatt. My party days aren't exactly a history that I'm proud of. It's one I'd proudly forget, if I were given the chance.

But now he knows at least part of that story.

And I'd really rather not have to deal with that.

The rest of the table moves on with their conversation. They start talking about soccer again, then basketball, and that drags Josh into the mix even though he still looks just as uncomfortable as he was before.

Eventually, the time to pay the bill comes, and we walk out to the parking lot.

"Hey." Wyatt races to catch up with me, keys to the SUV in his hand. "You okay?"

"Can we not talk about it right now, please?"

"Yeah." He nods. "Of course."

Michael and Zach belt out a tune at the top of their lungs, disturbing the people who are bold enough to pass by them.

Then Michael lets out this loud gasp.

"Karaoke!"

"Dude, oh my God! Yes!" Zach exclaims.

"Wyatt, Wyatt!" Michael races over toward us like a kid who's really proud of the dragon he just drew. "We want to go to a karaoke bar."

No, no, no.

I say, "Michael, you're drunk. We should get you back to the hotel."

"It's my bachelorette party—"

"Bachelor," I correct him.

"Bachelor party, and I want to go do karaoke, so that's what we're doing!" he declares. "Come on!"

"What should we do?" Wyatt asks.

"I don't know." I don't want to sound like I'm angry with Wyatt. I'm tired and I want to be in bed, even if it is only nine thirty.

But just because I want something doesn't mean that I get it.

Once Michael tells the other guys about karaoke, we've got four men in a car, demanding that we go to the nearest karaoke bar. I even look to Josh to help us out here, but he seems pretty excited about karaoke, and a car-wide vote comes down five to two.

So we're doing karaoke.

They've each got their favorites, but since it's Michael's special night, we end up at Duet Myself twenty minutes away because, and I quote: "That's the only karaoke bar that has Post Malone songs."

"This is a special kind of hell," I whisper as I put down Michael's card for the private room. The minimum is an hour, but that doesn't mean I won't try to squeeze us out early.

We walk to one of the private booths, which is brightly lit, with a sectional leather couch that stretches across two walls. It's only when the overhead lights are turned off that the neon decorations on the walls light up, posters printed with glow-in-the-dark ink, signs that paint the entire room in a deep purple glow. And then there's the small stage that takes up the last half of the room, with two big screens to show the lyrics and a wall-to-wall screen that seems to be playing random music videos on mute alongside lighting and strobe effects.

"Oh, this is wicked!" Michael races to the stage, picking up the microphone that isn't on, belting the chorus to a song I've never heard before.

The bar is pretty fancy, with their own app on an iPad on the table. We just have to scroll through the thousands of songs at our disposal.

Of course, Michael goes first. His first song choice is "Fireflies" by Owl City.

For a guy with a strong understanding of music and what it takes to not only build hit after hit but careers that will last the test of time, Michael is a really bad singer. I don't know if it's just because he's drunk, but his voice is gruff, and he holds notes for way longer than he needs to.

But that's the magic of karaoke, I guess: No one expects other people to be good singers.

We're just supposed to be here to have fun. I want to go home, though. Not back to the hotel, but back to Steerfield. I want to walk onto that mostly empty campus and lock myself in my dorm room until spring break is over.

I can't get a feel for what Wyatt might be thinking; he hasn't really spoken to me since we left the steakhouse. Even in the car he barely looked my way. What's going through that frizzy little head of his? Is he wondering about all the stupid things I did? Is he thinking about me stealing a car to hit the town, underage in every way? Does he think that I'm some kind of criminal? Is he regretting this whole thing?

I don't think it'd be possible for Wyatt to think less of me. I mean, look at how I treated him for the last half a year.

But I thought we were getting somewhere.

Finally, he looks at me, and that's when I realize I've been staring at him. He smiles that goofy smile that does something to my heart.

Like it thuds a little heavier in my chest.

Then he puts a hand on my thigh and gives me this look. Almost like he's asking, *Is this okay?*

I give him a soft smile back.

Yes, it is.

It's mostly the guys singing, the song choices ranging from Billie Eilish and Lorde to some old band called Rush. Josh even gets onstage with Zach to sing "Sunflower" from that animated *Spider-Man*. He *loves* that movie—we watched it at least five times on Netflix when it was added to the roster. It was cute at first, but it got tiring when he started to quote the movie while we watched it.

"You don't want to sing?" Wyatt whispers close enough that I can actually hear him.

"Never in a million years, Fowler," I reply. "You're the singer here—why don't you do it?"

"Pfft, yeah, right."

"Come on, this could be your audition."

"Not in front of all these people."

"What about a duet? We'll embarrass ourselves together."

"Absolutely no way."

Just as Ricky's rendition of Lizzo's "Juice" comes to a close, I grab the iPad and go right for the duet tab, picking the song right at the top. It isn't actually a duet, but it's close enough, and I have a feeling that Wyatt will like it.

I walk up to the front, Wyatt watching me with every step.

"What are you doing?" he asks.

The room is silently awkward while the song takes a minute to get started, and everyone is staring at me—including Wyatt, who still has this look of fear in his eyes.

"This is supposed to be a duet," I say into the microphone as the drums start to kick in. "But someone is too scared to come up, so let's give it up for Wyatt Fowler, huh?"

Everyone claps, even Josh, but Wyatt remains on the couch, hiding his face.

The first few notes of "Fool's Gold" by One Direction starts to play. I don't even know if this is a song he has any particular attachment to. It was just the first One Direction song that I saw on the list. I watch the screen, waiting for the words to light up so I know when to sing them.

I am not a singer. I can't carry a tune with a bucket, and I have two left feet.

But that doesn't mean I can't have fun onstage.

I serenade Wyatt, my voice low and too pitchy, but I hold out my hand, waiting for him to join me. I sway back and forth, but he still isn't budging. He looks mortified, giving that cringe-induced smile like he can't believe what's going on, like he's so uncomfortable but he doesn't know what else to do.

I don't care if he doesn't want to get onstage.

If I've got to be embarrassed tonight, so does he.

After the first chorus of the song, I step offstage, still singing, and take Wyatt's hand, pulling and pulling until he stands
up and I finally drag him to the front.

The lights are flashing, the color of the stage changing color
as I shove my microphone into Wyatt's hands.

There's a panic in his eyes, but then he looks at me. Right at
me, and no one else. The instinct kicks in, right when the next
chorus starts.

The words come like second nature.

He's not even looking at the screen.

Just at me.

His voice is just as magical as it was the other night, not a
hint of nerves to it. Soft, but strong in a way that projects some
kind of confidence that I have to guess is an act, at least in this
moment.

And when he sings the word *baby*, when he tells me that he
wants to sing to me, that he won't let me fall . . .

The world stops, and it's just the two of us.

At least, that's how it feels.

I'm so focused on him that I barely remember that I still
have lines to sing. I lean into Wyatt, sharing the microphone.
I don't want this moment to be over, even as we reach the end
of the song.

He's staring at me.

I'm staring at him.

And everything just feels right.

The song ends, and we step away from each other. Wyatt's
still holding on to the microphone.

Then the applause starts.

There are only five other people in the room, so it's not much, but they make up for it with the whooping and shouting.

"Yeah-heah!"

"Get a room, boys!"

Ricky whistles.

Josh just sits there, his legs crossed. He's got a soft smile on his face, but there's something so rigid about his body language. I don't know what to make of him. Wyatt wraps his arm around me and pulls me in closer. We walk down the stage together, leaving the microphone on the table because I think everyone is done.

We ride back to the hotel, most of the guys making small talk in the back seat.

Wyatt hands off the SUV keys, and Josh gets Zach back to his room. We all say our goodbyes, and Wyatt, Michael, and I take the elevator to the top floor.

"Thanks for indulging me a little, guys," Michael says as he wipes at his face, an obvious slur to his words. "That was amazing."

"Yeah, I had fun," Wyatt says, glancing down at me.

"Yeah . . ."

"Listen, Neil . . . buddy, I'm sorry for talking so bad about you." Michael throws an arm around my shoulder and leans his weight on me. "I hope you're not angry at me."

Angry? Why would I be angry? Because he felt the need to bring up old baggage I'd already let go of in therapy? In front of Wyatt, no less? That's the thing. I don't think I would've been nearly as upset with him if Wyatt hadn't been there. Everyone else in that room already knows what happened; they know what went on.

But Wyatt didn't.

And that matters.

"It's fine," I mutter.

"No, no!" Michael says, too loud. "What can I do to make it up to you? I might've ruined your relationship!" His drunken tone makes everything sound so serious.

"You didn't ruin anything," Wyatt adds, but I shush him.

"Actually," I tell my brother, "there *is* something you can do."

"Anything!"

"I want you to give Wyatt an audition for your label."

Michael doesn't even hesitate. "Absolutely!"

This may be a decision that he comes to regret in the morning, and maybe I should have him sign some contract with his blood or something. But I've got a verbal contract and a witness, so that's enough.

Plus, he seems sincere when he says, "You're amazing, Wyatt. Your voice, it's unlike anything I've heard before."

Wyatt's ears and cheeks go beet red. "Oh, um . . . thanks."

I've never seen him nervous like this before.

It's cute.

"We'll talk after the wedding." Michael pauses. "No, wait! I've got the perfect idea!"

The elevator door dings and opens to our floor. Wyatt helps me guide Michael out, each of his arms thrown around our shoulders.

"I made the mistake of getting one of my rising stars to be our wedding singer, but now she's going to be the US opener for the Boys Noise tour. We've still got the DJ, but Ashley wants live music for the first dance. You've got your guitar, right?"

"Yeah." Wyatt grunts.

"Good, you're hired."

"Wait!" Wyatt almost lets Michael slip out of his arms. "You're just going to hire me, just like that?"

"I've seen what you can do, my dude. I'll even pay you!"

"He'll take it," I answer for Wyatt. There's no way I'm letting an opportunity like this slip away.

"I don't know, I—"

"Nonsense, nonsense. You're hired. Pick a good song for the first dance. I want it to be a surprise."

"Shouldn't you run it by your fiancée?" Wyatt asks.

"Nah, she trusts me," Michael says. "You know, marriage is a two-way street. Gay people had it right when they called each other partners—you've gotta be partners, you know. You've got to trust each other."

Wyatt and I both look at each other, this strange look of exasperated joy on both our faces.

"You two have got that—I can tell. You're good partners. I mean, look at you now!"

"Yeah, thanks, Michael," I say.

"I'm serious." We lean Michael up, and he slides against the door, turning to Wyatt. "Neil is a good guy. Treat him right, okay?"

"I will."

"Good, or else I'd have to fight you."

I've never seen Michael like this before, but if he behaved this way sober, there's a chance we might've gotten along better. Though I suppose there's that saying: Drunk words are sober thoughts. I don't know, maybe there's more to Michael than I've thought.

Michael manages to get back into his room, and we say our good nights.

When the door is closed, Wyatt and I are both standing there in the hallway, and Wyatt turns to me.

"You did it," he says.

Me?

"*You* did it," I tell him.

"No, no. You did it!" He picks me up by my waist, which shocks me at first because I don't know what's happening, and I don't know if I like it. But he twirls me around in the hallway, narrowly avoiding this old couple who comes our way.

"Okay, okay." I laugh. "Put me down!"

Even though I don't want him to, Wyatt does just like I ask. It's even more awkward when my feet are firmly on the floor again because his hands are still on my waist, and we're looking at each other.

For a moment, for just a second, I think something is going to happen.

Our eyes don't want to find anything else but each other.

But there's no kiss.

Wyatt clears his throat, and instead of taking both his hands away, his left wraps into my right, and we start walking toward our room. It's still awkward—I bet we're both thinking about what just happened. But there's almost a comfort in the silence. Usually, my silent moments with Wyatt were so uneasy, the two of us sitting on opposite sides of the room, not saying a word to each other, ready to pounce on the other when we dared to breathe wrong.

Now, though, in the quiet of this hotel room—

Things feel right.

"I'm going to go call my parents, okay?" Wyatt says.

"Yeah, sure." I watch him step out onto the balcony as I

change out of my button-down shirt and slacks for the T-shirt and sweatpants I'd been wearing earlier.

I almost want to test my luck and grab one of Wyatt's shirts to wear, but I don't.

I do, however, steal one of his hoodies—from some brand called Goodfellow—because it's chilly in our room and I didn't pack any. Imagine that, a trans boy not packing the most essential item in all of our wardrobes. I give it a moment before I step outside, Wyatt's guitar in my hands.

He's not on the phone anymore, so I figure it will be safe.

"What are you doing with Niall?" he asks.

"Niall? You're not serious."

"It's his name."

"I should turn it into firewood just to save it the embarrassment of ever being called that again."

Wyatt stares at me, unflinching.

"Oh my God, I'm not actually going to burn it!"

"Don't joke about Niall."

"Well, take it." I hand the guitar off. "I thought we could think about songs."

"Is that my hoodie?" he asks.

"It was cold. Do you want it back?"

"No, no—it looks good on you."

The fuck does that mean?

"Do you have any ideas? For a song?"

"I just found out I was doing this ten minutes ago."

"So?"

"You're the worst."

"I know."

"I was thinking about Carly Rae, maybe 'Heartbeat' or 'Real

Love,' but those might be too on the nose. I know some Kacey Musgraves too, or Taylor Swift. I'm guessing 'All Too Well' is too depressing."

"You should explore, try different songs out. You've only got two days, you know."

"Shit, yeah." Wyatt focuses on the guitar, plucking at the strings, hissing when he doesn't get something right. In the months that I've watched him practice and play, he's never really slipped up before, not in a way that I've noticed, at least; and even if he has, he's never been this vocal about it. Is he stressed about performing? Is he scared? Does he want to back out? The deal was just for an audition, and I guess this could technically be that, though I'm betting he expected something more one on one.

"How do you know what to play?" I ask. "Like the strings?"

"It's easy when you memorize it, but there's an order." Wyatt scoots down the couch on the patio. "Come here?"

I take the spot next to him.

He hands me his guitar, and this time it feels more like some kind of rite of passage, almost like he's trusting me with his life even though I was literally holding this guitar seconds ago.

Wyatt scoots in closer, and I can feel his body wrap around me.

Then his hands are on top of mine.

Oh.

"Put this hand here." His left hand directs me to the neck of the guitar. And his right arm wraps around my body to guide that hand. "Each of the strings is a note. E, B, G, D, A, and E."

He lets me pluck them one at a time.

"Two Es?" I ask.

"Yeah, one is the highest, the other is the lowest."

He plays each individually, and I can hear the difference.

"But how do you know what to play?"

"Well," he chuckles. "I don't know if I have time to teach you everything, but . . . here."

He directs my left hand again. "You kind of number your fingers. Just use these three here." It's hard for my brain to focus on what he's saying with the heat of Wyatt's touch, his breath against my neck, the smell of his cologne.

"Okay." I let him guide me because I have no idea what he's talking about.

"Here, here, and here." I'm pretty sure I have fingers on the G, B, and E strings. "Now strum." He pats on my right hand.

The guitar lets out a smooth sound.

"You just played a D chord."

I strum a few more times, the sound coming out uneven when I move my fingers a little too much. But it is fun—that much I can admit.

"These strings are rough." After a few seconds, I can already feel the tingle.

"That's how I developed these calluses." Wyatt flips his hands over, showing me his fingertips. I never really noticed before how rough his hands look. Not that it's that noticeable, but the tips of his left fingers certainly look rougher than his right.

"I could just give you lotion."

"No way. It makes me a better player."

"Do you even have the science to back that up?" I ask.

He smiles at me. "Nope."

He lets me play for a little bit longer, messing around with the strings. He teaches me the A chords and C chords, but I forget them almost immediately and just start strumming haphazardly.

"This is fun."

"Clearly." He laughs to himself. "Hey, I, um . . . I hope your brother didn't make you too uncomfortable at dinner."

"No, you're fine. He just . . . he was drunk and being a jerk. Thanks for sticking up for me."

"Josh too."

"Yeah." I pause, biting my tongue.

"He's a good guy."

"I don't want to talk about Josh."

"Fair enough."

Wyatt leaves it at that. I can see this glow in his eyes and the slight dimples in his grin, the moles that dot his cheeks and forehead. There's even one right beside his left eye, barely noticeable until you're up close. The small, hooped earrings that I still can't get over even though I see them every day.

"Could I . . . ? I mean, you don't have to talk about it, but—"

"You want to know what he was talking about?"

I guess I should've seen this coming. At least I get the impression that Wyatt wasn't scared by whatever Michael hinted at.

"It's not bad. I didn't rob anyone. Or, you know, murder." I set the guitar down. "But yeah, things were kind of rough there for a bit. I don't really know why I did what I did, why I felt the need to be as wild as I could be; it was like the itch I couldn't scratch no matter what kind of balls-to-the-wall stuff I did. It was never anything *explicitly* illegal except for driving without a license. Mostly just sneaking out, working my way into clubs I was far too young to get into, crashing parties. My therapist told me it was because I wasn't getting the positive attention I thought I deserved, so I acted out to get the negative kind instead."

"Therapy?"

"It was a part of the whole coming-out, getting-on-testosterone thing."

"Do you think that had anything to do with it?" he asks. "You being trans?"

"Probably." It's funny to think that coming out *did* give me the attention I so desperately craved from Mom. The good and the bad. I felt I'd moved past that weird time in my life, where I couldn't stand to be around my family, when I didn't even feel safe in my own body, let alone my bedroom. Sneaking out, getting into clubs I shouldn't have been in because I knew the right people. I was fourteen and definitely looked it; no one was serving me alcohol; I never did any drugs. But, still, people noticed, and filmed videos of me, posting them. You really wouldn't think videos of the son of a hotel mogul would be *that* scandalous, but tabloids and YouTube paparazzi channels used to love me.

"That's why I came to Steerfield. Or, I guess, that's why I was sent to Steerfield. My mom, she . . ." I take a breath. "She thought that it'd straighten me out or whatever. Not in the sexuality sense, though it'd be pretty funny if she sent me to an all-boys school to try and make me cishet."

Wyatt and I both laugh uncomfortably.

"The stolen car . . . that was all a misunderstanding. I was trying to get a friend home. She was drunk and didn't want to leave her car, so I drove her."

"But you don't have a license."

"Sure don't! The cops pulled me over, didn't like the lip that

I gave them. And since my friend was passed out in the front seat, it was easy to misinterpret the situation. I had to do some community service to work that one off."

"Jesus, you're a little lawbreaker." Wyatt grins, laughing.

"I just remember feeling so alone in that house. Especially after my surgery, when Mom went back to work. She tried to be there for me, but there were days after the recovery at home started that I woke up all alone, and I was so scared." I remember being so lonely, so scared, my chest and body hurting so much. "All I wanted was my mom. It just sucked, you know? And I know it wasn't fair to take it out on her, I know that she tried her best, but . . ."

"Sometimes that's not enough."

I don't say anything to him.

"But you said she tried her best, though?"

"Any attention was good attention. Then, once I recovered, I went back to being ignored by my family. I tried to make it so I was impossible to ignore—and then they shipped me across the country just so they wouldn't have to deal with me. How fucked up is that?"

I feel Wyatt's hand on the small of my back, rubbing circles there. It reminds me of when I was little, when Mom would scratch my back when her nails were long. I always fell asleep on Dad's side of the bed, so he'd go to the couch.

"I'm sorry." I wipe my eyes with the hoodie sleeve. "For unloading all of that onto you."

Wyatt stays silent.

"I thought I got all this shit out in therapy, but I guess not."

"Neil." He says my name softly, like a prayer. "I hope you know that I like you a lot."

What's happening?

"And that being here with you the last few days, well . . . I'm just glad that we're friends now."

Oh. Friends.

"And I'm glad that you invited me on this trip. Even if your plan is totally batshit."

"Yeah. I'm glad we're friends too."

"Sorry, I'm, uh . . . not that great with words and feelings and stuff, I guess."

"Don't you want to be a singer?" I tease.

"I never said I was going to write the songs. But . . . I hope you know that you deserve better. I know loads of people will tell you family is everything or whatever. And it is, but that doesn't mean family has to be the people you're related to."

I'd considered that, of course I'd considered that.

For others.

But never really for myself.

"And, hey, you can come over to my house any time you want. On breaks or during the summer or whatever. I'm sure my moms would love to have you."

I give Wyatt a glance.

What did I ever do to deserve a boy so kind?

"Thank you, Wyatt," I say. "For everything."

I want to kiss him.

I want to kiss him until I run out of breath, until our lips are chapped, until our skin is rubbed raw. I want to kiss him like I'm dying, like he's the only other person I'll ever kiss again, like it's the last day on Earth and we've got hours to spare. I want to kiss him like I never kissed Josh.

I want to kiss him more than anything I've ever wanted.

But I don't.

Because I don't want to ruin a good thing.

I finally have someone I feel like I can be open with, someone I can tell things to, someone who understands. Wyatt has learned more about me in the last four days than most of my friends ever have.

The only one who comes close is . . .

Josh.

And look how that turned out.

He wanted me.

But I couldn't give myself to him.

Because I was afraid.

Because I was stupid and afraid.

I don't want to ruin things with Wyatt. I don't want to lose him as a friend.

I just got him.

So, I don't kiss Wyatt Fowler.

I don't kiss him even though I want to more than anything I've ever wanted before in my life. Even though I want to kiss him so much that my heart hurts, that my stomach is twisting into tight little knots that just won't slip loose. Even though I'm desperate to know what he tastes like, what his hair feels like in my fingers, what his body feels like against mine.

I don't kiss Wyatt Fowler.

Even though I want to.

Wyatt plays a little for me, his voice getting sleepier with each song. Finally he sighs, his wrist going limp over the neck of his guitar, and says, "I think I'm going to bed. I'm beat."

"Yeah, long day." Longer tomorrow.

He stands, carefully carrying his guitar back inside. "Are you coming?"

"I'll be there in a bit," I tell him. "Good night."

"Night." He closes the door to the balcony behind him. I stay outside, smelling the air. I'm trying to get my heart to calm down, to avoid admitting the truth to myself. I don't want to think about this, to think about how badly I wanted to kiss him tonight, to hold Wyatt's hand, to go even further with him than I've ever gone before. I don't want that.

But I do.

I know that I do.

And I can't stand the idea of these thoughts being alone in my head.

But who can I tell? Who can I talk to about this?

Not Wyatt, duh. Maybe Lindsay? But she'd judge me so hard. Not that it wouldn't be warranted.

Not Josh.

There is one person who might not judge me.

Well, he'll certainly judge me, but he'll probably be more sympathetic.

A five-foot-two strawberry-blond trans boy currently in New York.

Never have I been more grateful that Samuel is such a nocturnal creature.

He picks up the FaceTime call after a few rings.

"Hey, what's up?"

Clearly his phone is propped up against something, because both of Samuel's hands are occupied on this premium Xbox controller with all kinds of extra buttons that Samuel got specifically so he could, and I quote, "map my hotkeys more efficiently."

"I can call later," I tell him. There's a reflection in his glasses that shows off a blurry image of his screen.

"No way, I can talk and game. Where have you been?"

"It's been a busy few days."

"I can imagine." Samuel doesn't even look at my screen; he's entirely plugged in.

"What are you doing?"

"There's a raid, and my team fucking sucks so hard. You sure you don't want to get back into this? I could use a decent healer."

"I'm good."

"I could even teach you!" Samuel says. "They added catboys last year. You can be a magical catboy."

"Once again, I'm good."

Samuel smiles. "Your loss."

"Somehow I doubt that."

"So, what's up? Why'd you call?"

"I needed to talk to you about something."

"Yeah? Your mom freaking out again? Or did Michael back out of the wedding?"

"No, nothing to do with the wedding, really."

"Okayyy," he sings. "Are you going to stop beating around the bush?"

"I . . ." I open my mouth, but the words are lost again. How do I talk to him about this? How do I ask him these questions without giving myself away? "How do you . . . ?"

"How do you what?"

"Give me time," I say. "I have to think about how I'm going to ask this."

"Are you coming out to me? Neil, if you're going to tell me that you're gay, I already know that."

"I'm going to murder you." I have to remember to keep my voice low. I'm assuming Wyatt's asleep by now, but I don't know that for sure.

"You're the one being dramatic."

"Okay, so . . . how do you know when you're getting feelings for someone?"

"What are you talking about?"

"When you start to like someone, romantically . . . how do you know? You've had boyfriends and girlfriends before. You have a crush on Hoon."

"I've had exactly one of each," he says. "Who do you have feelings for? Aren't you dating Wyatt?"

"That's the thing . . ."

"You're going to dump Wyatt too?"

"No." I swallow. "Wyatt's the one I have feelings for."

Samuel's thick brow furrows, but his eyes never leave his monitor. "I'm so confused right now."

"The guy I think I like is Wyatt."

"Yeah . . . that's why you're dating."

"We aren't dating."

"What?" Then it's like the next minute or so plays out in slow motion. I watch the realization dawn on Samuel's face as he adds everything up. "Holy fucking shit."

I hear a thud, which I can only assume is him setting the controller down, and he finally stares at me in the camera.

"Holy fucking shit."

"Shut up."

"Holy shit."

"Samuel."

"What the fuck, dude?" Then Samuel looks away. "Oh shit, I'm dying."

"Nice to know just how important I am."

"Sorry, I waited in a queue for thirty minutes before enough people joined the party. I can't give this up."

"Right, I definitely know what that means."

"Wait . . . so the entire thing is fake. You and Wyatt, you're faking that entire thing?"

"It's a long story."

"You're doing it to get Josh off your back, aren't you?"

Well, I guess the story isn't *that* long. "Yeah, pretty much."

"God, you're like a supervillain."

"I'm doing what I have to do."

"Now you *really* sound like a supervillain."

"It was the best way to get Josh to forget about me, to get over his feelings."

"I'm not going to say you're wrong, but I'm also not going to say you're right."

"Whatever, I didn't call you just so you can judge my decisions, Samuel."

"No, wait. Wait." Samuel shakes his head, and I hear his characters shouting a spell from the speakers. "I'm sorry, I didn't mean to judge you like that. But you've got to admit that this is pretty wild."

"I know, I know." I put my free hand over my eyes. "I'm realizing I'm in over my head."

"That's one way of putting it," he says. "But . . . these feelings? That's what you called about?"

"Yeah."

"So the dating isn't fake anymore?"

"I don't know—that's the thing," I tell him. "A week ago, I couldn't stand his ass. He was annoying, uptight, always sticking his nose in my business. And now . . ."

"You're in love with him?"

"I'm not going to say you're right . . . but I'm also not going to say you're wrong."

"You've never really had a crush before?"

"No, not really."

"Even with Josh?"

"That wasn't a crush," I say. "That was just . . . two people who happened to be near each other and horny enough to do something about it. I blame my patches."

"Yeah. T will do that to you. But wanting affection is a fairly average human experience, dude."

"Can we please avoid the topic of Josh for the rest of this phone call?"

"Well, he's our one example here."

"He's not an example, he's just . . ."

"The only example, like I said."

"Whatever."

"Why do you think you like Wyatt now? What's changed? You said it yourself, you hated the guy a week ago."

"I don't know. I mean, nothing's *really* changed except . . ."

"You got to know him."

"I don't even think it's a crush. It's probably just gas, or my patches." Without even thinking, I go to carefully scratch my arm where the patch I put on this morning is still stuck.

"Well, you've always been a sucker for a guy with blue eyes."

"Wyatt's eyes are green."

"Interesting." Samuel hums.

"What?"

"The evidence is adding up."

"What evidence?"

"I'm not ready to present my findings to the court yet, Your Honor."

"I called you to help me. If you can't do that, then—"

"Okay, okay, let me just . . ." Samuel bites the tip of his tongue, and his eyes light up as the celebratory theme from the game plays. "Done! Puh-lease let this be a decent drop."

"Samuel."

"I'm getting to you, but the game was here first."

"Sam."

He knows I'm serious when I call him Sam.

"New enchantment, nice. Almost to level ninety too. Okay." Samuel finally sets the controller down. "I'm done."

"Thanks."

"Why did you even call me, Neil?"

"For advice."

"On this crush? And you think I'm the best person to help?"

"I don't know if it's a crush. I don't know what those feel like. And you're . . . my friend . . . I guess."

Samuel's hand goes to his chest. "I'm honored, even with the 'I guess.'"

"Shove it."

"Do you want my absolutely honest trans opinion?"

I have to stop myself from rolling my eyes. "Fine, yes. Give me your opinion."

"You called me for a reason when you didn't have to. There

was no reason for you to spill this secret to me, to call me when it's so late here on the East Coast. Because you already know your answer."

It's the most serious I've ever heard Samuel sound. He's usually such a goofball, so ready to crack jokes or say something stupid.

So it's a little surprising to hear his tone.

"Crushes are . . ." He sighs. "Weird. And bad. They're not fun. But they happen, and you can't really control how or when they decide to rear their ugly little heads. They're like IBS."

That's the Samuel I know.

"But you called me for a reason, admitted the whole fake dating to me when it was clear that you wanted to keep it a secret from all of us. I think you know you have a crush, and you just need someone to tell you what you want to hear."

"Well . . ." I'm still kind of in shock. "Thanks, I guess."

"You know, when your parents are therapists and you have your identity analyzed to hell, you learn a few things."

"Right."

"How does Wyatt feel about you?"

"What do you mean?"

Samuel stares at me. "What part of that did you not understand?"

"I—"

"Do I need to repeat it?"

"No."

"Then answer."

"You're being mean."

"Not fun to get a taste of your own medicine, huh?" Samuel has this shit-eating grin on his face. "Answer me, Kearney."

"I don't know how he feels. I can't read his mind."

"How is he acting around you?"

"I don't know . . . the normal way?"

"And what's that like?"

"Goofy, smiling a bunch, making bad jokes."

"Well . . . how do *you* feel about him?" Samuel asks. "And for the love of God, please don't say that you don't know."

"That's the thing, I don't. I mean, tonight? He made me feel . . . I dunno, warm? Appreciated? He sang for me, Samuel. The guy fucking played guitar and *sang* for me."

"Oh shit, that's hot."

"Yeah! You're telling me. And the whole fake-boyfriend thing is fucking me up too. Like he's holding my hand, and we're sitting close to each other, flirting in front of other people. I want it to be real, but I can't tell whether it is or not."

"I can see how that'd be an issue."

"So what do I do?"

"What makes you think that I know the answer?"

"Because . . . I called you."

"Pfft, that's *your* mistake." Samuel smiles.

"Please, just a *little* advice?"

"I already gave you everything that I know, Neil. You wouldn't have called me without a reason, and I think you know what that reason is."

I hate that he's right.

I didn't want to hear it, and at the same time, I know that I did want to hear it.

I have a crush on Wyatt Fowler.

"So what do I do about it?"

"Well, you can keep it quiet and let the feelings simmer until they boil over, probably in a very messy way that'll be impossible to clean up, hurting both of you in some way, shape, or form."

"That's dour."

"*Or*, if you'd let me finish, you could go for broke and tell him how you feel."

"Yeah, right."

"What do you have to lose?"

All I do is glare at him.

"Yeah, you're right. We got anxiety, bitch."

"Things are starting to get better between us," I say. "I feel like we're friends now. And I don't want to mess that up."

"What makes you think you'll mess it up?"

"Because I'm me."

"Right, yeah. That's a pretty good excuse." I hear Samuel let out a sigh. "Well . . . the best I can tell you is that you should try."

I sit there, waiting for whatever comes next.

"You know how you feel about Wyatt, maybe not totally, but you know that you like him. And you should do something about it. The worst that Wyatt can say is no."

"The worst he can do is reject me and never talk to me ever again."

"But do you *truly* think that will happen? You think Wyatt Fowler of all people will hate you and ignore you until the school year is over?"

"No." I know the answer immediately, because that isn't the kind of person Wyatt is. This version of a cruel Wyatt who hates me is something that my anxiety invented. I know that, but it's so hard to convince myself that it's the reality.

"All you can do is try, dude. That's all anyone is ever doing."

"I hate that you're right."

"What did you *want* me to say?"

"That I'm stupid and crushes are dumb and that I should shut up."

"But then you'd be disappointed, wouldn't you?"

I pause. "Yeah."

"There you go."

"I hate you."

"I hate you too." Samuel smiles. "I've got to do another raid, so I'm gonna hang up."

"Okay," I say. "Thanks for talking to me about this. And please don't tell anyone."

"My lips are sealed; just buy me dinner next week."

"Sure."

"Bye, dude."

"Bye." I end the call so that Samuel won't have to take his hands off his controller. And I sit there, simmering in my feelings, still hating that he's right.

Tuesday

APRIL 19

There's a knock at my door, slow and rhythmic. I've only been asleep for maybe three hours, and already it's morning.

"Neil, you awake?" Wyatt asks.

"Yeah."

"I have to pee."

"Well, come in."

Wyatt opens the door slowly, traipsing into the bathroom, and a few seconds later I hear peeing, followed by the flush and sound of running water.

"You know you don't have to ask every time," I say when he steps out of the bathroom. "You can pee whenever you want."

"I didn't want to walk in on you."

The easy solution is for us to share the room.

No, shut up.

Shut up, stupid brain. You're not involved in this.

"What are we doing today?" he asks.

I prop myself up on the bed, trying not to pay too much attention to the shirtless nature of the Wyatt Fowler standing right in front of me. It shouldn't even matter; we've seen each other shirtless plenty of times before.

But now it's different.

And I hate that I feel that way.

Though I certainly don't hate the view.

"Pictures," I tell him. "So put on your Sunday best."

"Where are we going?"

"Actually, I don't know. My mother never sent me the address."

That probably means that I should ask her, but if she never sent me the information, then maybe I have a built-in excuse for not showing up. I'm just a groomsman; do I even need to be there for some lousy pictures?

I glance at Wyatt. "Maybe we'll get lucky, and we can skip."

"I doubt that."

I climb out of bed, and Wyatt and I both move to the couch. I've convinced myself that I shouldn't have to even think about getting ready for these pictures until I have the address. For a moment there, I think that Mom must have forgot, or maybe she really didn't want me to come to the photography session, because it gets to be ten o'clock and I haven't heard anything. The light in California is great, but if you wait too long, it'll get too hot to take pictures. Everyone will look sweaty and oily, and Photoshop can only fix so much.

The closer it gets to noon, the more it feels like we've been spared. Or they're taking the pictures without us. Maybe I should feel bitter, but that just means I get to sit here on the couch with Wyatt, watching TikTok compilations on YouTube.

Except God doesn't love me that much.

I'm in the shower, music playing from my phone, when it's interrupted by a *ding!*

I duck my head out of the shower, careful to dry my hands off before I check.

Mom's sent me the address for the pictures, and when I read it on the screen, a sense of dread crawls up my spine.

And I can't help myself.

"Son of a bitch."

"So . . . this is where you grew up?" Wyatt asks as we stand at the gate to the driveway.

I asked the Uber driver to drop us off here. It's a walk up to the house proper, and the more distance I get to put between myself and walking back into that house, the better.

"Yeah."

"Where's the actual house?"

"Up the hill a little bit. It's not far."

"And why do I get the feeling that you don't want to go back in there?"

I glance at him. "And where would you have gotten an idea like that?" I ask him sarcastically. It's not that I don't want to go back in there, it's just . . .

No, actually, I don't want to go back in there. The last time I was here was over Christmas break, and I couldn't wait to leave. I tried to spend every free moment I could away from this house and the people inside, even if that meant just taking walks up and down the street. There were times when I couldn't be inside, no matter how much I tried. Too many weird feelings, too many memories that I'd rather not have.

"You know, we don't have to go inside."

"We kind of do," I say. I'd rather not be chewed out by Mother. I ring the bell on the callbox by the gate, and a second later, it crackles to life.

"Hello?"

"We're here, Mother."

She doesn't say another word. The gate just buzzes and slowly begins to open up.

Next to the driveway, there's a set of stairs built into the landscaping that makes the journey up the elevated property much easier, and much shorter. So of course I lead Wyatt up the driveway instead. No reason to get to the front door faster than necessary.

"How much of your family will be here?" Wyatt asks as we make our way up, passing by the lush green ferns and flower beds that Mother worked so ridiculously hard on. I'll give her this at least: When the house was first purchased, she had all the previous landscaping uprooted and moved. She wanted her own garden, grown herself, something she could be proud of.

"Us, Mother, Michael and Ashley, the bride's and groom's parties, grandparents," I say. "Think of it this way: The fewer people who are there, the more attention there is to put on us."

When we finally make our way up to the entrance, Wyatt gets the full effect of the house. Styled in a very modern fashion, the Bel Air home is just a few long white boxes stitched together. Sterile white walls, floor-to-ceiling windows, black trim, and confusing architecture—this was where I spent my first fifteen years.

And never once did it really feel like home.

"Wow, fancy."

"Yeah." I wish that we were here under different circumstances. It could be nice to stay in a house like this with Wyatt if we were on vacation or something. Plenty of space, a nice view, beautiful gardens, and a pool.

What's not to love?

Then it occurs to me that it sounds like I'm already planning vacations with Wyatt.

God, brain. Stop.

"I thought houses like this only existed in movies," he says.

"Bel Air architecture is something special." I doubt there are many places in the world where you'd see a home like this outside of California. There's something so West Coast about it. This is the same driveway and yard where I played, where I fell riding bikes, where I drew chalk drawings that were pressure washed away so that they wouldn't stain the pavement. Because everything needed to be erased, because the house needed to look perfect at all times.

I don't even know if I should ring the doorbell or not.

This isn't my house.

And yet . . . it is.

There's the sound of clacking, a splash of color on the opposite side of the frosted glass in the door.

"Oh, you're here!" Mother says, opening the door for me. She leans in to give me a soft hug and an air kiss so she doesn't ruin her makeup. "Good. We're in the backyard."

"Good morning," I say.

"Why are you so late?" she asks. "We started without you."

"I wasn't given the address."

"I'm sure I sent you all the information a few weeks ago."

I could prove her wrong, go back through my texts and show her that she never did. I mean, she never texts me, so it wouldn't even take that long. But Mother is never wrong in any argument she's a part of.

Never.

So it isn't worth it.

Most of my family is gathered off to the side while the bridal party takes their photos. I'm relieved to see Lindsay there in the mix. Michael looks a little worse for wear, but nothing some concealer hasn't covered up. He's talking with his friends while Nana and Grandpa sit in the shade on the patio. Nana's staring at me, and she hasn't once looked away since we walked outside.

"Hey, there you are!" Michael comes up and claps me on the shoulder. "Now we can finally get our set done."

"Sorry. I wasn't told what time. Or where."

"Eh, it's okay. Last-minute location change threw everyone off. We spent an hour in the hotel gardens before Mom decided it didn't look good enough."

"Hey," I whisper closely to him, making sure that Wyatt can't hear. He's distracted by how ostentatious the backyard is anyway, with the infinity pool and fountain and statues. You'd think we lived in a museum. "You remember what you agreed to last night, right? With Wyatt?"

"Yeah, of course," Michael says. It's a bit of a relief. I'd expected him not to remember, to go back on his promise. "Wyatt's still down, right?"

I nod. "We've already brainstormed some ideas."

"The kid's got pipes." Michael looks over at him. Wyatt's now talking to Lindsay about who knows what, the two of them laughing. "Does he have an agent? He need representation?"

Not exactly where I thought this conversation might go. I'd rather not be having this talk for Wyatt. He should be involved too. But I don't know how he feels about talking to Michael about this stuff directly either.

"He wants to be a singer," I say. "And he's amazing. He can play guitar too."

"I saw him carrying it around in the lobby when you both got here. If he's an indie kind of kid, I'm always on the lookout for those. They're popular online right now."

"He's got what you need."

Michael smiles. "Good. We'll see how he does at the wedding. Something tells me he's got a bit of stage fright."

"A bit." I look over at him again, still amazed by everything surrounding him.

Eventually, Ashley and her bridesmaids are done with their pictures, and it's our turn. The five of us line up all in various orders. I'm always on the end, though, the plight of every person five foot five inches and under.

We stand there, striking poses, hands behind the back, hands out front, arms around shoulders, feet spread apart. I can't imagine that these photos will come out well or interesting—but, hey, I'm not the one paying for them. Lindsay and Wyatt both watch me from the side, covering their mouths, staring. It's obvious they're laughing at me, but I can't even be angry at either of them. I'm sure I look like a huge dork.

Finally, we get to take a break, and it's time for Ashley and her parents to take some photos, so I walk over toward Lindsay and Wyatt.

"We're having a game night," Lindsay says right off the bat.

"Game night?"

"It was her idea," Wyatt adds.

"Besides, all the adults are getting drunk in the lounge tonight for the bridal party."

"I thought the bridal party had already happened?" Wyatt asks.

"No," I correct. "That was the bridal shower."

The confusion is visible on his face. "How many parties and brunches can one family have?"

"With this family," Lindsay interjects, "any chance to get drunk will be taken."

"I'm down," I say. "We can order some takeout."

It'll be a nice break from all of this wedding stuff, and Wyatt and I can finally get the night in that we wanted.

"Cool, I'll bring UNO." Lindsay relaxes against the half wall that's boxed in some fancy imported trees.

Wyatt raises an eyebrow. "UNO?"

"What?" She goes defensive. "It's a great game, and I'll kick both of your asses."

"Oh, you're so on!" Wyatt exclaims.

It's actually nice seeing them together like this. It's probably a weird thought to have, but I like that they get along, that they seem to like each other. Lindsay is important to me, so I want Wyatt to like her.

They get into talking about some Korean boy group called Stray Kids, and I sit there, listening to them bicker about which member they like more. We're called in for a few more pictures, some all together as a family, one set of me, Michael, and Mother together, then they throw Nana and Grandpa into the mix and I have to endure them correcting my posture and my smile.

"If you're going to be a boy, at least stand like one," Grandpa says, his arm thrown around my shoulder.

I want to sink.

All it takes is a few words, and I want to vanish.

To disappear.

I just have to make it through the next few hours, the next few photographs, then Wyatt and I can go back to the hotel, maybe get some food and go to the pool or something. Then we'll have a fun night with Lindsay, and everything will be good.

Just have to survive.

I have to stand there for what feels like hours as pictures from every angle are taken. At some point, I notice that Wyatt isn't standing around outside anymore, and I feel this worry in my chest. What did he see? What did he hear? Is he coming back?

When I'm finally allowed to take a break, I step inside, leaving my shoes near the entrance.

The house is so big, it takes me longer than I'd like to find him, walking around on the second floor, this look of confusion on his face.

"There you are," I say. "I was worried there for a second."

"Just trying to find the bathroom. This place is a maze."

"Yeah, sorry about that."

We're actually right near my old bedroom, so I lead him inside, directing him toward the en suite bathroom. The room is big but still feels so small. I open the doors to the balcony in my room, the one that overlooks the west side of the house. It's pretty much the end of the property line and provided the perfect escape over the security wall when I was sneaking out.

Sure, I got branches in my hair when I was climbing down the huge oak tree that's still growing strong now, but I did whatever it took to make it out of this house.

From here, I've got a good view of the houses that surround us, some forest, and, beyond all that, the city. This place that I used to call home.

Wyatt comes walking out of the bathroom a few minutes later.

"Come on," I say. "We should head back down." Don't want to be missed, not for even a second.

"That bathroom is huge! The bath looks like a hot tub."

"Yeah, it's big."

Wyatt stops as we stand in the middle of the bedroom. "I never really understood houses like this," he says.

"What do you mean?"

"What do you do with all of this space? What's the point?"

I shrug. "I dunno."

"I mean, this room is so bare and boring," he says. "Shouldn't a room look like someone? There's like zero personality here."

"Are you saying that I'm bare and boring?" I tease.

"Oh, I—" His cheeks go red. "This is your room?"

I nod, leaning against the doorframe while I stare at him. He looks so cute when he's flustered.

"I didn't, um . . ."

"I'm kidding," I say, walking back over toward him to flatten down the collar of his shirt. "Not about this being my room: It is. But I get what you mean. The worst part is that Mother hasn't changed a thing since I left for Steerfield, except for a new duvet. It's all the same."

"Wow . . . that's—"

"Depressing? Yeah."

Everything in our rooms was muted and drab so that none of the colors clashed. Rich hardwood floors we weren't allowed to run on, carefully crafted modern furniture that we could rarely sit on or use as it was intended.

"We couldn't even hang stuff on the walls," I tell him.

"Seriously?"

I nod. "I printed out this picture of Shawn Mendes and taped it to my wall one day. She yelled at me for an hour."

Surprisingly, Wyatt lets out this snort of laughter. "I'm sorry, I shouldn't laugh."

"What's so hilarious?"

"Just the image of you taping a picture of Shawn . . ."

"Listen . . . it was a phase," I tell him. "Leave me alone."

"At least I know you have a thing for musicians," he says quietly.

I swallow, every bit of moisture leaving my mouth.

Wyatt examines the room a bit further, looking at this god-awful deer antler statue painted black that still sits on the nightstand. The thing used to give me nightmares growing up.

"It's almost like being in an art gallery or something," he says, moving to sit on the edge of the bed. He even seems like he's being careful of how much he's wrinkling the sheets.

"That's probably the best way to describe it."

"I'm so used to houses with . . . I don't know, personality. I feel like when you walk into my room, you know it's my room. You know?"

I move to sit on the bed with him. "Yeah."

"Even your side of the dorm room, it screams Neil. With your weird abstract art prints and your fashion books."

I want to investigate further, ask him just what else he feels makes my side of the room declare that it's mine. But I save that question for later.

"It was never really easy growing up here."

"I can see why you'd want to escape." He looks up at the blank ceiling, and then back toward me. "You know, I've been jealous of you before."

"Really?"

"Before, knowing how much your family had, what they did. It was a lot to take in. And . . ." He stops himself.

"And what?"

"Just the feeling of knowing that if my parents had even just one percent of what your family does, that it'd make the biggest difference in the world to them."

I don't say anything.

Because I don't know what to say.

Wyatt continues. "Growing up . . . I guess I always kind of resented not getting things. It wasn't really until I was maybe ten that I really understood our situation, what we have, how hard my parents fought to make sure that I was provided for. I wanted my parents to be rich, so that we wouldn't have to shop at Aldi, and we could afford a bigger house, and nicer cars, and better toys."

Wyatt talks like he's walking on eggshells.

"But having this much, hoarding it, not living despite everything at your disposal—it just seems like such a depressing way to live. My parents might not have much, and I still wish they could have a fraction of what you have. But . . . then I look at how some of your family has treated each other this week, the stories about your grandparents, your mom, her friends."

There's a sting to Wyatt's words that I don't think he realizes is there. But the fact of the matter is that I'm in this situation too. Not that I can do much about it; I can't just deny who my family is, what they have. I'm a part of this problem. I'm the child of people who hoard their wealth instead of doing anything with it. Mother has employees who aren't paid fair wages, who go without health insurance.

And all of that trickles down to me, to my school, which is so easily taken care of and taken for granted.

It's hard to imagine what someone like Wyatt would see in a person like me.

Then again, I guess the inverse should be true.

But it isn't.

Here I am, silently wishing that he would lean over and kiss me, that we'd fall back together on my bed, the photography session left behind.

"We should probably head back down, huh?" Wyatt breaks the silence.

"Yeah, probably."

He stands up, and in the privacy of this moment, he offers me his hand. I shouldn't take it; I shouldn't punish myself further. Taking his hand feels like I'm agreeing to this contract that neither of us is truly aware of, and who knows what could happen if we both sign.

But I do.

I take his hand, and I let him lead me.

Well, I have to lead actually. Wyatt doesn't know where he's going. I take us out to the garden again, and it's like we were never gone. Lindsay is the only person who noticed our absence. The smile she gives me makes me think she thinks that something happened upstairs.

"Oh, Wyatt." Mother walks toward me as the photographer finishes up his final pictures of her, Michael, and Ashley together. "I had the most wonderful idea."

I don't reply. I just wait for her to finish her thought.

"We've got the photographer for another half hour; I want pictures of you and Wyatt together."

"Seriously?"

She gives me this confused look. It's not my fault that this is unexpected; she's the one who's never taken an interest in my life.

"I thought it would be nice to have, and besides, you both look so adorable right now."

I give Wyatt a glance, and he squeezes my hand lightly.

"What kind of poses do we do?" I whisper to Wyatt as we walk to our spot in front of the photographer.

"Just follow my lead," he tells me. "And act natural."

I roll my eyes. If he wants to take charge on this one, let him have it. For the first picture, Wyatt stands behind me, his hands on my hips. I don't know what else to do, so I just put my hands on top of his.

"Okay, okay." The photographer snaps some pictures. "How about something a little less prom night."

I turn around, resting my head on Wyatt's chest, then both of us stare at the camera with his heartbeat in my ears. I wonder what his face looks like right now.

"Good! Good!" The photographer sounds a thousand times more enthused.

"Pick me up," I whisper softly.

"What?" Wyatt asks through his teeth.

"Pick me up, twirl me around, do whatever, and act like you're the happiest person in the world."

I try not to panic as Wyatt hoists me into the air and we spin. I immediately become dizzy, grateful that my stomach is empty. I hear the clicking of the camera a few times, but I try not to lose focus as Wyatt looks up at me, this wild smile on his face. He makes me feel warm; he makes things feel easy.

He makes me feel wanted.

I realize that this is all just an act, that we're two people pretending to fall for each other for the sake of a person who isn't even here, and that, in maybe a week's time, this will all be undone, the two of us no longer actors in a play.

But doesn't that mean I should appreciate what we have while I have it?

Wyatt sets me down, and I put a hand to his cheek.

The camera clicks some more.

"Can I kiss you?" I ask.

"What?"

"Can I kiss you? It'll be good for the pictures."

My mind races with a thousand excuses. The pictures will inevitably be posted on Facebook, which Josh isn't on, but his parents are. So maybe he'll see them. Mother might show the pictures off to anyone who can't run away fast enough. Lindsay might offhandedly talk about how in love we are. I can post the pictures to Instagram, where Josh will *definitely* see them.

But these are just excuses.

I'm doing this because I want to kiss Wyatt Fowler.

He nods swiftly. "Go for it."

And I do.

I press our lips together, and it's as if the rest of the world just falls away. I can taste the lilac ChapStick that I let him borrow, the spearmint gum on his breath that he chewed on the car ride over. I let my hands find purchase on his neck, feeling the jump in his pulse as he kisses me back, wrapping his arms around my waist and pulling me in close.

I've gotten what I wanted.

So why does it feel so shallow?

I don't dare to open my mouth—that feels like a step too far, a violation of what Wyatt might find comfortable. But I'm fine with this kissing.

Eventually, we pull away from each other. Wyatt does it first, and then I realize what's happening, and as I come back to this moment, I realize that for the people around us, this wasn't anything special. They saw two boys who are in love with each other kissing . . . and isn't that what people who love each other are supposed to do?

As I look at Wyatt, my stomach sinks. Not for anything that he's done, not for an expression on his face. He seems happy, content.

So why does it feel like I just made a huge mistake?

I wish that I could say going back to the hotel makes things easier, but it doesn't.

After the kiss is over, I search Wyatt's face for any signs. Discomfort from the kiss, or joy that it happened. But there's nothing to read. He just seems like himself. Maybe that's supposed to mean that he doesn't care.

And why should he? He knows that this is all a ruse.

When we get back to our room, he takes his guitar out first thing, camping on the couch with his laptop, looking up the chords for various songs. I watch him work for a bit, then decide that maybe it's best that I leave him alone. I go to get us a very late lunch.

And, of course, I run into Josh in the elevator.

"Oh, hey." He looks up from his phone.

He's dressed in gym shorts and a tank top, this dorky

armband on his shoulder, his usual uniform when he goes on his nightly runs.

"Going for a jog?" I ask, as if that isn't incredibly obvious.

He smiles awkwardly. "Yeah. Had to get out of that hotel room for a bit."

"Me too."

"Did something happen?" he asks.

I want to say that he asks it quickly, like he's jumping on any opportunity to cause a rift between Wyatt and me. But he doesn't. The question seems genuine.

"No, just tired, is all." I lean against the elevator walls.

"I feel you. I'm not even in the wedding party and I'm exhausted." Josh pulls his phone out of his pocket, swiping up and smiling at a text message. My brain flashes with images of him and that boy he was having dinner with. I wonder if that's who he's texting, who's making him smile. And then I have to wonder why I care.

"Who are you talking to?" I ask.

"Oh, no one."

"No one?"

Josh gives me a look. "Yeah . . . is that okay?"

"Yeah, of course it is. Why wouldn't it be?"

"I don't know." Josh goes back to his screen. "You're the one acting weird."

"I'm not acting weird."

"You definitely are."

"Well, I'm not. So just drop it."

"You're the one who brought it up."

My eyes shift toward the floor number, counting down until we reach the lobby.

"You know," Josh says, "for what it's worth, you and Wyatt are really cute together."

Oh.

"Yeah?"

"Mhm. I'll admit that I was pretty jealous when I saw the two of you together, but it's clear you've got something special."

"Um . . . thanks."

The elevator door finally opens, and we both step outside.

"I'll see you at the rehearsal dinner tomorrow, yeah?"

"Yeah, of course." I watch him walking away. Then—and I have no idea why—I call for him again. "Hey, Josh?"

He turns.

"Uh . . . it was good to talk to you."

He smiles, a confused expression on his face.

"Good to see you too, Neil."

I watch as Josh plugs in his AirPods and runs off on his jog, avoiding the people on the sidewalk.

I don't have the energy to walk far, so I just grab Chipotle. By the time I get back, Wyatt is a little more wired, and he looks at me excitedly.

"You're back!"

"Sorry, the line was long."

"Forget the food!" His voice is overly excited, like he downed an entire pot of coffee before I got here. "I think I've got the perfect song to sing for the dance."

"Oh yeah?" I set our bag of burritos and chips on the coffee table as Wyatt pats the space next to him for me to take a seat. I wonder if he's thought at all about the kiss, if he's thinking about it as much as I am. Were my lips soft enough? Did my breath stink? Have I fooled myself this entire time into thinking that I'm a good kisser when I'm actually hilariously bad at it?

"What'd you pick?" I ask.

"Here. It was so obvious—I can't believe it's taken me hours to decide."

"What is it?"

"Just listen." He readies his guitar.

He strums a familiar melody with his fingers and his pick. He taps his foot to imitate the drum kicks, and after a few seconds, he starts to sing.

"I want to play this for you all the time, I want to play this for you when you're feeling used and tired—"

His singing is just as magical as the first time I heard it, the first time he sang to me. There's this intensity behind his eyes when he's playing, like it's his favorite thing in the world, a second home for him.

He only sings a few lines before the song and the guitar fade away.

"What do you think?"

"It's perfect."

While we're eating, Wyatt finds a Star Wars marathon on TNT that's supposedly lasting all week. I tell him that we can just watch them commercial free with my Disney+ account, but he's adamant that we watch it on cable.

Something about the commercials being a part of the magic? I dunno.

There isn't much magic to be found in the movie I'm being forced to watch.

"So, this is the first one?"

"Yeah."

"But where is Carrie Fisher?"

"No, that's *A New Hope*. This is *The Phantom Menace*."

"What does any of that mean?"

"This is the first chronologically. *A New Hope* was the first one released."

"I still don't get it."

"What could you possibly not understand?"

I actually do get it, kind of. It's just funny to watch Wyatt get worked up over Star Wars. We sit there, watching the movie, and I can feel my eyes glazing over at all the political talk. Then there's a loud knocking at the door.

"Yo! Buttplugs, open up!" Lindsay shouts. She stumbles her way in after I've unlocked the door for her. "I went to Target and grabbed as much as I could," she says, dumping the snacks on the coffee table. There's Oreos, Chips Ahoy!, gummy bears and worms, chips, popcorn, boxes of chocolate—which includes the most important candy ever, cookie dough bites. I grab that box before it even hits the table, stuffing it into the freezer to get nice and cold.

"What are you dorks doing?" Lindsay asks.

Wyatt grabs the bag of Cool Ranch Doritos. "Watching a movie."

Lindsay watches the screen, witnessing Anakin's podrace in all its CGI glory.

"What the actual fuck is going on?"

"Star Wars," he says.

"That's not Daisy Ridley or John Boyega."

"It's before those."

"Then it's not worth it. That long-haired dude isn't nearly as hot."

"That's Liam Neeson."

Despite her reservations, Lindsay plops down on the couch, ripping open the back of gummy worms before she grabs the remote. "Okay, the dorky shit is done." Lindsay turns the television off, then turns it back on when she sees how offended Wyatt looks. "The compromise is that I'm putting it on mute."

"Fair."

Lindsay digs around in her purse and pulls out this fresh deck of UNO cards.

"You stole those, didn't you?" I ask her, taking my now-chilled cookie dough bites out of the freezer.

Lindsay looks at me, this shocked expression on her face. "I resent that implication!"

"That's not a no."

"I didn't say I didn't steal them. I said I resented that that was your first thought."

"Unbelievable." I help Wyatt clear off the coffee table and take a pillow from the couch to sit on. "Watch your back, Wyatt. She's vicious."

"I've played a game or two myself." Wyatt takes the stack of cards, slicing the deck and folding it back together effortlessly. He perfectly shuffles the cards together, dealing the eight that we need and laying the played card on the table.

"Okay, I'm a little afraid now," Lindsay says, picking up her cards.

"Left of the dealer goes first," Wyatt says.

I've never seen Wyatt take anything so seriously. His studying and guitar playing comes close, but there's still a huge difference. Not that he's being a buzzkill, but I can see him biting his bottom lip, contemplating every card that he's playing before he plays it.

I want to tell him that it's just UNO.

Even though he's pretty adorable right now.

Wyatt's out first, because of course, and we decide to keep playing. He scoots over to me, leaning over my shoulder, looking at my cards.

"Oh, you've got some good ones," he says quietly.

"Don't ruin my hand!" I back away from him.

He gets closer, resting his head on my shoulder. "I was just looking. Don't get your undies twisted."

I roll my neck, hoping that I don't make any moves that might make him think that I'm uncomfortable, that his head is too heavy. I hope he doesn't think that, because I want him to stay here with me for as long as he wants.

I play a yellow four, and Wyatt hisses.

"Should've played that one." He points over my other shoulder to the red three.

"I know what I'm doing."

"Okay, okay!"

I go to play a yellow seven so I can maybe change the color to blue. I'm drowning in blue cards over here.

"I—" Wyatt shuts his mouth swiftly.

"Do you want to take over?"

"That's cheating," Lindsay says. "Don't let his ass win."

"I'll stop, I'll stop," Wyatt promises.

Of course, without his input, I'm able to lose the game that much quicker.

"I told you, that red four really fucked you over."

"It's not my fault." I show my hand. "Look at how much blue bullshit I'm dealing with over here."

Wyatt collects the cards, shuffling them back together. "Blame the player, not the cards."

"Shove it, Fowler." And I mean that with love.

Wyatt joins the game again, and we play four more games that last all the way through to the middle of *Attack of the Clones*. Wyatt wins all of them except for the second-to-last one, which Lindsay wins with a careful combo of reverse cards.

The next game, when I play a Draw Four card, Wyatt pulls out the rule book.

"Ah-ah, not so fast." Wyatt makes a clicking sound with his tongue.

"What?"

"Ahem." He clears his throat. "A Draw Four card may only be played in the event that the player has no other playable cards. If another player suspects the card has been played illegally, they may call out said player. If the card was indeed played illegally, the player who played it must draw four cards."

"Since when is that a rule?" I almost throw down my cards.

"Always has been." Wyatt shows me the rule book. "Let me see your hand."

"That's cheating."

"And if I'm wrong, I have to draw four."

I show him my cards, and of course, he's in the right.

"This isn't boyfriend behavior," I mutter under my breath.

"Not my fault you don't know the rules."

"Hate the player, not the cards." I mock with a version of his accent. All he does in retaliation is reach under the table, grabbing my free hand and holding it tight.

That shuts me right up.

"Okay, this isn't fair anymore." Lindsay starts pulling all the cards toward her when Wyatt wins the last game. "You're like an UNO machine. Where the hell did you learn to play like that?"

"UNO gets very competitive in my house. You either learn to play well or you have to do the dishes almost every night."

"I always thought it was just chance, or luck," I say.

He gives me this smug smile. "And that's why you lost."

"Bite me, Fowler."

He makes a big show out of chomping his teeth.

"Y'all are so gross." Lindsay looks on in disgust while she packs the cards away.

"Don't be jealous."

"Are you dorks going to keep watching your war of the stars?"

"It's not dorky," Wyatt says. "There's nothing wrong with Star Wars."

"Whatever you say." She slides the cards back into her purse. "I'm going to bed. We've got a long day tomorrow."

"Okay, good night," I say at the same time Wyatt says, "Night."

She waves and slips out of the room.

Suddenly, it's Wyatt and me again, sitting so close to each other. He hasn't looked at me; he's just watching the movie, leaning down far so he can rest his head on my shoulder, finally happy that he can turn the volume up. I want to say something, I want to say anything at all, but I don't know what I'm supposed to say. I don't know what would be right.

We should talk about the kiss. Maybe I should apologize for springing it on him without even giving him time to think. Maybe we should talk about where it leaves us. Maybe we should talk about how it leaves us nowhere, because this relationship is fake, and nothing was meant to come of it, and now I'm the one who's getting obsessive.

"Hey," I say, my voice quieter than I mean for it to be.

Wyatt perks up, looking at me.

"Want to go down to the pool?"

His brows furrow. "Isn't it closed? I thought it closed at nine."

I shrug. "We can still get in."

"Is that legal?" he asks.

"I will make it legal."

He gives me a confused look.

"Come on, I just quoted that Star Wars movie at you, and you didn't even fucking get it?"

Wyatt smiles that smile at me, and I feel this weight lifting off my chest.

Nothing secures the pool besides a closed door in the lobby that's easy to sneak around if you just go out a different exit and loop around.

During the day, the pool is gorgeous, warm brown hand-cut marble decorating the perimeter, awning areas with a cute pink trim that have these large bed-like lounge chairs with privacy curtains that can be pulled down. Closer to the pool itself, there's some stylish matching pink lounge chairs, all surrounded by lush, gorgeous greenery.

During the night, when the lounge chairs have been packed

away, when all the privacy curtains have been pulled, when there's no light but the neon glow of the pool water, it's strange, almost otherworldly.

I leave my shoes off to the side, rolling up the legs of my sweatpants and dipping my feet in the cool water.

"We're not going to get in trouble, right?" Wyatt asks.

"There's no one around." I pat the spot on the ground next to me. "It's just a pool. Plus I know the owner."

Wyatt folds up the legs of his pajama pants and slips his feet into the water next to me. For the briefest of moments, our knees touch, but Wyatt pulls away, probably thinking that I don't want that.

I do, Wyatt.

I really do.

It's dawning on me how awkward this moment might be. For what feels like an hour—but is really only probably a minute or two—we don't say anything to each other. We just sit here, leaning back against the water. Again, I want to say something, I want to do something, but I just don't know what I'm supposed to do right now. Things have been so easy with Wyatt over the last few days, so natural. Even earlier today, there were moments where things felt normal, like the kiss hadn't happened.

But now I'm worried I ruined everything.

"We're almost free, Wyatt," I tell him without even looking in his direction. "Just a few more days."

"Yeah, almost done," he says. "It's just the rehearsal dinner and wedding, right?"

I nod. "Then we get an extra day to do whatever we want."

"We can finally go see the Hollywood Sign."

I shoot him a glance. "Yes, I promise to take you to the Hollywood Sign."

"Swear on it?"

I put my right hand over my heart because that seems appropriate. "I, Neil Anthony Kearney, do solemnly swear to take you, Wyatt Fowler, to the Hollywood Sign this Friday."

Wyatt giggles softly. "It's a date."

A date.

Right.

His words, not mine.

What is that supposed to mean? Is it an actual date? Is he kidding? Playing along with our little game?

Why can't I read minds?

I just want to know what's going on behind those green eyes.

I can't wait for this wedding to be over. I can't wait to go back to Steerfield, back to the comfort of my dorm and my friends. The sooner I get back to school, the farther I am away from Mother and Nana and Grandpa and Michael. It'll just be me and Wyatt.

"The sky is really pretty."

The words take me out of myself at first. I'm not really sure if it's something he actually said, or if I'm having some major delusions.

But then Wyatt looks at me, his head still tilted up.

"Right?"

"Yeah," I say, meeting his gaze. "It is."

He smiles and goes back to staring at the stars. There's a plane flying above, a red light blinking among the stars, and the moon—it's barely full, like a little sliver has been sliced off the edge.

"I wonder what they call that," I ask to no one in particular, even though there's only two of us here.

"Hmm?"

"The moon phase. I wonder what they call it."

"It's a waning gibbous," Wyatt says with a smile on his face and confidence in his voice.

"How do you know?"

"I had this book as a kid. It had all this cool stuff about the planets and moons and the sun. I carried it with me everywhere."

"A regular astronaut."

"For a second I wanted to be. When I was a kid."

"Really?"

He nods. "Then I watched one of those movies where the astronauts get stuck in space and this one dude's tether thing broke off and he just kept getting farther and farther away and I thought, Hmm . . . space is really fucking scary."

"Your dreams crushed before they even got a chance."

"I've accepted that my feet will stay firmly planted on the ground, and I'm okay with that. An airplane is as high as I get."

"Right, because you did *so* well on the airplane."

We both laugh, the silence settling again after a moment or two. I notice how close his hand is, and I push mine closer, our fingertips touching. Wyatt looks over at me, and then down at our hands.

I pull away, putting my hands in my lap.

But then he reaches over, grabbing my left hand and putting it in his right.

It feels so hard to read his face. He looks happy and content—and yet, at the same time, I feel like I can see some bitterness, sadness, confusion.

"Can I talk to you about something?" he asks. "It's kind of personal."

Oh boy, here we go.

My heart starts to thud harder in my chest before I can even get any words out.

"Um, yeah. Sure. What's up?"

Does he want to talk about the kiss? Does he want to do it again? I'd do it again! Or does he want to tell me how much he hated it, how he never wants to see me ever again when we're back at Steerfield?

"Sorry, never mind." He bites at his lip. "I changed my mind."

"Are you sure?"

He nods. "Forget it."

There's sadness in his voice, and it breaks my heart. "No, no. Don't forget it."

I scoot closer to him.

"What's going on?"

"I . . ." He starts again, but his sentence drifts off into the night air.

"Hey." I reach over, putting my hand on top of his. "Whatever it is, you can talk to me about it, okay?"

"God." He laughs. "That was so cheesy."

"I'm trying to offer emotional support here, Fowler."

"I know, I know." He looks down at the water where it laps against the edge of the pool. "I've . . . I've been thinking more, about the gender thing."

I'm caught off guard.

"The gender thing?"

"It's been something that I've sort of been working through for a while."

"A while?"

"Yeah, a few years now actually. Kind of started when puberty became a thing."

"Yeah, same for me," I tell him. "Wait . . . if you've been thinking about this for a while, why are you just bringing it up now?"

He waits for a bit, looking back up at the sky. "I don't know. I think maybe you're the only person I trust with this."

"Oh."

"Sorry, that's sappy."

"No, no—I mean, yeah, kind of."

We both start to laugh awkwardly.

"We don't have to talk about it if—"

"If you want to talk about it, I've got ears, and enough experience with dysphoria to share between the both of us."

More awkward laughing.

"It was never like I felt like I was born in the wrong body, you know?"

"That's not always the experience with trans people," I tell him. "I don't like the phrasing 'wrong body' anyway—it feels gross."

"But the older I got, I don't know . . . the feelings got more and more complicated."

That sounds all too familiar to me, before and after going on T, finally getting my surgery.

"And when your body started to change—"

He doesn't have to finish my sentence; the expression on his face says enough. "I've thought a lot about how I want to identify, but I've always been so scared to do anything about it. I've stood in Targets thinking about buying skirts and makeup, but I can never bring myself to do it."

I don't say anything. This feels like his moment that he needs to explore.

"And sometimes, I like it when my face gets scruffy, and I like my armpit and leg hair."

"Ew," I say, knowing full well that I was thrilled when Mom felt I was far enough into my transition that she stopped making comments about me not shaving.

"Shush." He smiles at me. "I just . . . sometimes I feel like I want to be a girl; I want to change my body, to be softer. Other times I like my body how it is; I feel like a boy . . . whatever that's supposed to feel like."

Wyatt sighs.

"And then sometimes I feel like nothing, like this genderless blob that's just existing. I just . . . I don't know. I see someone like you or Samuel being so comfortable in your gender and I . . ." He trails off again.

"You're saying I transed your gender?"

"You're not funny."

But we both still chuckle, stealing glances at each other.

"If it makes you feel better"—I clear my throat "I still have dysphoria. There are still days where I feel like I can see my breasts, or I feel like my cheeks have filled back out, or when I'm convinced everyone around me still sees me as a girl, or the little voice in the back of my head is telling me that everything I'm doing is wrong. Putting on these patches and getting surgery wasn't some magic fix-all for the stuff going on in here." I tap my temple.

"Do you really still feel that way?"

"Not always, but sometimes. And you don't have to be a boy or a girl," I tell him.

"I know. I know that gender is more complicated than that and that everything exists on a spectrum and that's all good, but it's still confusing."

"For something that isn't real, it does wonders for the mental health. Have you talked to your moms about it?"

"How am I supposed to go to them and be like 'Hey, Mom, hey, Mama, I'm not a boy, not a girl either, don't really know what it'd be like in between those two, but I don't think that I'm that either.' I think they'll only be confused too. Supportive but confused."

"Valid." When I came out to Mom, I didn't really know what to expect. She'd been aware of LGBTQ+ causes and made yearly donations to various organizations—though I never knew if I should read those as her actually caring or her wanting the brownie points and the tax write-offs.

And after I came out, she threw me into all kinds of programs and support groups revolving around trans teenagers; she started taking me to doctors and basically outed me to my gynecologist without so much as a second thought.

To anyone else it might've seemed like she was a supportive mother, ready to take her son's transition seriously. But to me, it was overwhelming. She was making decisions for me, posting about me online without my consent. She never did her research into what it means to be the parent of a trans teenager, never went to support groups of her own.

Not to make this all about myself, but the fact that Wyatt came to me to talk about this, it makes me feel good.

I tell him, "You don't have to settle on a label now. You can just say you're nonbinary; it's an umbrella term too. Or not; you don't have to be just one thing. You can play around with pronouns too."

"Maybe. I don't even hate that, just not being on the gender binary. I don't even mind most pronouns. Back home I've accidentally been called 'she' by old men who see my hair from the back." He lets out another low, awkward laugh. "Can I ask you a favor?"

"Another favor," I tease. "Seriously?"

"Be nice to me. I'm emotionally vulnerable."

"Fine, fine. What's your favor?"

"Can you use 'they' pronouns for me?"

"Yeah, of course. Just me? No correcting anyone?"

"Just you for now. I think that's what I'd be comfortable with."

"Of course," I tell them. "Thanks for trusting me with this."

"Sorry to unload all of that on to you."

"Don't apologize. I've got some resources I can send you. There are loads of trans creators on YouTube whose videos might help make things less confusing. A lot of those videos helped me."

"Yeah, maybe. I think I just want to get a feel for myself."

"That makes sense."

I look at their lips, so close to mine, and I remember how good it felt to kiss them today, how badly I've wanted to kiss Wyatt again, how I want their hands on my body just like Josh's were, how I want to feel their skin against mine.

"Hey, um . . . Wyatt?" My mouth feels so incredibly dry right now.

"Yeah?"

Their voice.

I could just undo this, dive right into the pool or something, drag them in with me to distract them, to change the subject.

But no, I know I should do this. It feels like the right thing to do.

"I think that I should apologize," I say. "For the kiss."

"Yeah?"

"Yeah." I breathe in and out slowly. "I shouldn't have sprung it on you like that. I should've asked if you were actually comfortable."

"It was for the act, though," they say quietly, their feet moving back and forth in the water. "I understand."

"Well, still. I'm sorry."

They smile. "I accept the apology. As long as you accept my apology for it being a bad kiss."

There's this rise in my chest. "For what it's worth, I don't think it was bad."

"Really? I guess my first kiss was all right, then."

That makes me pause.

"Your first kiss?"

"Yep, that was all you."

"You've never kissed anyone before? Like, ever?"

"Is that a big deal?"

"Well, no, I just . . ." I honestly don't know what I expected. Wyatt never seemed like the type to me to really have boyfriends or girlfriends or partners. They never seemed to show interest in anyone at school; I never heard them offhandedly mention a crush or maybe a significant other who went to a different school. Except the weird adoration for Robert Pattinson that's peeked its head up some random times.

"Sorry for taking that from you."

Wyatt lets out an exasperated chuckle. "You shouldn't be. I liked it."

I'm going to combust, right here on the pool patio.

"I—uh . . ."

"Sorry," Wyatt says swiftly. "I didn't mean to make things uncomfortable."

"No, no, you're fine. It's just that . . . well, I liked it too."

"Yeah?"

"You're a good kisser, Wyatt."

We should do it some more.

Those should be the next words out of my mouth. Because I want to kiss them again, because that's what this moment is leading up to, it's so obvious. I want it, and I'd bet everything I own that they want it just as badly.

But I think we're both too afraid.

"Maybe"—their voice is still soft—"you could help me practice more, then."

It's not a question, that much is clear. I feel the heat in my cheeks, the fire starting in my brain, the alarms ringing in my ears. Did they just say that? They did, right? I'm not hearing things. They're staring at me, this soft smile on their face.

I open my mouth, and my tongue feels so heavy, so unbelievably dry.

"I'd like that." I struggle to form words, to believe that any of this is real.

But it is.

It has to be.

Wyatt and I move closer. I can't close my eyes, and neither do they. Maybe they want the same thing I want.

I want to see this happen; I want proof that this is happening, that I'm not having some fucked-up dream that I'm going to wake up from just before I get what I want so badly.

Wyatt looks so soft, their cheeks warm; I notice the moles that dot their face and the sparse hairs that grow between their eyebrows and above their upper lip, how long their bottom eyelashes are, the acne marks.

I wonder if Wyatt knows how beautiful they are.

I hope they do.

I need them to know that they're one of the most beautiful people I've ever met. Every part of them, inside and out.

Our heads tilt.

Our eyes close.

We lean into each other. Just like this morning.

"Hey!"

That's not Wyatt's voice.

And it's not mine.

We both shoot our gazes toward the voice at the far end of the patio, all the way on the other side of the pool. The security guard shines a flashlight right in our faces.

"What are you kids doing?" he yells.

"We should run," I whisper, taking my dripping feet out of the pool.

Wyatt turns to me quickly. "Huh?"

"Run!"

I grab my shoes, and I start running, almost slipping on the tile that surrounds the pool. I don't know if Wyatt is actually behind me; I hope that they are. All I can hear is the security guard shouting, "Hey! Stop!" and the sound of Wyatt's wet feet slapping the hotel floor.

"This way," I say, taking a left around the corner of the hotel.

We just have to get to the elevator before the security guard can catch us.

The sliding doors to the lobby open for us, and we race. I almost slip again in the lobby, my feet still pretty wet. Wyatt catches me, grabbing on to my free hand and pulling me forward, and we catch the elevator just as someone is walking out. We push through the closing doors, watching across the lobby as the security guard finally makes it inside, whipping his head around to see where we've gone.

The door closes, and we both finally relax against the wall of the elevator, staring at each other as we break out into laughter.

Wyatt doubles over and brushes their hair out of their face, still trying to catch their breath as the elevator lurches.

I don't know exactly what we're laughing at, but it feels like the right thing to do. It feels like the only thing to do as we ride to the top floor, the doors sliding open. I still wonder what's going through their head as we make our way back to our room.

We almost kissed.

That almost fucking happened.

And it would have if we hadn't been interrupted.

Are they glad we stopped?

They said they liked the first one.

I need to stop, I need to . . .

I need to pretend that this is Josh.

If I just pretend that Wyatt is Josh, if I just keep going with that same confidence I had when Josh and I were together, then I won't feel as nervous. I'd say that I've never heard of a more flawed plan, but the situation I've spent the past week getting myself into takes that cake.

The door to the room opens, and Wyatt steps in first. Even in the darkness, the mess that we made earlier is still visible, snacks and wrappers and crumbs left on the coffee table. I close the door behind me, leaning my body against it, watching Wyatt move quietly, still smiling at me softly.

We're both faced with the reality that we're alone again. Our eyes meet, and we stare at each other.

Just the two of us, in this room.

Before I even have time to wonder if we're going to pick up where we left off, if we're going to kiss again, maybe go further, or if we're going to ignore what just happened, go to bed, pretend that it didn't happen, Wyatt walks toward me.

Their hand finds my cheek so naturally as our lips meet again, as we lean into each other. Wyatt wants this as badly as I do; there's an eagerness to their kisses, almost like they're starved for something. It feels just like it did earlier. The taste of their mouth slightly chocolate from candy they ate.

I put my hands on their chest, feeling the way their heart speeds up under my right hand. It almost feels like it's ready to burst out from underneath.

It feels so natural to kiss them, like it's where we belong with each other. I fit so easily into them as they press me against the door, then I feel this sharp pain near the top of my ass.

"Ow!" I laugh into the kiss, and they pull away.

"Everything okay?"

"Yeah." I look back. "The doorknob was stabbing me."

We both laugh awkwardly.

"Maybe we could move somewhere more comfortable?" Wyatt suggests.

"Yeah, we should." I take their hand. I don't know if it's because

I know this is Wyatt's first time, or because this just feels like my natural position, but I take the lead, escorting Wyatt to the bed and pushing them down, straddling my legs around theirs.

"You're a good kisser," I tell them, pulling their lips toward mine again.

"I like kissing you," they say when we run out of breath, our chests heaving in sync. "I've wanted to kiss you for a long time."

I don't know why this surprises me.

What is a long time? Days? Weeks? Months?

I hate that my mind lingers on that question; there are a lot more important things to deal with right now.

What does Wyatt want?

To keep kissing, to draw the line here?

Or does Wyatt want more?

I know that I should ask them, but I don't want to break from their kisses. I throw my arms over their shoulders, feeling how soft their hair is on my fingers. I know for a fact they use two-in-one shampoo and conditioner, so there's no reason for their hair to feel as nice in my hands as it does. I'm not going to complain.

Wyatt lets out this soft whimper, and it's so adorable I can't help but smile at them.

"You're so cute."

It doesn't even feel like I'm talking to Wyatt anymore. We're just two people who have some kind of attraction to each other. And it feels like that's all that matters.

"What do you want to do?" I ask them.

"I, um . . . uh . . ." They stammer for a bit. "I've never done this before."

"You can call it sex, Wyatt. We're not twelve."

"Right." Their face feels so hot next to mine. "I've never had sex before."

"I can show you how, if you want."

Wyatt doesn't even hesitate. "I do."

"Okay." I push them down to lie flat on the bed, and I kiss them, again and again and again. I kiss them like we're going to die, I kiss them like there's no air left in the room, I kiss them like they're the first and last person that I'm ever going to kiss, I kiss them like we're the only two people left on this planet whirling through the galaxy.

I kiss them like the world is on fire.

Things are awkward at first.

And in the middle.

And at the end.

Wyatt has never used lube; they've never rolled a condom on before. I'm just grateful that I still had a few stashed in my bag. Maybe from last Christmas? In the moment I don't care where they've come from, only that they're not expired.

I guide Wyatt slowly, assuring them that we can take our time.

They're clumsy, unsure, scared that they might be hurting me, but I try to reassure them every step of the way. It feels good. They feel good.

There's something so different about seeing them naked, on top of me. We stare at each other, unable to catch our breath, sweating. They keep whispering my name, singing just to me.

It doesn't last long, but I'm okay with that.

And because Wyatt is the perfect person, they ask how they can help me finish, and I guide their hands again, slowing, thoughtfully, carefully. Twisting, crooking their fingers just the right way.

They stare at me as I struggle to catch my breath.

And just as I'm about to ask them what they're thinking, they say it without being prompted.

"You're so beautiful."

There's so much to learn about a person when you're naked in bed next to them. Like with Wyatt, I can follow the moles that decorate their face, and I can trace them all the way down their chest, to their thighs, down to their ankles. And I can see the birthmark on their hip that's shaped vaguely like the state of Washington, and I can see the same kind of stretch marks that I have, though Wyatt's are probably from their growth spurts, almost like they're strokes painted by a masterful artist, and I can see that they're uncircumcised.

And they can see my scars in their full glory. Their hands trace my stomach, and I don't feel ashamed; I don't feel this urge to cover myself. It's obvious that Wyatt isn't afraid of them, that they aren't a big deal, and, at the same time, they are. Wyatt makes me feel . . .

Appreciated.

Like I don't have to hide a part of myself.

The cleanup is awkward too, sharing an illuminated bathroom as we wipe away the evidence of what we just did. And as much fun as a shower together might seem, it feels too early. Josh and I never showered together, mostly because the showers at school weren't nearly big enough.

The entire experience is awkward, but the thing is: I don't care.

I feel closer to them; I feel like we understand each other a certain way now. I feel privileged to be the only person to have seen them like this. And it feels like an honor that I got to show them so much of myself.

Wyatt showers first, then it's my turn, and I can't stop myself from smiling like an idiot. And I don't really know why. But I don't mind one bit. I'm glad that Wyatt is still in the bedroom when I get step out, the humid air escaping with me.

"I, uh . . ." Wyatt hesitates, sitting there on the edge of the bed, talking to me while I crawl under the comforter. "Good night, I guess."

They stand.

"Where are you going?"

"To the couch," they say. "To sleep."

I smile at them. They're so cute.

Silently, I pat the spot next to me on the bed.

"Are you sure? Like, is that okay?"

"After what we just did? Yeah, it's okay."

It only has to be awkward if we let it. There doesn't have to be this beat between us; we don't have to let the wall come back up.

At least, I don't want it to.

Wyatt gives me that grin as they climb into the bed next to me. There's plenty of space on this king-sized monstrosity, but we still find our way to each other, and I stare into those green eyes.

"That was okay, right?" I ask them.

Definitely the wrong question.

I shouldn't give them room for doubts, but I can feel the doubts creeping their way back in.

"Yeah. It was."

Wyatt bites their bottom lip, a clear sign that they're thinking about something.

"Tell me," I say.

"What does this make us?" they ask. "Like . . . with the whole fake-dating thing, I don't really see where this leaves us."

"Well, it doesn't feel like faking anymore," I tell them.

I don't know if I'm ready for this conversation. I don't regret what we just did. I don't regret that we crossed this line into something more.

But I just don't think I'm ready.

Maybe we shouldn't have done this.

"We can talk about that when we're back at school," I tell Wyatt. "Let's just make it through the wedding first."

"Oh, okay. Yeah, sure."

There's no mistaking the disappointment in their voice.

I would give them an answer if I had one, but I don't. I don't know how I feel, if I want a partner or if I want Wyatt to continue to be a fuck buddy. There's something in their gaze that tells me that they want me.

And I do too.

But it feels like I shouldn't.

Because I don't deserve it.

Suddenly, this entire night feels like one giant mistake. I crossed a line with Wyatt, a clear line that kept our relationship the way that it was. We moved on from friends . . . probably.

And I don't know how I'm supposed to feel about that.

My heart wants to say yes to being partners—even if that word feels so heavy—to ending the fake part of this relationship.

But I can't.

And I don't know why.

"Good night, Neil," they whisper softly.

"Good night, Wyatt."

Our hands find each other as we close our eyes. After a few minutes, I can hear Wyatt's soft snores, the ones that I'm so used to hearing from across the dorm room, the ones that usually serve as my soundtrack to falling asleep. Except now they're right up against me.

I can't quiet my mind. I can't tell myself that things are going to be okay, because I don't know if they will be, and I hate that uncertainty.

I just got Wyatt as a friend.

And tonight, it feels like we pressed the button on the countdown to when this whole thing will implode around us.

The people that I love leave. Always. They leave me alone, they ignore me, they ship me away just so they won't have to deal with me.

So isn't it better to push them away first?

Wednesday

APRIL 20

I wake up with my arms around Wyatt.

Sometime in the middle of the night, I guess I must've just latched on to their back and refused to let go.

They don't even seem to mind.

I guess my body was used to sleeping in the same bed as Josh, curling around him. I can feel their soft breathing against my chest, the steady rise and fall. I don't know what time it is, and I don't want to know. I don't ever want to leave this bed with them in it. Because the second we do, things are going to change.

I can feel it.

There are feelings now, obviously.

And feelings are never good.

I don't know if I have it in me to break their heart. I don't want Wyatt to look at me the same way that Josh did when he told me he loved me, when I had to take his world away from him.

Why did I do this?

Why did I let this happen?

Fuck.

I could've turned them down; I should have shut this down before it ever got this heated. I should've never kissed them, never taken them down to the pool. I should've begged Lindsay to stay in our room last night so that we never even would've thought of this as an option.

I don't feel ashamed of the act, of what we did. I loved kissing Wyatt; I loved seeing them so vulnerable. I liked teaching them, guiding them. The problem is that I want it to happen again; I want it to keep happening. But I don't know if Wyatt wants to just be friends with benefits.

To be honest, I don't know if I want that either.

I want more.

I want all of Wyatt, or I want nothing.

And right now, nothing seems like the much safer option.

Wyatt's better off without me anyway.

I feel Wyatt stir underneath me after who knows how long, and they carefully turn around to face me. I want to get closer to them; I don't want to forget how their body feels underneath me like this.

"Good morning." Their voice is slow, rough, tired, perfect.

"Morning."

They reach up, rubbing the sleep out of their eyes. "How'd you sleep?"

"Good," I lie. Because it's easier to tell them that than it is to admit that I barely slept at all, that I wanted to be awake as we lie here together so that I could remember more of them, more of this moment.

They smile that perfect smile. "Good."

I smile back at them. I want to be happy right now, and I'm trying my hardest.

"What time does the rehearsal dinner start?" they ask.

"One."

"Seriously? Isn't that a little early for dinner?"

"We've got to run through the rehearsal part first," I tell

them. "That'll probably take forever. Then we get to have dinner, some dancing."

"Sounds like fun. I like dancing."

"Just save the first one for me?" I don't know why I keep saying stuff like that. It's only going to make things harder.

Wyatt smiles. "Of course."

"What time is it?"

"No idea." Wyatt rolls back over, grabbing their phone off the nightstand. "Nine sixteen."

"Any chance you want to grab breakfast?"

I can't deny that it feels like things have changed now.

Maybe the sex was a mistake.

No, scratch that.

Sex was definitely the mistake.

It feels like I don't know how to talk to Wyatt anymore, and I don't know what to do about that. It wasn't like this with Josh, at all. We were fine the second we finished. We just got right back to watching whatever movie it was we were watching before it happened, and then the next time we were alone, it happened again, and again. Eventually, Josh asked me what we were doing, and that was when we agreed that it'd be no strings attached, strictly a friends-with-benefits situation.

Now, with Wyatt . . .

I don't know.

And I desperately wish that I had the answer. Does anything have to have changed? Can't we be normal with each other? What kind of conversations do we have now? What kind of conversations did we have before?

What do I do?

"Hey."

I feel this light kick under the table, and I look across the table at Wyatt.

They really wanted what they labeled "purposefully bad breakfast food," which meant that, in a city filled with literally hundreds of restaurants dedicated to amazing breakfasts and brunches, we ended up at an IHOP, where everything is sticky and the air is filled with the smell of cooked potatoes and too-sweet syrups.

"You okay?"

I nod. "Yeah, I'm good."

"You've hardly touched your food," they say.

Because my stomach is in knots, and it feels like the second I swallow a bite, I'll just throw it back up. "Just not hungry, I guess."

I don't know if Wyatt can tell that something is wrong, that part of me does wish that I could take it back, while the rest of me wants to repeat it all over again, to let them kiss me again.

"I love hash browns," Wyatt says unprompted, proving their point by shoveling the rest of the hash browns on their plate into their mouth. Then they start singing "I love hash browns, I love hash browns" in this country accent that almost makes it sound like they're mocking themself.

"Maybe you should sing that at the wedding," I suggest.

They smile at me. "I doubt your brother would appreciate it."

They go back to eating, and I go back to staring at them wordlessly. I hate how they make me feel; I hate that I feel so comfortable around them, and that my heartbeat speeds up when they're near, that I want more of them. I mean, seriously, how many people just break into song about how much they like hash browns?

Why can't I have this?

Why can't I let myself have this?

What am I afraid of?

Of hurting us?

Hurting myself?

Hurting them?

When Wyatt finishes eating, we walk back to the hotel. When we're out the door, Wyatt takes my hand in theirs, swinging back and forth. I guess they're more confident in this entire thing than I am.

It sounds messed up, but I almost wish they were more uninterested than I am. That they'd hated last night and never wanted to do it ever again.

I don't want to break their heart, to tell them that we can't do this. It'd be so much easier if they could hate me, if they'd break my heart instead.

So much easier.

It's eleven thirty by the time we get back to the hotel, which leaves us enough time to get dressed for the rehearsal and go to the hotel gardens. The entire space seems to have changed in the span of days, with areas being cleared or moved, and cut off from the rest of the guests. There's an even larger tent being built up in the center of the venue too. And off to the far side, closer to the large fountain, there are rows and rows of white chairs that everyone involved in the wedding is now situated around.

Mother is there, along with Nana and Grandpa, Michael and

Ashley (obviously), Lindsay along with the rest of the brides-maids, Zach and the other groomsmen, Ashley's little sisters, who will be the flower girls, and a cousin who will be the ring bearer.

When Mother spots me, she walks over. "Neil, there you are. Where have the two of you been?"

"We just stopped to get breakfast; we didn't realize—"

"I wish you had told me," she says, the annoyance obvious in her tone. "These next two days are going to be important. You need to make sure you are early everywhere you are needed. Am I understood?"

"I— Yes, ma'am."

"Wyatt, you can have a seat in the back row."

I let go of Wyatt's hand, letting it slip away from me.

"And you, come with me." Mother leads me by the shoulder to the front of the venue. God, I hate this so much. I can only dream of skipping this entire thing, flying back to Charlotte on my own, hiding in my dorm room. Wyatt can find their own way back; they have a return ticket.

"Good, everyone's here," the priest says. My immediate family isn't exactly religious, but I think Nana might've objected if we didn't have a priest doing the ceremony. "We can go ahead and get started on placements."

For the next hour, we're told the steps of the ceremony, from Grandpa escorting Nana to their seats down to Ashley being led down the aisle by her father. Then we actually have to prac-tice each step a few times. I feel like if Mother wasn't here, we might've been stuck doing it once or twice, but we do each step no less than seven times to ensure that they're done perfectly.

My job is to escort Mom down the aisle, then join Michael

and the other groomsmen. "Slow down," she mutters to me as I lead her to her seat beside my grandparents. "You're walking too fast."

There are times when I imagine that our relationship is a normal one, that she treats me like a mom should treat their kid, that she didn't spend my childhood throwing money at me to get whatever I wanted because that was apparently what she thought a parent should do, as if she hadn't somehow found a way to support my decisions about my identity without really ever talking to me about it or defending me when other family members said I was being ridiculous or going through "a phase." Sure, maybe her sending me to Steerfield saved me from making big mistakes, from going down the wrong path, but she'd never recognize that it was her fault in the first place. And it feels like she'd recognize *me*.

I look over my shoulder at Wyatt, a somewhat uninterested look on their face, but they still look happy to be here. When there's a break for the bridesmaids, Lindsay goes over to them, and the two of them start talking and laughing.

I like that they like each other.

Not that Lindsay and Josh didn't get along with each other, but there's a lot more warmth between Wyatt and Lindsay.

All the more reason to not break things off, to let this continue, to tell myself that I can love Wyatt just fine, that we'll be good for each other—

Mother snaps her fingers rapidly. "Neil, pay attention."

"This doesn't involve me," I say.

"We're right after your grandparents. You need to know when they're walking so you can be on time."

"As if anyone would notice," I mutter.

"What was that?"

"Nothing."

"Right, nothing." Mother goes back to the center of the crowd. In every orchestra, there can only be one conductor. We have to run through the whole affair several times, walking back and forth down the aisle to get all the beats right. I end up standing next to Nana and Grandpa a few times while we wait.

"You fill out that suit nicely, son," Grandpa says, and I don't know if I should take it as a compliment or not.

"I think the bridesmaid dresses would've fit you better," Nana adds.

Because of course she has to.

"Well, I think a casket would've fit you better, but we can't always get what we want." I want to say this as loud as I can, but it comes out a whisper. Because this isn't the time for me to make a scene, to defend myself against her transphobic bullshit.

I have to be the good son this week.

The perfect child.

"How is everything going?" Wyatt's voice in my ear makes me jump, and I grab my chest.

"You scared me."

"Sorry."

"It's going about as well as I expected it to," I tell them, leaning back into them.

"That bad, huh?"

"Yep."

Mom claps her hands. "Okay! I want to see Michael and Ashley up front so we can see how they'll look."

Michael steps forward, but Ashley stops him.

"Actually," she says, "I'd like to get a quick view of the

ceremony. Can we have someone stand in while we watch the whole playthrough?"

"Of course," the priest says. "Any volunteers?"

Mother motions to me. "Neil, you and Wyatt stand up there."

I freeze. "Us?"

"There isn't another Neil here," she says with this sarcastic tone. "Get up there—we don't have a lot of time before dinner."

I want nothing more than to take Wyatt's hand and pull them back into the hotel so we can hide in our room for the rest of the day, but there's no denying the eyes staring expectantly at us now, or the judgmental look that Nana and Grandpa are giving as two male-presenting people stand at the altar. Wyatt and I take our stance under the arch in front of everyone.

The priest runs through his spiel—rather quickly, after a curt look from Mom. Wyatt and I both put our hands together. I have absolutely no idea why—it just seems like the natural thing to do here.

"Dearly beloved, we are gathered here today to celebrate the joining of these two families—"

I stare down at Wyatt's hands around mine, their grip so warm and strong.

When I look at them, into those deep green eyes, my heart hurts. My heart hurts the same way that it hurt when I looked at Josh when he told me that he loved me. And my heart has to be hurting for a reason; it has to be telling me something. I can't expect Wyatt to get involved with this family. I can't expect Wyatt to get involved with me.

I don't want to live in a world where Wyatt Fowler hates me.

But maybe that's the cost I have to pay now to avoid a much worse hurt later.

"And then the groom will say 'I do.'" The priest motions to me.

"I do," I say dutifully.

Wyatt says it with more conviction . . . and that just about breaks me.

This isn't our life. It isn't.

And it never will be, no matter how badly I want it.

The dinner is a chaotic affair held in the banquet hall of the hotel. Every single person who is here for this wedding is present. Kids are running around; adults are eating and drinking a little too much before the early morning tomorrow.

I don't know what's going on with me. Between this morning and Mother fussing at me, dealing with Nana's stares and Grandpa's comments that aren't *quite* transphobic but still feel like they are, the heat and my empty stomach adding up to one hell of a headache, Wyatt has attached themself to my hip when I just want a little bit of space as we enter the banquet hall absolutely filled with people. They try to hold my hand as we walk in, but I slip it away.

They look at me and ask, "Are you okay?"

No, I'm not.

"Just a headache, sorry."

"No worries. Maybe you just need some food."

We move to our table, which seems to be where the teenagers have been exiled. Lindsay and Josh are already both there, along with a few of Ashley's relatives who can't be more than maybe twelve or thirteen.

"How was the rehearsal?" Josh asks.

Why am I even here?

Between sitting next to Wyatt, and being only a few seats away from Josh, I feel hot, like my clothing is getting too tight on my body. Am I having a panic attack? Is that what this is?

No, right?

I've never had a panic attack before, even in the days leading up to my surgery or when I came out to Mother. At least, I don't *think* I've ever had a panic attack.

But isn't it so much more than that? Isn't it the heat of the lights above me and the constant talking that only seems to be getting louder, Wyatt's touch on my knee and the tingle at the back of my head, the gurgle of my stomach and the irritation from spending my entire morning getting yelled at by a woman who doesn't even seem to like me?

I just want to be done with the day.

The sooner, the better.

"It was okay," Lindsay says. "God, I sweated in my dress, though. The wedding is going to be miserable."

"Yikes." Josh's eyes go wide as he takes a sip of his water.

"And Wyatt and Neil got married!"

Josh trips up on himself, knocking his glass of water over on the table, where it spills all down the front of his pants. "Married? Aren't you both a little young?" he says between struggling to absorb the water with his napkin.

"She's joking," Wyatt says. "We had to stand at the altar so they could do a test run of the vows, I guess."

"I don't know." Lindsay smirks like a cat. "You both said 'I do.' The priest read all the marriage stuff—sounds to me like that's legally binding."

"It isn't," I say bluntly. "We're not married."

And we're not dating.

We're not together.

Lindsay gives me a quick glance before she grabs a napkin and helps Josh with the brand-new water stain on his pants.

"I think I'd better go change," he says. "It looks like I peed myself."

"Probably for the best," Lindsay says. "Here, I'll cover you." She slips the sheer cardigan off her shoulders and hands it to him. When did the two of them get so friendly with each other? They've only ever met, like, three times before this week.

"Thanks." Josh stands up. I'm not sure why he thinks that it's less awkward to move around with a cardigan held awkwardly in front of his crotch, but whatever. Lindsay does her best to help cover him as they make their way out of the banquet hall.

"What's going on?" Wyatt asks when Lindsay and Josh are out of earshot.

"Nothing."

"You seem upset."

"I'm not *upset*."

Wyatt isn't even saying anything, but I hate that they're looking at me; I hate that they're so obviously concerned. They shouldn't be. They shouldn't care about me at all. I'm not worth it.

"It's *nothing*."

"Okay! Geez, don't bite my head off."

"I'm not biting your head off!" I say.

"Yeah, you are." There's a moment of silence between Wyatt and me, the rest of the room going about like everything is normal, like their lives aren't falling apart in front of them. "I'm fine."

"You don't seem fine."

"Don't tell me how I feel."

"Okay, sorry." They put a hand on my thigh.

"Please, just stop touching me."

Wyatt takes their hand back, and they give me this wounded expression.

This isn't fair.

This isn't fucking fair.

God, why can't my brain just fucking be normal?

"I'm sorry, I just . . ."

I feel like I could cry.

"If something's going on, we can talk about it."

"Fine, yeah," I say, letting the napkin in my lap fall to the floor. "Let's talk."

Might as well go ahead and get this over with. Wyatt can go back to sleeping on the couch; we can make it through the wedding tomorrow, fake an emergency, and they can spend the last days of spring break with their parents. And when we get back to school, it'll be like this week never happened. They'll hate me again, and I'll let them, because that's the natural order of these things.

We walk around the corner of the banquet hall, closer toward the elevators where no one seems to be. At least, if anyone does walk by, they don't have to be in our business.

"Do you want to go up to the room?" Wyatt asks when things are a little quieter. I can already feel my heart slowing down a bit. Maybe it was just the dining hall. The heat of the lights, the constant talking.

"No, I can't. I just . . . I needed some space."

"Okay." Wyatt puts a hand on my shoulder.

"Please stop touching me."

They take their hand back. "I just thought . . ."

"I don't need you to think right now, okay?"

Their brow furrows. "What's gotten into you?"

"I just—I need some time. And you breathing down my neck isn't helping me." I cover my face with my hands and let out this low groan.

"Is something wrong?"

"What was your first clue?"

"Why are you acting like this? You were fine yesterday. What happened?"

"The kiss," I blurt out, my mouth not moving quickly enough to stop the message from my brain. "And the sex, and everything, Wyatt. Everything happened."

"I don't . . . I don't get it. Was it bad?"

No.

And that's the problem.

"Whatever. It doesn't matter."

"It does," they say. "If there's something going on, I want to talk about it with you."

I take my hand back. "Don't you get it? *I* fucked up. I shouldn't have brought you here. It was all a mistake."

I can hear the elevator as it opens and closes, people riding to their floors, getting off in the lobby.

"It was a mistake to bring you here. It was a mistake to plan this entire act. What the fuck was I thinking? What does fake dating you earn me? Clearly Josh has already moved on; he doesn't give a fuck that you're here. What are we even doing?"

"Neil."

"No, just, get away from me. Please?"

I try to steady my breathing, but my chest feels tight. It's like the short period when I wore a binder, before I did the proper research, when I put myself in danger by binding too tightly for too long.

That constriction.

"I made a mistake," I tell them. "I shouldn't have dragged you into this."

"What are you saying?" they ask me.

"Whatever this is"—I point back and forth between the both of us—"it's got to end, now. No more fake dating, no more fake kisses, no more hand-holding, no more anything."

"Did I do something wrong?" they ask again.

No, you didn't do anything wrong, Wyatt, except make a coward fall in love with you.

"Yes, you did," I lie.

Their shoulders slump forward. "I wish you'd tell me what it is."

"That doesn't matter—"

"It does to me," they say firmly.

"Whatever. This is over. You can perform at the wedding, and we can act like we're together until we go back to Steerfield. Then we never have to talk about it again." I step away from Wyatt, fully prepared to go back to the rehearsal dinner.

"No." Wyatt steps in front of me.

"What?"

"No."

"You can't just say no." I try to step around him, but Wyatt is quick.

"That's not good enough, Neil."

"I don't care."

"You're my friend, and I'd like to know what I did. What changed?"

"Oh my God, just drop it. This was all a fucking act anyway!" I finally move past Wyatt and around the corner, where I run headfirst into my mother, standing there with her arms crossed.

My blood freezes.

Because the look on her face tells me that she's heard every single word.

"I came to see why you'd left in such a hurry," she says. "But I can see the two of you are busy."

"We aren't," I say.

"You faked this whole relationship?"

"Is that true, Neil?" Josh asks. I don't even know where he came from. One second the elevator door was opening, and the next, he was there, with a new pair of pants and Lindsay standing next to him.

"Yes, Neil. What's going on here?" Mother stares at me and then Wyatt. "You're not dating this boy?"

"God, stop. Just stop."

"And how am I going to explain this to everyone?"

"You don't fucking have to!" I say a little too loudly. Heads turn in our direction. "Not every fucking thing has to be about you!"

The faucet has been turned on.

"Oh, but that's impossible, because *everything* has to come back to you. Because you don't know how to actually be a mother, you just throw money at me and hope that it fixes all of our problems. And when it won't, you'll take any chance you can get to embarrass me."

She stares at me. There's this look of disbelief on everyone's faces.

I didn't even mean for the words to come out, but now that they're out there, I can't say that I'm sorry.

"Neil Anthony Kearney, you cannot talk to me that way!"

"Maybe if you acted like a mother, I'd treat you like one! Moms don't ignore their kids. They don't ship their kids across the country because they don't want to deal with them. They don't let their kid experience transphobia on the daily from their own fucking family while parading that kid all over the news like they're the greatest fucking ally ever. And that's all you've done for years, Mom. *Years.*"

That's when her face twists and I see the wet glare in her eyes.

Oh shit.

Fuck.

No, no, no.

Fuck.

I need to get out of here.

I press the elevator button, and when nothing happens, I press it and press and press and I keep pressing it until the door finally opens, ignoring the sound of Mother's heels as she runs somewhere. I don't know.

I fucked up.

I fucked up so monumentally. I fucked up so hard.

"Neil." Wyatt stops the door from closing, cramming their way into the elevator.

I watch as the door finally closes. Josh is still standing there, staring at me.

Then he's gone.

And the elevator begins to move.

"What is going on?" Wyatt asks.

The million-dollar question.

"I don't know anymore. I don't fucking know. I just . . ." I want to cry, I want to scream, I want to hit something. I'm so angry with Wyatt, and I'm angry with Josh, and I'm angry with my mother, and at Michael and Ashley and Lindsay and my grandparents and everyone.

Except I'm not.

I'm angry with myself.

I'm the one who fucked up. I'm the one who let this happen.

"I messed up, Wyatt."

"You didn't." They step closer, wrapping their arms around me.

Their embrace feels warm, comforting, grounding.

Like I'm home.

Except I don't deserve their warmth, their comfort. I don't deserve any of it.

"I did."

And I can't undo it.

"Everything's going to be okay."

"No." I push away from them. "Don't you get it? Can't you see how fucked this entire thing is? I dragged you all the way across the country so I could do what? So I could show up the boy whose heart I broke? Doesn't that disgust you?"

"Neil."

The elevator opens, and I don't even check to see if it's our floor; I just run out.

"Neil!" Wyatt calls my name, stopping the elevator just in time to slide between the closing doors. "You can't keep running away."

"I'm fucked up, Wyatt. You were right when you said that I'm no different from my mom. I'm shallow. I'm selfish. I pulled you into this shit when I shouldn't have. And I'm sorry."

"You don't have to apologize."

I pull the key card from my wallet, pushing it in the lock and pulling the knob. But it doesn't give. I try again, and the door doesn't budge an inch.

"Fuck." I struggle to slide the key back in, but it slips from my fingers and falls to the floor. I stare at it, on the carpet, the logo of the hotel printed neatly. Everyone knows. Mom, Lindsay, Samuel, Josh. Everyone knows how much of an idiot I am, how badly I fucked up.

And I deserve it.

I deserve it for how I treated Josh.

Because he deserves better.

And so does Wyatt.

They pick up the key card slowly, sliding it into the door and opening it with ease.

I stumble into the room, going I don't know where. To the balcony, to the bed to bury myself in the sheets, to hide in the bathroom and drown myself in the tub. All better alternatives than standing here, talking to Wyatt, making them wait while I break their heart.

"Neil—"

"Don't ask me what's going on. Don't do that again," I whisper.

"What's going through your head?"

"That I'm a huge fuckup."

"Because?"

Because I fell in love with you. Because I'm in love with you. Because I'm pushing away everyone because I don't want to be loved. Because I don't want any of them to hurt me first. Because I don't deserve either of them. They deserve so much better, maybe even each other. And I don't deserve anything but loneliness because all I do is hurt people.

It's what I'm good at.

I learned from the best.

"You shouldn't have come here," I say. "Your parents should've said no."

"But I'm still here."

"Then you should leave."

"Is that what you want?"

Don't ask me questions right now, please. Because I'm going to give the wrong answers.

"It's not like it matters. You were only here because I promised you I'd get you an audition."

"Neil—"

"I'll tell Michael that he still owes me. You'll get—"

Wyatt strides toward me, their long legs carrying them across the room to me in just a few steps. "I don't give a shit about the audition, Neil. I care about *you*." They put their hands to my cheeks. "Yeah, that might've been a plus, but this wasn't about the audition. Ever."

I stare up at them. This person who I think I love, this person who I kissed, this person who I let inside to see all the ugly bits of my brain, this person I could see myself spending the next year with, this person who I want to hold on to for forever and never let go.

"That's the problem," I say, my voice a little calmer. "You love me more than I can love you."

It doesn't even occur to me that I used the L-word just now.

"I don't believe that's true," they say.

I put my hands on theirs, pulling them away from my face. "Doesn't matter what you believe—it's the truth."

"That's a matter of perspective."

God, that sounds so cheesy, and so perfectly Wyatt Fowler.

"This was all an act," I say. "It wasn't supposed to be something more. Just the two of us faking our way through this."

That's all it was.

An act.

"I think . . ." The words don't want to come out. "I think that I need you to leave."

Wyatt bites on their bottom lip so hard that the skin beneath it turns white. I'm almost scared that they'll bite right through, and they'll start bleeding everywhere.

And then they nod.

My worst fear.

"Okay."

Stop, I want to tell them. Fight back, argue with me, do something!

They don't, though.

"I'll let you pack," I say. "And I'll order you a new ticket and a ride to the airport."

"Okay."

"I'm sorry."

"I don't want an apology," they tell me.

Fair enough.

I slip away from Wyatt, leaving them standing there in the living room. I need to be alone, even if the only thing separating us is a flimsy door. And as I reach to close it, they open their mouth.

"You're wrong."

I pause, not saying a word.

"This was never an act for me."

I let their words sink in, and I turn away so they won't see me cry.

Then I close the door.

I give Wyatt time to pack by themself, and while I'd love nothing more than to crawl under the duvet and sleep until my flight in a few days, I have to do something.

But that doesn't mean I can't also sit in bed while I do it.

The earliest flight is tonight around eleven, which means that Wyatt won't have to sleep here while they wait.

Good.

The sooner they get out of California, the better.

Just as I'm finalizing the purchase, I get a text from Lindsay.

LINDSAY: Hey
LINDSAY: Is everything okay?

I don't reply to her. Instead, I screenshot all the information Wyatt will need, and I text it to them. Then I just lie there, in bed, wondering what the fuck I've done.

It'll be for the best.

Wyatt will go home; they'll go back to their parents; they'll be angry with me, bitter. When we get back to school, they'll never want to talk to me ever again. I'll just have to survive those two months with them while we share the dorm room.

Though, who knows, maybe I can throw enough of a tantrum to get moved.

It didn't work the first time, but I never offered to pay someone.

Oh, right.

The payment.

I drop Wyatt two thousand dollars via Apple Pay; that seems like a fair amount for putting up with me for a week. But a few seconds later, my phone buzzes with the rejection of the money.

Are they serious?

I pay them again, and it bounces back once more.

I sigh, crawling out of bed and opening the bedroom door, ready to demand that they take the money. But when I look into the living room, it's totally empty. Their suitcase is gone, their guitar, laptop, phone, charger, shoes.

They're actually gone.

Everything except their suit, which is still bagged up, hanging in the coat closet.

They did it.

They left.

Isn't that what I wanted? Wasn't this the answer? The only way out?

I thought that getting them away from me would make things better, easier. I thought that it would stop my heart from hurting. But staring at the empty space that they occupied, knowing that they're somewhere out there, maybe down in the lobby, or in an Uber on their way to the airport . . .

It hurts me.

• • •

I don't go back down to dinner.

I can't bear to be around everyone. I can't stand the thought of talking to Lindsay, telling her what actually happened, what went on this week. Or looking at the pain on Mom's face from the words that I said. The confusion from Josh. How I could be so cruel to him when all he wanted to do was love me?

I'll apologize to Michael in the morning, ask him if I can skip out on the wedding, explain to him that he'll need a new wedding singer for his first dance, apologize for all the trouble that I've caused.

I haven't left the bed since I realized that Wyatt is actually gone.

I've opened my texts to them, drafted a few apologies, explanations, but none of it works, none of it fits. How could they ever forgive me for this? How could they ever forgive me for how I treated them before?

Even scrolling through old text messages, there's nothing there but a silent contempt. Asking each other for notes, me telling them I'd be out late, them saying to be careful coming in because they'd just swept.

I'd tracked dirt in on purpose that day.

God, I'm an awful person.

Then I think about the last words Wyatt said to me.

This was never an act to me.

I keep replaying that moment again and again in my head. I was supposed to turn around, apologize then and there. We'd kiss and realize our feelings for each other and fall over each other getting back to the bed, still miss the rehearsal dinner.

But that wasn't what I did.

I lost, and that's that.

• • •

I don't know what time it is that night when I'm woken by the knocking at the door.

I slip out of bed, disoriented, and I can feel a headache forming. I pull on a sweatshirt while the knocking continues.

"I'm coming. Hold on."

I don't even register that I should check the peephole to see who it is. There are a lot of people in this hotel who I'd rather never talk to ever again.

And one of them is on the other side of the door.

"Neil, I know that you're in there. Your location on your phone is turned on." Lindsay pounds on the door some more.

I open the door just as my next-door neighbor opens his.

"Young lady, will you please keep it down?" the older man fusses at her.

"Oh, stuff it, grandpa." Lindsay strolls into the room, and I close the door behind her.

"No, please. Come on in."

She's still dressed in her rehearsal dinner dress, her hair a little looser around her shoulders, so it can't be *that* late. Everything's still a little fuzzy from the nap.

"What happened?"

"What do you mean?"

"Well, your mother stormed back into the banquet hall in tears, and it took her friends half an hour to get her out of the bathroom because she was crying so hard, and you and Wyatt were *faking* this entire thing? Just so you could get back at Josh? And where did Wyatt go? I saw him leaving the hotel with all his things."

"You saw Wyatt?"

"What's really going on here, Neil?"

"It was an act. This was all an act. I dragged Wyatt into this scheme so that I could get Josh off my back, convince him that he should move on, forget about me." I let the words spill out of me so quickly that I'm surprised that Lindsay can even understand me. "Then things got complicated. I asked him to leave."

I hate to use the wrong pronoun for Wyatt, but I don't want to out them, and little bells would go off in Josh's head if he suddenly heard me using they/them.

Lindsay stares at me, her arms crossed as she leans against the counter in the kitchen.

"You fake dated your roommate."

I nod.

"What the fuck is wrong with you?"

I don't answer her.

"Seriously, like . . . who thinks to do that?"

"I panicked."

"You're an idiot."

That much I know is true.

"And your mom?"

"She found out too," I tell her. "But then . . . I don't know, things kind of snapped, and I told her off."

"I was there for that part. It really messed her up, Neil."

"You think I don't know that? I just . . . I'd had enough."

She moves to the couch where Wyatt slept, sitting on the edge of the cushions, her arms still folded. "I mean, Neil, I know that she isn't the easiest person to get along with, but she's your mom."

"That doesn't mean anything," I tell her. "Especially when she doesn't act like a mother."

I don't want to get annoyed with Lindsay, but I'm really not in the mood for a lecture about how I should forgive my mother. I don't have to forgive her for anything.

"Have you actually talked to her about how you feel?"

"You know just as well as I do that she doesn't listen."

"You could still give her a chance."

"And you can leave if you're going to keep asking me about her."

"Okay, okay." She holds her hands up defensively. Then she sighs. "What are you going to do about Wyatt?"

"What do you mean?"

"I mean, it's clear that you're in love with him. So what are you going to do?"

I sputter, almost choking on my own spit. "What are you, you can't just—"

"Please, Neil. I saw the way you two looked at each other. It's obvious you're in love, even if you were faking at first."

"It doesn't matter," I say, finally making my way over the couch, slumping down next to her. "Wyatt deserves better. And now he's not coming back."

"What makes you think that he deserves better?"

"Because the only reason I dragged him here was to show up Josh."

"You really think that?"

"I *think* I need to go back to therapy," I say, only half joking.

Lindsay laughs quietly, leaning back on the couch. "In this family? We could all use a lot of it."

I let out a low groan, covering my face with my hands.

"I fucked up, Lindsay. I fucked up big-time."

"Yeah, I know."

"No, I mean . . ." I pause. My next words come so easy, and I think that's what scares me the most. "I love Wyatt, a lot."

"Why don't you think you deserve him?"

"Because of how I treated him, how I treated Josh, how I used them, the things that I said to them both." My own family, my own fucked-up past, the way I let my own parents' relationship influence me and how watching their love fall apart over the course of years has me so fucked up.

There are a lot of reasons that someone like me doesn't deserve someone like Wyatt.

"It was easier that way," I say.

"Why? What made it easier?"

"Isn't it easier for him to hate me now? What if we break up? What if things go wrong? What if we fight and argue; what if we're married one day and he decides that he wants a divorce, that he hates me. It's just . . . it's easier this way."

"So, you'd rather deny yourself potentially years of happiness with this person that you love all because you think it might go wrong one day?"

"It's easier."

That earns me a firm slap on the back of the head.

"Ow!"

"You're a fucking idiot."

"Whatever."

Lindsay stands up. "You both love each other. I can feel that. I could *see* that. You're so in love with each other it makes me want to throw up, and you ended it because of some future that might not even exist."

"I—"

"Neil." Lindsay breathes in and out slowly. "Love is a risk, okay? Every single person in love takes a risk every single day of their lives. And yes, there are relationships that end. People break up. They get divorced."

"You're not selling the image here."

"But they last too. They get married, they stay together, they're happy."

"But what—"

"You've got to stop asking 'what if,'" she tells me.

"Easier said than done."

Lindsay sighs. "Yeah."

What if Wyatt doesn't want me back? What if they've decided that they don't want to talk to me anymore, that they never want to see me ever again?

"Fear is natural, dude. If you're afraid of losing someone, that must mean they're important to you. Right?"

Her words make sense.

And I feel so stupid for not seeing it sooner.

"I'm a fucking moron." I could vomit.

"Yeah, yeah, you are." Lindsay starts to rub circles on the small of my back. "But it's not too late to apologize to him."

"What time is it?"

Lindsay grabs her phone from her bag. "Eleven thirty."

My stomach sinks.

"It is too late."

"His flight already left?"

I nod.

"Then have the best time that you can this weekend; maybe even leave after the wedding. He'll still be waiting for you in North Carolina." I try to stop the shaking of my hands. "I fucked up."

"Yeah, you did." Lindsay stands, grabbing her things. "You *really* want my advice?"

I watch her as she makes her way back over to the door.

"Why ask? You're going to give it anyway."

"Cute." She gives me a fake laugh. "Talk to Josh. I think the two of you have some things you need to work out before you talk to Wyatt again."

I hate that I know she's right.

It's what I should've done in the first place.

"He's not the paranoid weirdo you made him out to be," she says. "He's a good guy, Neil. With a big heart and a lot of love for you."

"I know."

"Good. Talk to him tomorrow, okay?"

"I will."

Lindsay opens the door slowly. "I'll see you in the morning?"

"Yeah."

"Good. Get some sleep."

I listen as she closes the door, her footsteps vanishing down the hallway. And as I stand up, going back to bed, crawling under the covers, staring at the skyline in front of me, I know what I have to do.

I grab my phone, staring at the messages that I've drafted for Wyatt.

And I go to their contact information.

My fingers hover over the CALL option.

But knowing what you have to do and actually doing it—those are two different things.

"I know that I'm probably the last person you want to hear from right now, and I realize that you're on a plane, and that you're not going to hear this message until you get back to North Carolina, but I wanted to call you anyway. I wanted to say that I'm sorry, I'm sorry for everything. For how I treated you for so long, for making fun of you, and your clothes, and being so mean to you. And for dragging you all the way out here just to prove a point to Josh, and for making you put up with my family for an entire week, and for . . . and for scaring you off, making you leave. I'm sorry, Wyatt, and if it takes me the rest of my life for you to forgive me, then that'll be fine. I just don't think that I can go without you in my life. You make me feel good, and loved, and warm, and I hate myself for not realizing that sooner. I only hope that you'll be willing to start over, to go back to being friends or whatever you want to be. Or maybe you'll never want to see me again, and that'll be okay too. I just couldn't let you go without knowing how sorry I am, and I just hope that you'll be able to forgive me in some way. I just . . . yeah . . . I think that I love—"

"We're sorry, but you've exceeded the length of this voice mail message. Please hang up and dial again if you wish to leave another."

Thursday

APRIL 21

I wake up missing Wyatt.

It only took a single night of them sleeping beside me to make me feel like this is where they belonged. Then I remember last night, and I snatch my phone off the nightstand.

But the screen doesn't turn on.

Dead.

"Shit." I dig around for the charger.

Maybe Wyatt texted me; maybe they called. Maybe they've forgiven me, and they'll be at the wedding, waiting for me, coming to get their suit, performing at the reception.

When I'm out of the shower, my phone is charged enough for me to use it, but there are no new calls or texts from anyone, not even Mom. The more I think about what I said to her, the deeper the hole in my gut goes. I meant it . . . but that doesn't mean that I should have said it.

I hurt everyone. That's what I do best, I suppose.

And right underneath that is being late.

I dress in a T-shirt and jeans, pulling my shoes on at the door and grabbing my suit bag. Racing down the hallway, I barely catch the elevator as the doors begin to close.

"Hold it!" I shout, and a hand reaches out, catching the doors. "Thanks."

"Yeah."

Josh stands on the opposite side of the elevator.

I should've let this one go.

I thought a lot about everything that I would say to Josh last night, going over all my feelings in my head, preparing my arguments that might help me come out the other side with at least a *shred* of dignity. But being in front of him now, I'm unprepared. I figured we'd talk after the wedding, when things were a little less stressful, maybe at the reception.

An elevator doesn't exactly seem like the best place to talk about everything that happened.

"Big day," I say, my words so soft that I'm scared he won't hear them at first.

But he does.

"Yeah. Ready for it to be over?"

"Definitely."

I hate how far we've gotten from each other.

"Where's Wyatt?" he asks. "Still getting ready?"

I decide to be honest for the first time in a long time—although I'm also mindful that Wyatt didn't want me to share their new pronouns with anyone else.

"Um . . . no. He left last night." I still hate using Wyatt's incorrect pronouns.

"Oh. That's a bummer."

"Yeah."

Josh shuffles his feet. He looks good in his suit. I'm not sure why he's expected at the wedding so early; maybe it's just easier to be down there with Zach.

I realize: This is my moment. The longer it stretches on, the longer we're in the elevator, I can feel that this is when it's supposed to happen.

I just don't know how to start the conversation.

I stand there, silently hoping that the elevator will take on more people, but it doesn't. It's just the two of us as we make it to the ground floor, the doors sliding open.

"Guess I'll see you at the ceremony, then?" Josh says, giving me a short wave as he walks out of the elevator.

I stand there, watching him for so long the doors threaten to close on me.

I stop them with my hand and shout, "Josh! Wait!"

He turns, watching as I stride toward him.

"Can we talk, just for a second?"

He stares at me, and there's this light in his eyes. "Sure."

It takes a little walking around to find a place where we can talk privately, but eventually I take him to this lounge area not too far from the pool, with comfortable seats where you can relax. Except there's no relaxing right now. My heart feels like it's ready to burst out of my chest. Josh watches me and my leg bounces up and down, my hands twitching nervously.

I take a deep breath.

"I owe you an explanation."

"Okay."

"The reason that Wyatt was here—at least the reason that I told myself he was here—was that I wanted you to get over me. And I thought that if I invoked our little Pull-Out Clause, then you'd get over me."

"Right. I kind of gathered all of that last night," he says, and then he stares at me expectantly. Except the thing is, I have no idea what to say next. There are a million things I could apologize for, so I don't know where to start.

"And . . . I don't think I can begin to understand how monumentally fucked that was for me to do."

"I'm inclined to agree with you."

I give him a sharp look.

Then, surprisingly, Josh lets out this low laugh. He scratches at his head uncomfortably, and then I can't keep myself from laughing either.

"Hey," he tells me, "you said it, not me."

"Doesn't mean that you have to agree."

He smirks. "Well, if it's got feathers and it quacks, it must be a duck."

"What?"

"Nothing." He shakes his head. "I should have seen that there was something going on. I mean, you *hated* Wyatt before all of this went down. I was pretty suspicious."

"Yeah."

"So what was the plan here? Pretend to date Wyatt, get me to get over you, then keep up the act at school?"

I rub my hands on my knees. "I didn't really think much further ahead than this week."

He laughs again, and there's no mistaking that smile.

I smile at him. "You know, when I hear it out loud like that, I realize how stupid that sounds."

"Yeah, yeah, you're an idiot." Josh reclines in the chair.

I can't argue with the evidence.

"I guess, um . . . I guess the reason that I wanted to talk to you out there . . . is so I could apologize to you."

I wait for him to say something, anything, to give me the signal to move forward. But I guess his silence says enough.

I go on. "I treated you really poorly, even before we . . ."

"Ended things?"

I sigh. "Yeah. You poured your heart out to me, and I kind of—"

"Took a shit all over it?"

"Isn't this *my* apology?"

"Yeah, but you're bad at it."

"Fair enough." I breathe again. "I'm sorry, Josh. I really am."

"Well, Neil, I'm not going to fault you for things that you weren't comfortable doing."

"You're going to make this as hard as possible, aren't you? I'm sorry for the things that I said to you last week, how cruel I was to you. You're one of my best friends, and I think that I was just afraid. I don't know."

"A classic self-sabotage."

"Pretty much," I say. "I don't want to sound mean . . . but I wasn't in love with you. I couldn't give you what you wanted. I couldn't say it back to you. And I think that I didn't understand my own feelings."

Josh nods.

I keep talking. "It wasn't going to be a case of wrong place, wrong time. I'm just the wrong person. And you deserve someone who can love you back."

"I can see that now." Josh sighs. "I owe you an apology too. I should've respected your boundaries, believed you when you said you didn't have feelings for me. But you shouldn't say what you just said like you're incapable of love."

"What do you mean?"

"You love, Neil. And I don't like watching you pretend that you don't."

I'm not sure what to say to him.

"You're too hard on yourself," he presses.

"Maybe if I wasn't such a fuckup, I'd get to ease up."

"You make mistakes—we all do. We're human."

"Okay, Philosophy 101. I mean, there's no denying I'm a fuckup. Look at the damage I've caused."

"Yeah . . . that scene with your mom was brutal to watch."

"I'll be lucky if she ever wants to talk to me again," I say. "Same can be said for Wyatt. I like hurting people, I guess."

Josh looks at me seriously for a second before saying, "I'm going to tell you something, and I want you to try to not get mad at me at first, okay?"

I nod.

"You really hurt me. It really sucked, those things that you said to me. And seeing you and Wyatt together so quickly, it was enough to convince me that there were some serious differences in how we saw each other."

Each word is like a stab in my gut, twisting the knife deeper and deeper.

But I have to listen to this. I have to know how badly I hurt him.

"I cried the night that we ended things, and I cried the night after. I hid in the bathroom on the plane and cried. I had to explain to my parents what happened to us. And I had to spend a lot of time thinking about why it never worked between us, why we couldn't have had something more, if I had done something wrong. It sucked, Neil. It really, really sucked. All I wanted you to do was to treat me like a person, but you couldn't even give me that while you broke my heart."

I don't say a word because I don't know if I'm allowed to.

"I loved you, and I still love you." Josh licks his lips. "It hurt to see that you'd moved on so quickly, especially with someone you'd told me you hated. Like, I really couldn't remember a single positive thing that you'd said about Wyatt."

He takes a breath and releases it. I don't say a thing.

"Deep down I probably knew that it was fake." He chuckles softly. "I mean, really. The plan was pretty ridiculous."

"Yeah." My mouth feels so dry.

"But when I saw the two of you together, that changed."

"What do you mean?"

"I mean, I believed it. I believed the two of you were in love. I realized there was something that Wyatt could clearly give you that I couldn't. Maybe it was space, or maybe it was time. Maybe it was a different type of love. I don't know. But . . . I could tell."

"I don't even know if that's true," I say. "When I look at you, I still have all those memories of the things that we did together, the dates we went on, the nights we spent with each other. I still feel something for you."

"And I'm still in love with you. I don't know where you got this idea that it'd only take me a week to get over you, but . . . yeah, no. But I also know that we're done."

"Do you think that we can go back to being friends?" I ask.

This might be the answer I'm most afraid of. If all this ends with Josh deciding he can't be a part of my life anymore, and that I can't be a part of his, I don't know what I'm going to do.

"I don't think I'm ready for that right now," he says. "I mean, it's only been a week."

Oh.

"But I want to be friends again."

"Yeah?"

"Yeah. We've just got to get there. Slowly, I think."

"Yeah, yeah. Of course." That's better than nothing.

"Feelings are weird. So, it's okay for now." Josh leans in closer. "I still can't believe you dragged Wyatt into all of this."

"I seriously don't know what I was thinking."

"Maybe it was for the best?" he offers. "I mean, you two seem to like each other a lot."

"Can I ask you something?"

"Yeah."

"When you . . . when you realized you were in love with me, what was that like? How did that happen?"

"You're asking me when I fell in love with you?"

I nod. "What was it like?"

"You realize that love's not really a thing most people whittle down to a single moment."

"Yeah, but like . . . what was the best moment?"

Josh lets his head hang in shame. "You're actually hopeless."

"So you don't know?"

"Jesus Christ, Neil. Remember that LEGO Y-wing that you bought me?"

"Yeah."

"We had this missing piece, and you turned my room all over, looked under everything and everywhere until you found it."

I think I looked for a full hour.

Josh couldn't finish the stupid thing without the piece.

"That was when I think I first realized that I loved you in more than just the platonic sense."

"So, love is looking for LEGOs?" I say. "Got it."

"Yeah, you can look at it that way," Josh says. "But I see it more as it's knowing what the other person needs and doing whatever it takes to find it, because somehow your own happiness has become inseparable from theirs. Because it makes you so damn happy to see them happy. And it makes them happy to see you happy."

Oh.

That sounds . . . familiar.

"I think . . . I think that I'm in love with Wyatt."

"Did you tell him that?"

I give Josh a glance. "Don't you think he'd still be here if I'd told him?"

"Right, yeah."

"I love him," I say. "And I think that I fucked things up."

"Did you apologize? I know that's never been your skill set, but it looks like you're learning."

"Over the phone." I turn on my screen again. Still no calls or texts. "I guess I'll have to wait until we're back at school to talk to him. If he even wants to talk to me anymore."

"Well." Josh stands up. "If I'm talking to you again, maybe there's hope. I mean, I know the full diagnosis of someone who's fallen for Neil, and Wyatt was definitely showing the symptoms. Poor guy."

"Do you really think so?"

"Yeah, I do." Josh holds out a hand for me to take.

"Can I ask you *one* more question?"

Josh raises a brow. "You're pushing it, Kearney."

"That's not a no?"

He smirks, so I take that as permission to ask.

"Who was that handsome guy you've been hanging out with?"

"Wouldn't you like to know?" Josh lets out this low chuckle. "Come on—we've got a wedding to attend."

There's still this guilt in my stomach as I get dressed in my suit. Wyatt hasn't responded—they haven't called back or sent a text. And walking around the venue, getting ready to be a groomsman, of course I'm going to run into Mom.

She's racing around, making sure every last detail is perfect, that the flowers are arranged just right, that all the lights in the tent for the reception are lit, that the orchestra has its music cues.

I keep avoiding her gaze, trying to work up the courage to go and talk to her, to apologize for the things that I said. But I can't bring myself to do it. I shouldn't feel guilty for what I did, because it was all honest. It's been years of feeling neglected, like I was second best, like I didn't deserve a spot at the table where my own family was sitting.

I still feel awful, though. I don't regret the things I said.

But I *do* regret how I said them.

I can't bring myself to talk to her when I see her. Because I'm a coward.

I stay where I am, out of the way, out of her line of sight.

"Hey, Neil." Michael pops in from behind the curtain.

There's actually a bridal shop that shares a nicely landscaped alleyway with the hotel that Mother rented the space from. The owner cleared out their entire back of the store so that everyone could get ready here, and even set it up nicely for us. Vanities lit up in this orange glow, lots of couch space to relax on, some bottled water and snack packs that won't cause any bad breath.

"What's up?" I finish buttoning up my dress shirt.

"Can you help with this?" Michael walks in, his bow tie hanging loosely around his neck. "No one else knows how to tie this, and Mom is busy."

"Yeah, sure."

I pop Michael's collar, readjusting the bow tie so I can tie it properly. Perks of always having to dress myself for Mother's galas. It's easy for my hands to wrap around the knots naturally.

"How's that?"

"Good." Michael adjusts it a touch. "You'll have to teach me how to do that."

"It's easy." I go back to putting on my own suit, slipping into my blazer, tying my own bow tie around my neck.

"So, uh . . ."

Here we go.

"I heard that Wyatt left."

"Yeah." God, on the list of people I don't want to talk to about all of this, Michael is near the top.

"I ran into him in the lobby last night. He said he wouldn't be able to perform at the reception," Michael says. "Did you two break up?"

I look at his reflection in the mirror. "I don't actually know."

"Well"—Michael runs his hands along my shoulders, smoothing out any wrinkles—"I hope you can patch up whatever happened."

"Me too. I'm sorry about Wyatt canceling."

"It's okay. The DJ is ready. We'd prefer something live, but beggers can't be choosers. Mom is ticked, but . . . you know." Michael takes a pause in front of the mirror, looking over himself again. "You seemed happy with Wyatt."

I open my mouth, ready to say something. But no words come out other than: "Thanks."

"You know I've got to talk to you about Mom, right?"

Here we go. Someone else doing the work for her.

"You hurt her feelings last night, Neil."

"Believe me, I know."

"Have you thought about what you're going to say to her?"

"I need to apologize."

"Well . . . yeah."

"Is it fucked up that I don't know if I'm sorry?"

Michael pauses. "You're not."

"I regret how I said what I said . . . but I don't regret saying it. It's the truth, Michael. She's been an awful mother to the both of us."

"Well, to you. I've got Dad to thank for most of my poor upbringing."

"So you're admitting she's a bad parent?"

"That's not fair, Neil."

I immediately feel my heart leap in my chest, beating faster and faster. "What do you mean?"

"I mean, she tried her best to do what she could for us, you know?"

"No, I don't."

"Neil—"

"Don't do that to me, Michael."

"I'm just saying—"

"No, you weren't there. You weren't there for years. You don't get to tell me how good of a parent she was."

"I'm not saying she was good," Michael says. "And that's not fair—she helped raise me too."

"You still don't know what you're talking about," I tell him. I don't want to sound upset, but I don't like that Michael is standing here telling me that Mother did a good job at raising me, that she was a good parent, that she did what she could. "I don't want to hear this."

I turn around, ready to leave the room and this conversation far behind me.

"Neil, wait."

"You don't get to tell me how to feel about her, Michael."

"I'm not telling you how to feel," he says. "I'm just saying that you maybe don't know as much as you think you do."

"Well, I'm sorry that she hurt me, and that I'm not over it. I'm sorry that you're so well adjusted after Dad royally fucked you up."

"That's not fair either, Neil."

"What do I care? Clearly you're doing so well for yourself."

"And it took me so long to get to a place where I felt healthy in my relationship. If Ashley hadn't been as kind and as patient as she is, then we'd be doomed. Because it was so easy for me to see Dad in the mirror, and I bet that it's easy for you to see Mom, isn't it?" Michael lets out a bitter laugh. "I'm not perfect; I made mistakes. But I went with Dad because I thought he needed me. The divorce fucked with him too. It fucked with all of us."

Why am I even having this conversation? I'm not interested in unpacking our parents' divorce, or which of them would have possibly been the better parent. Once the papers were signed, Dad barely talked to me. And after my transition, he stopped.

"We've all made mistakes," Michael says. "Some forgivable. Some not. Ultimately, what Dad did to you, the things he put Mom through—it's not worth forgiving. That's why he's not here. But there's a reason Mom is here."

I look at Michael long and hard. There's something in his expression, something that I can tell he hasn't told me yet.

"What's going on?" I ask.

"It's my fault," he says.

"What?"

"That you were sent to Steerfield, that you're so angry with Mom."

"What?" I repeat.

"It's my fault."

I stare at him, unable to fully process what he's telling me.

"Are you fucking serious, Michael?"

"She didn't know what to do, dude. You were so much trouble; she didn't know what to do with you. And after you were arrested, she was so scared of what might happen to you. I knew about Steerfield because of Josh. So I suggested it."

"You're the one who sent me away?"

"If that's how you want to look at it."

"How the fuck else am I supposed to look at it?"

Michael's getting frustrated. "You can look at it however you want, but you were out of control. Sneaking out of the house, getting into clubs. You mouthed off whenever you got a chance, skipped your classes, stole a car. I've never seen a fourteen-year-old more out of control, I mean   seriously."

I can't say a word because I know that he's right. I was a hellion, a wild child.

Out of control.

I felt the world owed me everything, that everyone owed me something. But that's not how the world works.

Michael continues. "She came to me, asked me to lunch. I didn't know what she wanted to talk about, but she came to me for help. Wondering if I could talk to you, if I knew what she could possibly do to help you, to get you back on a good path. Because that's what you do when you love someone, Neil—if you see them going down the wrong path, you do whatever it takes to get them off that path."

I wait for him to finish.

"I suggested Steerfield. I knew that it was a good school, one of the best boarding schools in the country, and I told her it might help you. You already knew Josh, sort of, so you would have a friend. I thought it would help."

"Why didn't you say anything to me about it?"

"Because I knew you'd be pissed," he says. "You don't know what she's been through. She tried her best to be a good mom to the both of us. She did what she could."

"How do you know?"

"Because I saw what she did for us, things that you didn't see. I saw her fighting to be the good parent; I saw her desperate for our affection, to be better than Dad ever was. I saw her trying." He takes a breath. "And if you want to compare them, she was definitely the better of the two."

I watch Michael moving, his body language so rigid, his hands making tight fists. I want this to not have changed anything. I want Mom to still have been in the wrong, to be the villain of this story, the bad guy who is defeated at the end.

But that's not the truth.

I was the bad guy.

Okay, the reality is probably something closer to none of us being a villain or a hero. We were just people doing their best, the best with what we had.

We still are.

I don't like it.

"I know that you don't *want* to talk to her, but you need to talk to her."

I don't say anything. I just let Michael walk toward me. He puts a hand on my shoulder, his touch warm.

"For yourself, and for her."

I nod slowly, and Michael's hand disappears. I hear the door open behind me, and close. Suddenly, I'm alone with my feelings, with new knowledge about my mother, this person who I've spent most of my life resenting, angry at because I thought she shipped me away without a second thought, because I thought she threw money at me because it was the simplest way for her to parent.

But maybe there was more to it. I have to admit that.

Because there was always more. The nights that we'd actually get to spend together, watching *90 Day Fiancé* together because we were both obsessed, or going out to get dinner, shopping together, whispering mean things about strangers or gossiping about Michael and Dad.

The door behind me opens again, and I turn, expecting to see Michael there.

But Mom is standing there, surprise on her face when she realizes that it's me.

"Oh, Neil." She pauses. "I thought that Michael would be in here."

"Nope, it's me."

There's this beat of silence that seems to last forever but, in the reality that isn't my mind, probably only lasts a second or two.

"Have you seen Michael? I need to ask him something."

"He just left."

"Okay."

Mom moves like she's going to leave.

"Mom?"

She stops, not really turning to look at me, the door squeaking as she opens it farther. "Yes?"

Another case where I don't know what to say. You'd think that I'd have this down pat by now, between Lindsay, Josh, Michael, and now Mom; how many emotionally wrought conversations can a person be expected to have in a twenty-four-hour period?

"Can I talk with you?"

"Can it wait, Neil? There's a lot going on."

"It'll only take a minute," I tell her. "I promise."

"Okay." She closes the door behind her. You'd think based on her tone that there was nothing going on between the two of us. "What is it?"

"I'm sorry," I tell her. I don't want to mince words. "I'm sorry for the things that I said to you last night."

Mom clears her throat, and she goes to sit down on the nearest seat, an armchair draped in what looks like a white sheet. She looks good today: a simple black dress, strings of pearls around her neck with matching earrings, fancy, but not fancy enough to drag the attention away from Ashley. Her dark brown hair is wavy, pulled over her shoulder.

"The things that you said to me last night, they really hurt my feelings, Neil."

"I know."

"The only people who have ever talked to me like that are your father and my parents." She pauses. "But you know that, don't you?"

"Michael told me the truth."

"About what?"

"That it was his idea," I say. "To send me to Steerfield."

Mom has this soft smile that's still so sad. "Why don't you sit down?" She pulls the chair across from her closer, and I do as I'm asked. "I think it's time we sat down and had a conversation."

"Okay."

She waits a beat, holding her hands together while the gears turn behind her eyes.

"I know that I haven't been the best parent that I could be to you, or to Michael." She lets out a small sigh. "I always told myself that I was going to be a better parent than mine were. I promised myself that I'd never make my children feel unloved, that I'd listen to them, that I'd treat them with the respect that they deserved. I'd give them everything my parents never gave me."

I've never actually heard Mom talk this much about her parents before. It wasn't that it was a forbidden subject in our house; it's just that they never came up, like she avoided the topic entirely. The most it felt like they ever came up was when Mom would throw out that they were coming for Christmas or Thanksgiving dinner.

And she never sounded happy about it.

"I just wish that you'd leveled with me," I say to her. "When I came out to you, you didn't seem to care at all. You just threw me into programs and surgery without doing your research, without bothering to learn about trans people."

"I know."

"And sending me off to Steerfield without just *talking* to me," I say. "That's all I wanted, was for you to talk to me, to pay attention to me."

"I know, I know." She looks at me. "I barely know my own son. And I never gave you or myself the chance to get to know you."

"Can I ask you something?"

Mom doesn't say anything, but I take her glance at me as permission to continue.

"Why don't you ever stand up for me?" It's the one thing I've wanted to ask her the most. She's been so vocal about me being trans, posting about me on her social media when it benefited her, making big deals about donating to trans charities, but when it came to something as simple as standing up to her own family about my transition, about using my name and the correct pronouns, it was always silence. "I think above all else, that's what hurts the most, that you never stand up to Nana and Grandpa when they say their transphobic shit."

It doesn't take long for the water to appear in her eyes. "I know that nothing I can say will excuse what I let them get away with," she admits.

I stay silent.

"I was afraid of them then, and I still am today. And I know how silly that might sound . . ."

"Not really; I've met them."

"I know that I shouldn't be. They can't control my life anymore, but parents have a way of hanging over you, even when you don't want them to." She pauses. "I'm sure you know that already."

She breathes out slowly through her nose.

"It's not an excuse, and I don't want it to be one. But I'm still their daughter."

"I understand that," I say. "But it hurts. To see you stand there and let them treat me the way that they do. It's almost like you're signing your approval."

She nods carefully. "I know. I know that. There's a lot that I have to apologize for."

"But you aren't the only one who's made mistakes," I say.

"No. I'm not. But I'm the parent, and you're the child. And obviously, I failed at my job."

"Mom—"

"No, you don't have to say anything, Neil. I know that I failed you, and that I've hurt you. I know that I failed as a parent, that I did the wrong things. And that I'm not the only one here at fault."

"You're not," I tell her. "I was an awful kid. Still am."

"You're not awful," she starts to say. "Well . . . okay, you had your moments. We both did the wrong things. And we hurt each other a lot."

"I'm sorry," I tell her again. "For everything. For the things that I've said to you, for sneaking out, for everything that I've said behind your back, for the way that I've acted at this wedding."

"I deserved my fair share of it." She gives me a sad look. "There aren't really words that I can say to make it up to you, for the things that I've put you through, and what your grandparents have said to you."

"And there's nothing I can say after what I've put you through."

She laughs. "Do you think a mom and a son have ever had a conversation like this before?"

"If they had, then we'd probably know what to say to each other."

"Fair enough." She reaches over, putting her finely manicured hand on my knee. "I'm sorry, Neil."

"I'm sorry too, Mom."

"We can talk more after the wedding."

"I think that'd be nice," I say.

This doesn't feel fixed. It'd be hard for a single conversation to repair sixteen years of trouble between the both of us. But it feels like we're on the right road, at least for the time being. Who knows, our egos could get the best of us, and everything could unravel. But I like the idea of having honest conversations with my mom for the first time ever.

"Now . . ." She straightens, pulling herself together. "We need to talk about Wyatt."

"God, I really don't want to do that."

She ignores me. "You faked the whole thing?"

"Mom."

She holds her hands up defensively. "We don't have to discuss it; we don't have to talk about it. I just wanted to know why."

"Isn't that discussing it?"

"Don't be a smartass, Neil." She says the words with a smile. "The two of you were cute. I totally bought the lie." She gives me a slap on the knee.

"Really?"

"You fooled me."

"Yeah, well . . . I fooled myself too."

"What do you mean?"

"I let feelings get in the way," I tell her. "I don't want to talk about it anymore."

She's got that look in her eyes that tells me she isn't ready to let this go. But she relents. "Okay . . . but I've got ears if you ever want to talk."

"Thanks."

"Can I say something else to you?"

"If you want to, yeah. I guess I could use any advice you have."

"When you're seventeen, or sixteen, or eighteen, or even twelve . . ." She pauses. "Basically, when you're your age, everything feels like the end of the world. Everything feels so big, like it's going to impact you for the rest of your life. But that's just a part of life, a part of relationships. Fucking up, apologizing, learning what you can do better, what you should do different. Being scared of messing up just shows that you care. There are some things you need to be careful about, decisions you need to think long and hard about. But you also need to let yourself have your feelings, to stop being afraid of going after what you want, of going out and getting it."

"That's easier said than done."

"Yeah, it is," she says. "But in twenty years, do you think you'll regret not talking to Wyatt?"

I don't even hesitate. "Yes."

"Then fix it."

"He's not going to forgive me. I hurt him," I say. "And I'm scared."

"I think we've learned a lot about apologies in the last ten minutes." She breathes carefully. "But in my experience, I've learned that the things worth doing are what scare us the most."

I look up at her, at the honesty in her eyes.

"And falling in love is one of the scariest things in the world," she continues. "The both of you were cute together, even if Wyatt didn't know how to dress."

"Mother . . ."

"Is his closet *made* of flannel?"

I can't stop myself from laughing. "Yeah, kind of."

"He *is* sweet, though, and most importantly, he has manners. Most people don't know the difference between a salad and a dinner fork."

We both laugh together.

"Give him a chance and apologize. You never know what might happen. And you know I'm not a woman who apologizes frequently."

"Yeah . . . I know." I stop myself. "That I need to apologize."

She gives me a glare. "You should. He's a good kid. At least from what I saw." And then, very suddenly, she stands up, smoothing out her dress.

"How ready are you for this to be over?"

Mom rolls her eyes and exhales loudly. "You have no idea." She holds out her hand and I take it. "Come on—we've got a wedding to get through."

I don't know if I feel better or worse. There's so much running through my head, with Mom and Michael and Wyatt. I don't know what to think, what to feel.

Before the wedding begins, I find myself a quiet spot in the garden, pulling out my phone, finding Wyatt's contact information again. It rings, and it rings, and it rings.

"Hello?"

I take a very shuddery breath.

"Neil?"

Their voice makes me stop, and for a moment I think that they might be in front of me.

But they aren't.

"Neil?"

"Wyatt."

"Hi."

"Hi."

We both hold there in silence for a moment. Has it only been a few hours? It feels like it's been months since I've seen them. That's when I realize how much I miss them.

"Hey," they say again.

"Listen, Wyatt . . . I'm really sorry. For everything, for what I said to you, how I pushed you away."

"Yeah, I got your last message."

I want to ask them what they think, what's going through that head, what they want to say to me. But I'm scared of their answers.

Isn't that what Mom said, though? If it's scary, maybe it's worth doing.

"How do you feel?" I ask. "About us."

"I think . . . I think I need to think," they say, their accent slipping out. "For a bit."

"Okay, yeah."

"Tell Michael I'm sorry I couldn't make it to the wedding."

"It's okay. He still wants you to audition."

"Yeah, maybe."

That's when I see Mom racing toward me, this look on her face. She's motioning with her hand, mouthing words like "Come on!" and "Now."

"I think I have to go," I tell them.

"Yeah, of course."

"I'll see you soon, right?"

"Definitely."

I don't want to let them go. I don't want to hang up the phone. Because I might lose them if I do. What proof do I have that they'll come back to me? What proof do I have that I won't fuck this up again?

I think that Mom was right.

Maybe part of being in love is the fear of fucking up, and doing whatever you can to make sure you don't.

"Goodbye, Neil," they say softly.

"Goodbye, Wyatt."

It doesn't feel like goodbye, though.

Not yet.

I'm going to make sure of it.

The call ends, and I slip my phone into my pocket, double-checking that it's on silent before I walk toward Mom.

"Who was that?"

"Wyatt."

"How is he?" She crosses her arms.

"Sounded pissed," I say.

She doesn't say anything; she just sits down next to me on the concrete bench.

I can't deny that it's a good feeling, having Mom here next to me. It feels like such a simple—albeit strange—gesture. But it feels nice, like we're mother and son again.

"There's always the chance that he'll be more accepting in person?" she offers. "Maybe he just needs some time to himself, mull things over."

"Yeah . . . right."

I just keep thinking about the thing that she said earlier.

About being brave, about how something must be worth doing if it scares me so much.

But I guess it wasn't worth doing.

Then again, was a phone call the thing that scared me the most?

No, what scares me the most is leaving this entire wedding behind, flying all the way back to North Carolina just to see them again, just to show up on their doorstep and kiss them until I can't breathe anymore. That's what scares me. Loving Wyatt Fowler scares me.

Showing them that I love them scares me a billion times more.

"Sorry, Mom," I tell her, standing up.

"For what?"

"I think I've got to go."

"You're leaving now? You can't just walk out. You're a groomsman."

"I've gotta go." She's still shouting my name as I race through the garden, past guests still making their way in. "Sorry! Sorry!"

I've got to work fast.

I make it up to my hotel room, looking for the perfect flight on my phone while I ride the elevator up. There's one in an hour and a half, not completely booked, not direct, but the next one leaves in three hours and I can't wait that long, even if I'd be landing in Charlotte around the same time. My brain doesn't understand that, though, so I buy the ticket; the price doesn't matter.

I just need to get to them.

I just want to get back to Wyatt.

I want to get back home.

I throw as many things into my carry-on as I can, barely taking the time to peel myself out of the suit. The important things like my phone and laptop. We have the room until Sunday; maybe there's some universe out there where I manage another flight back here to get everything.

But it's just clothes, skin care, shoes.

That can all be replaced.

And Wyatt can't.

For Wyatt, this will all be worth it.

Getting onto the plane isn't easy. I feel like I run from one end of the airport to the other just to get to my gate.

At least without Wyatt here I can use my PreCheck.

The flight is long, night coming so much faster now that I'm racing toward the East Coast.

Which gives me too much time to think about what I'm going to do. How I'm going to do this. An hour in, my heart finally settles, and I start to think about how stupid this is. Wyatt's going to see me, slam the door in my face, tell me that they never want to see me again.

I don't even know their address, which is what leads me to dragging out my laptop to use the shitty plane wi-fi.

At the beginning of the semester, we had to fill out emergency-contact forms for our roommates. Most stuff could be handled by the school, of course, but it was just an extra precaution. The last thing I wanted to do was give Wyatt all my contact information; this was the kid who'd ruined my semester, taken my single room away from me, and I didn't want to give them anything. But our counselor dragged out that old "you both signed a contract with this school" rule. So I had to fill it out.

And now I'm so glad I did.

It takes a bit of looking in my student portal, but I find his parents' contact information, plus the address of their house. It's not that far from school, maybe a twenty-minute drive.

We land in Fort Lauderdale for our layover. I have an hour and a half to get some food from a Steak 'n Shake in the airport, but as I sit there, staring at my food, I realize that I don't have an appetite anymore. If only it was In-N-Out.

I chew on the fries, but other than that, nothing seems to sit well on my stomach.

Even music doesn't seem to be a good distraction. It's just noise in my ears until I find "All That" by Carly Rae Jepsen in my *Recently Played*. I don't think I've ever listened to any of her music on my own, so I have Wyatt to thank for this. I can't stop thinking that this could be one big mistake. But it's my mistake to make, and I have to know what's going to happen.

I open my phone, looking for someone to talk to, but my options are limited. Lindsay and Josh are probably still at the wedding, and calling Mom right now feels like I'm asking for trouble.

So, I tap Samuel's number.

"You what?" is all they can manage after I've filled them in. "You're, like, actually my hero, you know that."

"Shut up."

"I'm serious, this is amazing. God, I can't wait to tell the guys." I can hear the tapping of their keyboard on the other end of the call. Still gaming.

"Don't mention anything just yet." I still haven't won Wyatt back, and it'd be super embarrassing to have to explain it to them afterward if this goes south.

Which it won't.

Because I believe it.

"Is that literally all you called to tell me?" Samuel asks me.

"Yeah, I guess. And I think I was looking for some reassurance. And, you know . . . you're my friend."

"Who are you, and what have you done with Neil?"

"I'm trying this whole new emotional-honesty thing."

"Sounds overrated."

"You're telling me." We both laugh quietly.

"Well, if it's any consolation, if a guy raced all the way across the country just to come and see me, it'd be hard for me not to fall for him."

"Hoping for something with Hoon?"

"No, he's with his family. They're important too, I guess."

"Right."

"Okay, I've got to bounce now. We finally got a tank for this dungeon."

"I'm just going to nod and pretend like I know what you're talking about."

"Whatever, wear a condom when you fuck! And remember to pee after—"

Samuel doesn't get to finish his thought before I end the call. There wasn't much said about the whole situation, but I do feel some relief after hearing Samuel's voice.

I try to quiet my brain from everything that might happen, everything that I'm about to do. How are they going to react?

Will they turn me away? Will we kiss right there in their drive-way? There are too many possibilities, too many variables that I can't predict. I don't like it.

This could all be one big mistake.

But I've got to take this risk.

For Wyatt.

For myself.

I've got to know.

The landing takes forever; my hands are shaking while grip-ping the back of the seat in front of me. I need to get off this plane; I need to get to them.

It's already ten thirty because of the time change.

I'm going to be showing up on their doorstep in the middle of the night, which probably isn't going to win me any points with their moms.

Shit, I didn't even think about how they'd react to the boy who broke their son's heart standing on their doorstep.

It's not too late to go back.

Except that it is.

Charlotte International isn't so busy on a Thursday night, especially with it being so late. It's already past eleven o'clock by the time we're allowed to leave the plane and I make my way to the pickup area. The Uber I ordered is waiting for me.

"Neil?"

"That's me," I say, settling into the back seat. Thankfully, the driver doesn't seem to want to talk all that much; he just asks me about the flight, if I live in Charlotte. I give short answers. I don't mean to be rude, but my mind is racing with everything that's happening. I'm tired after an entire day of travel seemingly shoved into a few hours. From one end of the country to the other and then some.

I'm tired, but I feel buzzed. I don't even know if I could sleep if I tried. I follow the map on my phone every step of the journey, cursing silently at the red lights and traffic that we manage to catch. Eventually, we get off at an exit, and onto another highway that stretches out with dark woods on either side of us. Right, Wyatt doesn't technically live in Charlotte, just outside it in Mint Hill. We drive for a long time before getting off on another exit, and things start to look a little more residential as we pass by the stereotypical exit stops like the gas stations and McDonald's. I've never been to this area before. My North Carolina experience begins and ends at Charlotte.

We drive for a little bit longer. I guess I never really pictured where Wyatt might call home, but the neighborhood looks, well . . . normal. Trees decorate the sidewalks, and the houses look nice, lights on in some, most of them dark. Cars are parked on the side of the street. There are two people walking a dog.

It seems so quiet, calm. These houses aren't mansions; personality seems to radiate off them, even in the darkness. There are lawn decorations, flags, toys left out in front yards, swings, gorgeous flowers and trees, lawns trimmed imperfectly, some decisions that clash against each other.

I can tell that these are more than houses; these are homes.

"Here we are," the driver says as he pulls up next to the car parked in front of the house. I double-check the number on the mailbox before I let the driver go. I watch as his taillights get farther and farther away, eventually turning a corner.

Then I'm alone, with nothing but my bag around my shoulders.

Just a boy, standing in front of the house of the person whose heart he broke, hoping that they'll hear me out, listen to what I have to say.

I can do this.

I walk up the steps, the porch creaking under my feet. There are no lights to be found on the first floor, but one of the windows on the second floor is lit up. I can only hope that that's their room.

I knock lightly, figuring that's better than ringing the doorbell.

But I can't hear anything on the other side. No one moving around, no one coming down any stairs.

I knock again, but I'm scared of waking Wyatt's parents.

There's still no answer. Either they can't hear me or they don't want to answer the door at eleven fifty at night. Can't exactly blame them.

I hop off the porch, going to the front lawn in perfect view of their window, and then I pull out my phone and dial their number.

"Hello?"

Their voice doesn't sound tired. Maybe I didn't wake them up.

"Wyatt."

"Neil."

"Go to your window."

"What?"

"Go to your window," I repeat.

They let out this sigh. "Please tell me that you're not in my front yard at midnight."

"Technically it's not midnight yet," I say as I see the shadows in their window move, pushing back the curtains. And there they are.

I know that it's only been a day, technically two, but it feels like forever since I've seen them.

"What are you doing?"

"I'm here for you."

"What?"

"I came back for you."

There's the barest hint of a smile. I don't think they want me to see it, but I do.

"You're such an idiot."

"Yeah, well . . . never claimed I was smart."

They vanish from the window, but I can still hear their breathing on the phone. "What about the wedding?"

"I skipped it."

"How could you skip it?"

"I felt like it."

Eventually, the front door unlocks and swings open along with the screen door in front of it, and they're standing there, staring at me from up on the steps.

I don't know which one of us hangs up first; all I know is that they're standing in front of me again, finally.

"What are you doing here?"

"I needed to see you."

Their voice is quiet. "For what?"

"So that I could say that I'm sorry."

They stand there, against one of the pillars that supports the overhanging roof of the porch, their arms crossed.

Say something.

Anything.

Please.

"You came all the way here to do that?"

I nod.

"How'd you even get my address?"

"The emergency contact form from school."

"I seriously can't believe you," they say with the barest hint of laughter in their voice. The problem is that I can't tell if it's the kind of laugh you make when you find something endearing, or if it's the kind you make when you're so uncomfortable with what's going on in front of you that you don't know what else to do. "Did your Uber already leave?"

I look around for a bit. "Do you see another car here?"

They hold back another laugh. "Come inside. It's cold."

I follow them into the house, through the front door and into the open living room. There's a plush, worn-out couch where Wyatt sits on the far end. There's a fireplace that looks like it hasn't been used in a long time. A television, huge coffee table, recliner. There are some toys strung out, and some textbooks. The kitchen connects with a dining table decorated with even more textbooks, notebooks, and an open laptop. The decoration seems cheap, kitschy. It's ugly, but I think that's part of the charm.

I don't know where to sit, so I join them on the couch, at the opposite end.

Wyatt stares for a bit, first at me, then down at their feet. They're folded in on themself, tucking their feet. They seem comfortable here.

I wonder what that feels like.

"You seriously came all the way here just to talk to me."

"I . . . Yeah."

"I really can't believe you."

I can't tell if that's a good thing or a bad thing yet.

"I just, I had to see you in person. I had to—"

Wyatt stops me with a hand. "Listen, Neil. Can we talk about this in the morning? It's late."

I stare at them, my mouth left open.

"Yeah, yeah. Of course."

"You can stay down here, just for tonight. I'll tell my moms what's going on so they're not freaked out in the morning. Then you might want to . . . I don't know, look for a hotel or go back to school early or something. Sorry."

"No, it's okay. I mean, I showed up on your doorstep unannounced. That's pretty stupid."

"Is that all you packed?" they ask, looking at my backpack.

"Yeah."

"Got any pajamas in there?"

"Nope."

"Okay, let me go grab you something to wear."

"Thanks."

Wyatt stands up from the couch and walks through the same archway they entered through. A minute later, they come down with a pillow, a blanket, and a hoodie and sweatpants for me to wear.

"Here you go." Wyatt leaves them on the coffee table. "There's a bathroom in the hallway, under the stairs, just a toilet and sink so . . . yeah. You can shower tomorrow."

"Sure." I look at the clothes. "Thanks."

"No problem."

We can't look at each other, not yet. We don't know how to talk to each other again, not after what I did. I thought that me showing up here would magically fix everything, that we'd kiss and go up to their room and sleep in the same bed and everything would go back to the two of us being happy.

"I'll see you in the morning," they say, turning off the lamp on the nightstand.

"Good night, Wyatt."

"Night, Kearney."

I can't explain why, but that hurts.

Wyatt vanishes back into the hallway, going up the stairs again. I change into the clothes quickly so that there's no chance of one of Wyatt's moms or their little sister walking downstairs and seeing a half-naked teenager they don't recognize standing in the living room.

I make the bed, biting back tears. Because I'm not going to cry.

I'm not.

Except I can't keep it back.

I fucked up things even worse somehow. It was foolish to think that just coming here would solve things, that what I said to Wyatt could be magically undone by me just showing up.

I should've known better.

But I didn't.

Because I never know better.

Friday

APRIL 22

When I open my eyes, there's a child staring at me.

She looks like an adorable little kid straight out of a sitcom or something, with dark brown skin, and her hair pulled into little puff balls on top of her head. She's even wearing pajamas that have the sisters from *Frozen* on them.

For a second, I think that I've got to be dreaming.

Why would there be a child here? How'd she get into my hotel room? What's happening?

Then I remember that I'm not in a hotel room—not yet anyway.

"Hi," she says. When she opens her mouth, I can see that one of her front teeth is missing.

"Hello."

"Who are you?" She leans on the coffee table.

"What a rude thing to say to someone so early in the morning." I'm mostly joking—I've never known how to talk to kids. They're just so . . . small. And weird. I stare at her. "Who are you?"

"Are you Wyatt's boyfriend?"

"Why would you—"

"Lana, why are you bothering the nice man?" a voice comes from the kitchen, followed by this very tall white woman with tied-back blond hair. She's got a bowl in one hand while she whisks with the other.

"He started it!"

"I can assure you that I did not," I mutter, sleep heavy on my voice, even to my own ears. I sit up, staring at the house in front of me. It's a lot nicer looking in the light; there's a lot of color. The little girl, Lana, grabs the remote and takes the spot at the end of the couch, open now that I've moved my legs.

She turns to Netflix, turning on one of the Pokémon shows.

"What's your name?" Lana asks me.

"Neil."

"I'm Lana."

"I heard." I look around a little more. There are more pictures on the wall than I originally thought there were. A few more toys strewn around that I'm guessing belong to Lana. Or maybe Wyatt still likes playing with Barbies. I'm not going to judge.

"Why are you here?" Lana asks.

"You know, that's a question I'm starting to ask myself too."

She stares at me. "What?"

"Nothing." I pull the blanket away, rubbing my eyes before I stand up and stretch.

"Those are Wyatt's clothes."

"He let me borrow them," I say, remembering again that Wyatt wants to keep their pronouns between us for now.

"Are you Wyatt's boyfriend?" she asks again.

"Lana!" the woman from the kitchen shouts again. "Stop asking so many questions."

"That's one of my moms."

"I figured." I guess now's no better time to meet at least one of Wyatt's parents. I trudge into the kitchen, my feet shuffling on the floor. I didn't realize just how badly traveling for an entire day would wear me out.

"Good morning," the woman at the stove says.

She looks a lot like Wyatt. Same smile, same eyes, same frizzy hair.

"I'm Melanie." She leaves the food on the stove for just long enough to walk over to me, shake my hand. "I'm Wyatt's mama."

Mama. Got it.

"I'm Neil, Wyatt's . . . friend."

"Yeah, we've heard a lot about you."

"Well, that can't be good."

She goes back to the food: sizzling bacon and scrambled eggs that smell heavenly.

"Sit down, sit down. Wyatt's still asleep, probably won't be awake for a while." Melanie moves to set a plate of toast on the table. "The boy sleeps like a log when he's on break."

"Yeah, sometimes I'm worried he's not going to wake up for his classes."

Melanie laughs at that, but not the kind of laugh you make when you actually find something funny, more the kind of laugh to make someone feel comfortable.

"Can I help you with anything?" I ask her.

"No, no, just sit down. It'll all be ready in a few minutes."

"Actually, um . . . can I use your bathroom?"

"Sure. Down the hallway there, on the right."

I make my way down the hallway, getting a good look at all the family photos that hang on the wall. There are a few of Wyatt with Melanie, them on a dock holding what has to be the smallest fish in the world on a fishing line, the two of them in the mountains. Then there are pictures of Wyatt and a taller Black woman where Wyatt looks maybe twelve or thirteen; I'm guessing this is their other mom. One of a young-looking guy holding an infant. I'm assuming that's Wyatt and their birth father.

Wyatt doesn't look too different now; it's more like their entire body just got stretched out horizontally, and the rest stayed the same. Maybe with frizzier hair and more body dysmorphia.

I find the bathroom tucked under the stairs, pee, wash my hands, and return to the kitchen.

"Lana! Breakfast!"

I hear the television turn off, and Lana races into the kitchen, her feet slapping on the linoleum.

"Can I sit next to Neil?" she asks.

"I don't know," Melanie says with that wonder you use when you're talking to a kid. "You should ask him, not me."

Lana turns to me without skipping a beat. "Can I sit here?"

"Sure thing."

What, am I going to tell a little kid no?

She pulls her chair out and climbs into it. I think Wyatt said she was four? But she seems pretty independent for a kid her age. Melanie sets out the rest of the food, and I wait until she's made her own plate and Lana's before I take some eggs and bacon.

As Lana is chewing on the end of a piece of bacon of her own, she keeps staring at me with these wide brown eyes.

"Lana, it's rude to stare," Melanie says.

"It's okay," I assure her.

"You're pretty," Lana blurts out, and Melanie laughs. "Your eyelashes are nice."

I laugh too. "Thank you."

"So, Neil . . . Wyatt told us that you spontaneously showed up at midnight and were just staying till morning."

"Right, yeah. I'm sorry about the late arrival."

"It's okay. Wyatt's guests are our guests. You can stay as long as you'd like."

"Thank you. Hopefully it won't be too long." I wonder how much Wyatt told their parents about me, the things that I've done and said. I get the vibe that they're all pretty close with one another.

I don't get the feeling that this is a woman who hates me for breaking her kid's heart, for making them go home early, for basically kicking them out of the state of California. Then again, maybe a part of southern hospitality is treating the boy your child hates with some level of kindness.

"So how was the wedding? I thought you wouldn't be coming back to school for a few days."

"Yeah, some stuff happened."

"It was surprising when he asked us to come get him, so late too," she says. Again, it's hard to read what she's getting at through her tone.

"Sorry about that." I put my fork down, my appetite gone just like that.

"He didn't tell us much. We figured that something had gone wrong, but we weren't going to push it. Did the two of you have a fight?"

"You could say that."

"Do you want jam on your toast?" she asks, dropping the subject just like that.

When we're all done eating, Wyatt still hasn't come downstairs, which is only making my anxiety about the entire situation spike even worse. What am I going to say to them?

"Why don't you help me with the dishes?" Melanie asks, and it's definitely not a request. "It's usually Wyatt's job."

"Sure, I don't mind."

We store the extra food in the microwave while Lana sits and watches us.

"I rinse, you dry?"

"Sure."

"What brings you back to North Carolina so early?" Melanie asks me.

Guess we're diving right on in.

"I came to talk to Wyatt," I tell her. I try to make sure it doesn't sound like a lie, which is ridiculous, because it isn't, but still, there's something about this woman that scares me. I was mean to Wyatt, then a little over twenty-four hours later I'm sleeping on her couch without her knowing, so she has every right to be cautious about me.

Melanie chuckles. "Yeah, we covered that. But what are you here to talk to him about?"

I hesitate, unsure of what I should say.

On the one hand, I've known this woman for fifteen minutes. On the other, she has this energy that, while frightening, makes me feel like I could tell her anything.

"I want to apologize to him," I say.

"Would you be willing to tell me what happened? Wyatt was so beat up when we picked him up, and he barely came out of his room yesterday."

"I . . . made some mistakes," I say, careful of my language around Lana. "And I want to make it up to Wyatt."

"And you think that showing up on our front porch in the middle of the night was the way to fix that?"

"You know, the entire flight here I really thought it would be. I had these dreams of Wyatt, like . . . embracing me or whatever, being so happy that I came all the way here to see him, left the wedding early, all that," I tell her. "I think the reality is setting in."

"Well, good. Reality can be good," she says, rinsing the soap off a spatula. "But you know, dreaming is good for the heart too."

"I just hope Wyatt can forgive me."

"Come on now, you've got to be a little more hopeful than that," Melanie says as she rinses a plate of the yellow stains left from runny eggs. "God, you teenagers. You make one mistake, and you think it's the end of the world."

"It doesn't help that it does feel like the world is going to end," I tell her. "Love isn't exactly an easy feeling to navigate."

"Oh, so you're in *love* with Wyatt?"

I sputter, dropping the fork I was drying. "No, I mean. That's not what I meant, I—"

Lana laughs at me. "Neil loves Wyatt!" she chants.

I shoot her a look.

Melanie comes to my defense. "Lana, be nice!"

"Things are . . . complicated right now," I say, picking up the fork and putting it back in the sink.

"Are they actually complicated? Or are you making them complicated?"

"I don't get what you mean."

"Just . . . be kind to yourself," she says. "You're seventeen?"

"Sixteen."

"You've got your entire life ahead of you, Neil. Don't be so afraid to take what you think might make you happy."

"But what if it doesn't?" I ask her.

"But what if it does?" There isn't an ounce of hesitation in her voice. "Isn't it so much better to know for sure, to have what you think might make you happy, rather than let it go?"

"I . . ."

I don't know. In theory, yes.

I just can't get over this fear.

"If you don't go for what you want, you'll never ever get it. But if you do go for it, well . . . you never know what might happen."

"It might not even matter," I tell her. "It all depends on Wyatt."

"Not necessarily."

"I've talked to him, and we've not really gotten anywhere. I don't even know what I could say to him that might start things over."

"Well . . . maybe words won't work. Have you tried showing him instead?"

"How would I do that?"

"Now, I can't give you all the answers," she says. "But who knows, maybe you could express your feelings better that way? You're not exactly a wordsmith, kid." Melanie looks at me and smiles. "I call 'em like I see 'em."

She could be right, though. I don't know; I wish that the answer were easier. I wish that words could be enough to show them that I'm sorry, that I want them back, that I want to undo what I did.

I hear footsteps on the stairs, and my blood freezes. Wyatt shuffles into the kitchen, dressed in a drab gray T-shirt and loose sweatpants.

"Well, good morning to you." Melanie reaches across from me, turning on the microwave. "Mom's at work, but we found another fourth for breakfast."

"Mornin'." Wyatt yawns, taking a seat at the table.

"Wyatt, Neil slept on the couch last night," Lana says bluntly.

"Yeah, he did," Wyatt tells her, sleep still heavy on his voice.

"Does that mean that he's in trouble?" Lana asks. "'Cause when Mama is in trouble, Mom says that she's going to make her sleep on the couch."

Wyatt covers their face, but there's no mistaking the grin plastered behind their hands.

"No, he's not in trouble."

Well, that's something.

"Lana, go watch TV."

"Okay!" Lana races back to the living room.

And just as Melanie puts the last dishes on the drying rack, she wrings out the sponge, leaving it in the sink. "Shoot, I think I left wet clothes in the washing machine." Just like that, she strolls out of the kitchen, leaving the two of us there, mostly alone. Lana is currently distracted by princesses on the television.

I open up the microwave when it won't stop beeping, and bring Wyatt their food before I sit down next to them.

That feels like the right move.

"How'd you sleep?" Wyatt asks, biting off the end of a piece of bacon.

"Fine," I say. "Your sister woke me up."

Wyatt laughs. "She likes new people."

"Clearly."

We sit there for a bit, Wyatt not touching their food again. It almost feels like they're waiting for something. But I can't read their mind to know what I should say. If I *could* read their mind, then I probably wouldn't be in this mess.

"Look, Wyatt—" I start to say at the same time they say: "Neil . . ."

Then we stare at each other, unsure of who should go first.

"You," I tell them. If they start with how they're feeling, then maybe I can figure something out.

"I, uh . . . I kind of wish that you hadn't come here."

Oh.

I didn't think it was possible to feel worse than I already did, but this is a new low.

"You told me to leave, and I did. So the fact that you came to me, it kind of feels like this slap in the face."

"I get that."

"Do you?"

"I . . ." I hesitate. "No, I guess I don't."

"I thought that things were finally getting better between us, that we were becoming friends—"

"We were! We are!" I tell them. I can't stop the desperation in my voice. "I only came here so that I could apologize to you. In person, not over some lousy phone call."

Wyatt looks up, and we both see that Melanie is standing in the mudroom between the kitchen and what I'm guessing is the laundry room, humming to herself.

"Oh, don't mind me," she says. "Just folding some towels!"

"Mama, that's one of Mom's dresses."

"Oh, right." She looks at the garment in her hands. "Got confused."

"Let's go outside," Wyatt says. They stand, and I follow, grabbing my shoes from the living room. The backyard is spacious; there's this tall wooden play set that I guess is for Lana. Wyatt walks right over to it, taking a seat on one of the swings that hang off the side. There's another open one beside it, so I take that one.

"So, you came all this way to apologize?" Their voice is quiet, and they won't look at me; they're just looking at their own feet as they kick softly at the dirt.

"I felt like that'd be right."

"You know, it really sucked," they say. "I feel like I gave you so much, and then you just got angry with me for no reason. You ignored me until you yelled at me without even telling me what I did wrong. Do you know what that feels like?"

"I do, actually."

They raise their brows.

"Because I did the same thing to you that I did to Josh," I tell them. "And what I did to my own mother, and what I do to a lot of the people around me."

"Well . . . I'm glad you realized that," they say.

The words feel cold, but they're true. What evidence do I have to support what I'm saying to them?

"I don't know if I believe myself either," I tell them. "But I'd like the chance to show you."

They look up at me.

I take a breath. "I'm really sorry, Wyatt. I'm sorry for being so cruel to you over the last year. I'm sorry for the things that I said to you, for the way that I caused you to feel. And I'm sorry for yelling at you, for making you feel like you did something wrong when the problem was mine and only mine. I just think that . . . I think that I was afraid."

"Why were you afraid?"

"Because usually when I let people in, it doesn't exactly end well. But I shouldn't have let that influence how I feel about you."

I look at them, and the way that they're staring at me. It's so hard to read their expression.

"You can't just keep pushing me away," they say. "If you want this . . . if you want to be together, then you can't hide yourself from me."

"I know."

I feel a hand on my lap, their hand taking mine.

"I want to see all of you, Neil Kearney."

I want to appreciate the softness of the moment, but I can't stop myself from laughing.

"What?!"

"That sounded so cheesy," I snort.

"Fuck off." Wyatt swings sideways, toward me, knocking me off balance. They've still got this smile, though. "I was trying to be romantic."

Maybe laughter is the best medicine.

"So . . ." I don't want to ask this question, but I can't stop myself. I need to know. "Are you interested in going back, to like before?"

"Well, if you mean am I interested to going back to faking a relationship, sleeping together, and you yelling at me, then no. I'm not interested in that."

"Right."

They find my hand again. "But I am interested in finding *something* else with you."

I look at them. "Really?"

"I think we can go slow, ease ourselves back into it. If you'd be okay with that."

I look at their hand around mine, and I take it, squeezing them softly. "I think that I'd be very okay with that."

"Good." They smile at me. "I like your face, Neil Kearney."

"I like yours too."

Things are still a little awkward when we head back inside. I'm still in this space that I'm unsure of, that I don't know if I'm welcome in. Even if Wyatt and I are repairing things, it's still weird to be a boyfriend in your boyfriend's parents' house for the first time. Especially when you showed up on their porch twelve hours ago.

And if this goes any further, we need to have a conversation about how Wyatt wants to identify, because I don't know how they feel about the word *boyfriend*.

Not that Wyatt and I are boyfriends. Not yet. We're taking it slow.

Slow.

Not boyfriends yet. Just . . .

I don't even know what you'd call us.

When we get back inside, their mama asks them for help with something, no doubt something she could probably do on her own. She probably just wants to grill her child. But that gives Lana ample time with me.

"Can I show you my room?" she asks when I go to hide in the living room to give the two of them some privacy. Except

Lana's question isn't exactly a question. She just takes my hand and leads me up the stairs to her room. It's painted this soft pink, with a bookshelf filled with picture books, butterflies on her bed and painted on her walls, a big Barbie dollhouse with a few dolls sitting inside, some clothes and blankets strewn on the floor.

"And this is my unicorn." Lana shows me. "She poops slime."

"Why would you want a toy that poops?" I stare at the neon-colored plastic unicorn. Sure enough, when Lana feeds the unicorn this little packet of powder and presses down on its stomach a bunch of times, the unicorn poops out neon-green slime in my hands. "Lana, this is disgusting."

"Is not, it's slime!"

"Your toy pooped in my hand." I show her the evidence.

"And this is my favorite teddy bear." She moves on, leaving me to deal with the slime in my hands. At least it's mostly solid.

God, I hate that I had that thought.

"This used to be Wyatt's, but he gave it to me." I can see how the fur seems faded, and there's familiar red stitching on the leg left from a repair job. I wonder if Wyatt fixed it themself.

"That's sweet," I say. I grab an empty plastic container from the floor, leaving the slime in there and wiping the residue off my hands.

"Are you and Wyatt boyfriends?" she asks bluntly.

Got to love how kids have no filter.

"I don't really know," I tell her. She hands me the teddy bear.

"You should get married; I want another brother. Because if you get married, then you'd be my brother."

I laugh. "I'll get started on the wedding planning."

"Good. Do you want to see my tea set?"

"Sure."

There's a soft knock at the door, and Wyatt peeks their head in. "Am I interrupting?"

"Just having some afternoon tea," I say, leaving the teddy bear on the bed.

"Lana, can I borrow Neil for a second?"

"Are you going to go make out?" Lana sticks her tongue out like she's disgusted.

"No, just want to talk to him for a bit."

"Okay!"

I stand up, making sure there's no leftover slime on my hands before I follow Wyatt down the hall.

"I talked with Mama. She and Mom are already okay with you staying until we go back on Sunday. If that's cool."

"Yeah, should be okay," I say. "I've got to call Mom, see if she can get my suitcase and mail it back to me."

"It sounds like the two of you made up."

"We're on the right track, I think."

"That's good. Is that backpack seriously all you carried?"

"I needed to make the flight."

"Unbelievable." Wyatt hangs their head, shaking it. "Well, you can either sleep on the couch, or—"

They open a door at the end of the hallway, and there's no mistaking this room as anything other than Wyatt's bedroom. It's small, longer than it is wide, with their bed tucked in one corner. There's a desk where their laptop sits, an acoustic guitar and a larger electric one with an old-looking amp tucked in the corner. There are posters all over the wall, advertising for Hayley Williams and Phoebe Bridgers and Lil Nas X and Harry

Styles and Day6 and a bunch of others. Some pictures too, all taped to the wall.

"We've got an air mattress; you can sleep in here."

"Already trying to get me into bed?"

"Shut up." They chuckle. "You can sleep in here or have Lana wake you up every morning on a lumpy couch. Your choice."

"This could be comfortable. The couch wasn't that bad, though," I say, moving toward their bed, sitting on the edge. "Though, if I'm a guest, shouldn't I get the bed?"

"Don't press your luck, Kearney."

I imagine this scenario where I pull them down to me and we fall onto the bed. They're on top of me and the tension is high, and we kiss. They smell sweet. But we're taking things slow. I have to remember that.

Slow.

I pull away.

"So, this is your room?" I ask.

"As far as I'm aware."

"Shut up."

I look around, taking it all in. Then I notice that there's something behind their door, hanging on the wall. "What is that?"

"Oh, you don't have to—"

I move too quickly for them, though, closing their bedroom door, and right there, on the wall behind it, there's a huge One Direction poster. Niall, Liam, Harry, and Louis are staring at me because it's from that one album after Zayn left.

"Why do you still have this?"

"I can explain."

"Is this what I'm going to have to compete with?" I tease him.

"Please. As if you could ever compete with Harry Styles."

"Wyatt Fowler!" I am full of mock outrage. "I'm offended."

"Good."

"What about that guy, on the drums?"

"Dowoon?" Wyatt peers at the wall. "Not a chance."

"So there's no one hanging from your wall I can compete with? Good to know."

"Shut up." We settle back into this silence, and it feels more comfortable than it does awkward.

"I like your room," I finally say. I go back to their bed, sitting down on the firm mattress. "It looks like you."

"Thanks, I guess."

"It's definitely a compliment."

"I know." They sit down next to me, and our knees touch. This time, neither of us pulls away.

"Have you talked to your moms at all?" I ask.

"About what?" they ask. "There are a lot of secrets."

"The gender thing."

"Nope. I probably won't until I absolutely have to."

"Fair enough. Gender is scary."

"You're telling me."

Wyatt leans in, and their lips press against mine. The kiss is soft, short, but it's enough. I put my hand to their cheek so I can feel their soft skin. How did I ever convince myself that I wasn't in love with Wyatt Fowler?

"Are you kissing me because you don't want to confront the complications of your gender identity?" I ask when we pull apart.

Wyatt smiles. "That obvious?"

I lean in to kiss them again, but before I can, the door to Wyatt's bedroom swings open, Melanie standing there.

"Hey, I saw the door was closed. Everything okay?"

Wyatt and I shoot back to our places on the bed, and they nearly fall to the floor trying to get away from me. "Yes, ma'am, everything's okay."

"Good. We should probably leave the door open just in case something bad happens, right?"

"Yes, ma'am."

"Good idea." And with that, she leaves us there.

I turn to Wyatt, and they turn to me, and we both just start laughing. I cover my face to keep hiding my embarrassment.

"Oh my God."

"She's going to kill me," they say.

"She'll kill me first," I tell them.

I look at them on the bed, smiling, looking like they belong here. I know that things aren't going to be easy, that we're taking these steps again, that we're starting over. All I can hope is that we can follow the path correctly this time, that I can make this second chance worth it. Because I want to.

I want to prove to Wyatt Fowler that I love them.

And I think I have an idea.

Wyatt's other mother, code-named Mom—but she insists that I call her Amanda—comes home around six, after an entire day of Wyatt and me basically being forced to stay in the living room while Melanie works on her own homework and we watch over Lana.

At least it's nice to share a space with them.

Despite us being under their mama's watchful eye, I still feel comfortable on the couch with them, and it feels like we're not faking this. I guess after a week of fooling people, it's still hard to get a grasp on what's real and what isn't.

Dinner is served, which turns out to be pasta with spicy Italian sausage and garlic bread, and afterward, it's still my job to help with the dishes, though this time it's with Amanda. She's a Black woman, shorter than her wife, with her curls in tight coils that hang over the sheared sides of her head.

"You two seemed to be very comfortable on the couch earlier," she observes.

"Oh, um . . . yes, ma'am." I wonder if I'll ever feel comfortable talking to either of their parents, or if I'm condemning myself to a relationship of being completely awkward around them, making a fool of myself at every turn.

"Good." She hands me a wet pot. "Wyatt likes you a lot. He was telling us all about your trip on his phone calls."

"Really?"

She nods. "You'll have to come over more weekends, visit, have dinner."

"I'd like that. I've never really had a place to go on the weekends."

"Wyatt also told us a few things about your family. Life doesn't need to be like that."

"Thank you," I say quietly. "Things are getting better, I think. My mother and I had a good conversation."

"Well, I'm glad to hear that, Neil. Now get your butt in the living room—it's *Jeopardy!* time."

The rest of the night is us in the living room. Lana's put to bed, while Melanie turns on *Jeopardy!* and we all watch from the couch. Well, I watch, but the three of them get pretty into it. Amanda kills it with the most correct answers, with Melanie close behind her and Wyatt in last. (Seriously, Wyatt's parents bust out an app that keeps track of their scores.)

"Better luck next time, Wyatt." Amanda pats them on the knee, a grin of self-satisfaction on her face.

"European history always throws you off," I say. "I told you that you needed to get a tutor."

Melanie and Amanda both laugh. "We said that same thing, but he claims no one at Steerfield is offering."

"Because they aren't!" Wyatt insists.

It's so nice to watch the three of them together, acting like a family is supposed to act. I was always convinced that I'd never get the chance to have this, that it wasn't mine to have.

But who knows? Maybe it isn't that far out of reach.

Melanie and Amanda go to bed, and while Melanie is skeptical of leaving us alone, Amanda insists, pushing her wife up the stairs as Wyatt and I are left on the couch. Wyatt turns on the TV, but I'm not paying attention to it. We don't have to say a word to each other as we sit there; we just enjoy the company. At one point, they're brave enough to grab a pillow and set their head in my lap. I let my fingers find their hair, playing with the soft strands.

I like this life. I like sitting here listening to the sound of their breathing while some awful reality show we picked on cable plays on a low volume. I like having nights with their family and watching *Jeopardy!* with them. I liked watching over Lana while Wyatt sat next to me, glancing up every now and then and smiling at me.

I don't deserve it.

But it's mine.

Eventually, we go to bed, and Wyatt lets me borrow more clothing to sleep in. We make up the air mattress because neither of us thinks it'd be the smartest idea if I was caught in their bed in the morning.

The mattress is almost level with the bed, though, and the only space to set it up is right beside it, so it's close enough.

"Hey, Neil?"

Their voice comes through the darkness of the room.

"Yeah?"

"I'm glad that you came here."

I can't quite see them, but I can make out their outline. I can so easily picture the smile on their face.

"I'm glad too."

Saturday

APRIL 23

"What do you mean you're leaving?" Wyatt asks at the breakfast table.

Okay, probably not the best way to start off a morning.

"I have a plan," I tell them. "I need to do something, and I need *you* to do something for me."

"Okay." They eye me, obviously skeptical. "What?"

"Can you have your parents bring you back to Steerfield early? Tonight."

"Why?"

"Because it's just something that I have to do."

"And everything's okay?"

"Yeah, I just have to keep it a surprise."

They put their hand on my thigh under the table. "I'll see you tonight, I guess."

After packing what few things I bothered to drag out, I say goodbye to the Fowler household. Lana hands me the jar of poop slime, claiming that I can't possibly leave it behind, and Amanda and Melanie tell me they look forward to me coming back. I thank them both for their hospitality, and Wyatt walks me to the Uber.

"I could drive you back, you know," they tell me.

"I've got to do this alone," I tell them. "But it'll be worth it."

"And I can't bribe you to tell me what you're doing?"

"Give me a kiss and I'll think about it."

They do just that, a short kiss on my lips.

"Okay, bye!" I wave, climbing into the Uber.

"You said that you'd tell me!"

"I said I'd think about it, and I decided not to tell you."

"Jerk!"

And with that, the Uber drives away.

I've had this plan for a few hours now, and I really think that it'll be something special if I can pull it off. I fell through on my promise to take them to the Hollywood Sign, but I can still give them that first dance.

The Uber drops me off at school, and I have to go to the office to sign the form that I'm back on campus before I go to my room. It's still the same as before, nothing different besides missing some clothes and things that we took to California.

I didn't give Wyatt a time when I definitely should have.

I also should've asked their parents to make sure that Wyatt's here tonight, but here we are. I only have a few hours to make this work, so I need to get started. I shower and get dressed in clothing that actually fits me before I go back out into the city. Well, I still pull on Wyatt's hoodie. I like the way it feels.

My first stop is Michaels, where I load my cart with fairy lights and fake plants. It doesn't even matter to me if they match—I just need the decoration. Then I go to Target, and I buy white sheets, except they don't have a ton of plain ones, so I end up getting some with tiny dots and faded stripes. It doesn't matter; it'll all look good in my head. And on my way out of Target, I grab a wireless speaker and some thumbtacks, a very strange haul.

This should be easy, this will be fun, and Wyatt will love it. They will.

They have to.

When I'm back at Steerfield, I get to work on transforming our room, using the thumbtacks to pin the sheets to the wall in various layers.

This will probably be what Wyatt is most angry about; they've always been adamant about not being charged for damages to the room.

But I can only hope it'll be easier to ask for forgiveness than it will be for permission.

As I'm hanging up the last sheet to the wall, blocking off a good portion of the room, my phone vibrates in my pocket.

A text from Wyatt.

> WYATT: Parents are bringing me down around seven
> ME: Sounds good.

But before I can hit SEND, the screen switches to a phone call, and the words *Do Not Answer* light up the screen.

I definitely have to change that now.

"Hello?"

"Well, hello to you too," Mom's voice chimes in. "Thanks for letting me know you landed safely."

"Sorry," I apologize, and kind of mean it. "Things were a little hectic."

"I can imagine," she says. I swear I can hear a smile on her lips. "Well, Michael wasn't exactly thrilled you left early, but I explained things."

"I owe you one."

"You owe me more than that. Your brother too."

It feels weird to be able to laugh with this woman I loathed for so much of my life. But now it feels like we're on the right track. Finally.

"How is Wyatt?"

"Fine. Surprised when I showed up on his doorstep."

"Makes sense," Mom says, and then she goes quiet, things getting awkward again. "I just wanted to call, make sure you were okay."

"Yeah, I am."

"Mhmm . . ." More silence. "I'm glad that we had the chance to talk, Neil."

"I am too."

"I hope that you'll come home more often?"

"Yeah . . . I think I'd like that," I say to her. "Maybe you can come to Charlotte."

Another smile. "I'd like that."

"I can show you Cook Out."

"Now that I'm not sure about."

More laughter.

"I've got to go, make sure the hotel is all cleaned up. But I'll talk to you tomorrow, okay?"

"Yeah, sounds good."

"Love you."

"Love you too, Mom."

And just like that, the call ends. I could almost fool myself into thinking that the entire thing was made up. I've literally never talked to my mother like that before, and she's never spoken like that to me either. It's weird, abnormal, odd. But I like it; I like feeling that we're on the other side of something now.

And now I've got to get to work.

• • •

I make the room perfect, right up until the last second, when Wyatt is texting me that they're back on campus.

ME: come alone
WYATT: You aren't naked, right?
ME: perv
WYATT: That doesn't answer the question.
ME: NO!
ME: i'm not naked, weirdo

There are a few more students at Steerfield, some who came back early like us, though most will arrive tomorrow. When the room was getting too hot, I left the door open, praying that no teachers or staff would come by to see what I was doing. I got a few weird looks, but nothing bad.

With seconds to spare, I start the song, making sure it loops. Wyatt walks in just as Carly starts to sing the words.

They take it all in.

The plants, the lights, the sheets. I did my best to make it look like the tents at the wedding, with some extra ideas from Mom's Pinterest board. The sheets paint the walls a soft white, though with the hanging lights, they've turned a warm orange. I probably didn't need the flowers and plants, but I felt like it sold the image of a dream wedding.

"What is this?" they ask, standing there with their suitcase in one hand and their guitar in the other.

"Well." I stand there in the middle of the room, trying not to look awkward as hell. "I promised you a dance. And you never got it."

"Neil—"

I step closer to them, holding out my hand. "Can I have this dance, Wyatt Fowler?"

They smile at me and set their things down, closing the door behind them before they take my hand.

"Only if I can lead."

"Of course."

They take me to the center of the room. Our hands are outstretched together, and their left hand is on the small of my back. I follow their steps, which isn't much more than shuffling back and forth with each other, but it feels nice.

It feels like home.

They feel like home.

I put my head against their chest, listening to the thudding of their heart along with the music.

Maybe it's cheesy, a little too on the nose as Carly Rae Jepsen sings about a boy showing her that she wants him. But the song tells Wyatt everything I want them to know. That I want to be their friend, that I want to be a home, that I want to show them that I care about them any way that I possibly can.

And I hope that they can find the same in me.

I never really knew what it felt like to fall in love before.

That's what I told myself, at least.

I'd never let myself feel those feelings. I told myself that they were bad, that they would only end in tragedy, that I'd only get my heart broken.

But I'd gladly let Wyatt Fowler break my heart.

As many times as they want to.

We look at each other, and our lips meet, our mouths open. My hands find their cheeks as I pull them in closer and closer.

I love that Wyatt's kisses already feel familiar to me.

"I can't believe you did all this," they say when we pull away for air.

"I owed you a dance," I reply. "I wanted to make it special."

They take in the atmosphere again. "I'd say that you made this special."

And then we kiss again, like the world is ending.

I don't think either of us wants to sleep alone, so we pull our mattresses onto the floor, sitting them side by side, covering them with a sheet from the wall. Everything is still left up, but I'll deal with that tomorrow.

Right now, I just want Wyatt.

Clothes are shed, lips meet again, and our hands explore each other, touches light like we're afraid the other will break.

But we won't.

I know it.

As we lie down next to each other, out of breath, I stare at Wyatt on the bed next to me, and they turn on their side so they can look at me as well.

"What are you thinking?" I ask them, brushing the hair away from their face.

"That I feel good," they say.

But that can't be all.

"What else?"

"What do you mean?"

"You bit your lip," I say, my finger tracing their chapped lips. I'm going to have to get them a moisturizer if kissing is going to become a more regular thing.

"I don't want to say it."

"Say it," I tell them. "You're not going to scare me away."

"Are you sure?"

I nod.

"I . . . I love you."

I can't stop myself from smiling at them, at how nervous they look, how their entire face is flushed red, looking even darker in the faint orange glow of the lights. I laugh because I don't know what else to do, because they make me so happy that I think I'm overfilled with joy, that it needs some way to get out of me.

"What?"

"Nothing." I lean in, kissing them again. "I love you too."

ACKNOWLEDGMENTS

This book almost never existed. After I wrote *I Wish You All the Best* but before I decided that the next book I needed to write was *The Ghosts We Keep*, there was *The Feeling of Falling in Love*. (I know that's a weird timeline, stick with me here.)

For years on end I struggled with Neil and Wyatt's story, the two of them staying the same, but the circumstances of their love changing. Neil was cheated on and sought revenge; the week in California was a road trip from Boston to Florida; the book was dual point-of-view; the title was a lot longer and a lot worse. I wrote draft after draft of this book. When I say there are hundreds of thousands of words I wrote sitting in various folders and writing programs across four or five different computers, it's no exaggeration.

It feels like it's nothing short of a miracle that I managed to write this book, that I finally cracked Neil's story, that I finally found the right words to express all the feelings and emotions that come with falling in love.

But it's here! Finally, it's finished and you're holding it in your hands, and the work is done. Of course, with working on a book for nearly five years, there comes a list of people that I have to thank, so without further ado . . .

My friends always come first. Huong, Corey, Cam, Robin, Kat, Remi, Pav, Adriana. I definitely complained about this book a lot less than the last one. But still, your constant support over the course of these last few years has meant the world to me.

Lauren: the dream-agent, who knew that this book had to bake a little bit longer before it was ready. I'm glad that we waited, and working alongside you continues to be the best experience I could've asked for.

And David and Jeffrey, who helped realize the true potential of this book, helping me weed through messy notes, unrealized ideas, character motivations that made no sense, and plot threads that needed a lot of tender love and care.

To Maeve, who designed the perfect cover for this story before I even dreamt about what it could look like, and to every person at Scholastic who worked behind the scenes to help bring this book to life with their time, effort, love, and care.

Then there are the authors who I feel lucky to call friends, people who inspire me to work harder and push myself further with each and every story I tell: Becky, Adam, Camryn, Sophie, Cale, Julian, Alice, Sabina, Amber, Rachel, Adib, Jay, Nita, Mark, Aiden, Jason, Claribel, Casey, Lana, Natalie, and anyone else who I'm almost definitely forgetting. It's easy to feel like you're alone in an industry like this, but y'all make it worth it to still be here.

To each of my readers, whether you've so graciously followed each of my books or this is the first of mine that you're picking up, thank you so very much for your support.

To every romance story I've ever loved.

And to every trans person who ever believed that they didn't deserve a love story. This book is dedicated to you, to every trans person who thinks that they're too complicated to love, who maybe saw a bit too much of themselves in *I Wish You All the Best* and who wanted a love story of their own.

To Austin and Rachael—see, I didn't forget you this time! And Teagan, my conversations with you keep me going, they're so insightful and introspective. Now if only you could change your own diaper.

To my Dad, I feel like I said everything I needed to say in the last one, so I'll keep this simple: I miss you, and I wish you were still here. We all do.

And lastly, to Mom. Your continued support and love and care means the world to me. I feel like I've run out of words, so I'll keep this one simple too. I love you, a lot. And I hope you never doubt that.

ABOUT THE AUTHOR

Born and raised in a small town in North Carolina, Mason Deaver is an award-nominated, bestselling author and designer living near Raleigh. Their acclaimed YA novels include *I Wish You All the Best* and *The Ghosts We Keep*. Besides writing, they're an active fan of horror movies and video games. You can find them online at masondeaverwrites.com.